# THE TEMPLE OF THE WILD GEESE

*and*

# BAMBOO DOLLS OF ECHIZEN

Originally published in Japanese as *Gan no tera* by Bungei Shunju, Tokyo,1961
and *Echizen take ningyo* by Chuo Koron-sha, Tokyo, 1963
Copyright © 1961, 1963 by Fukiko Minakami
English Translation © 2008 by Dennis Washburn
First English translation, 2008

Library of Congress Cataloging-in-Publication Data

Minakami, Tsutomu, 1919-2004.
[Gan no tera. English]
The Temple of the wild geese ; and Bamboo dolls of Echizen / Tsutomu
Mizukami ; translation by Dennis Washburn.
p. cm.
ISBN-13: 978-1-56478-490-2 (alk. paper)
ISBN-10: 1-56478-490-8 (alk. paper)
I. Washburn, Dennis C. (Dennis Charles), 1954- II. Minakami,
Tsutomu, 1919-2004. Echizen take ningyo. English III. Title. IV.
Title: Bamboo dolls of Echizen. V. Title: Bamboo dolls of Echizen.

PL856.I5G313 2008
895.6'35--dc22

2007040574

This book has been selected by the Japanese Literature Publishing Project
(JLPP), which is run by the Japanese Literature Publishing and Promotion
Center (J-Lit Center) on behalf of the Agency for Cultural Affairs of Japan.

Partially funded by a grant from the Illinois Arts Council,
a state agency, and by the University of Illinois, Urbana-Champaign

www.dalkeyarchive.com

Printed on permanent/durable acid-free, recycled paper
and bound in the United States of America

# THE TEMPLE OF THE WILD GEESE

*and*

# BAMBOO DOLLS OF ECHIZEN

TWO NOVELLAS

*by*

TSUTOMU MIZUKAMI

( Tsutomu Minakami )

TRANSLATED WITH A POSTSCRIPT BY DENNIS WASHBURN

Dalkey Archive Press
Champaign and London

# The Temple of the Wild Geese

# I

Kishimoto Nangaku, whose paintings of birds and wildlife had won him acclaim among Kyoto art circles, passed away in the autumn of 1933. He died in a back room of his sprawling residence, which sat enclosed by a black wooden fence on a corner of Higashi no Tōin in the district of Maruta-machi.

Nangaku's death was caused by a combination of severe chronic asthma and old age. In his declining years, when he was wasted and thin as a praying mantis, it seemed that all that remained was his strength of will. Those disciples with him at the end all agreed that when he died, it was as if a withered, worm-infested tree had fallen. Because they had known Nangaku when he was still a man of vigor and vitality, when he had sported with more than his share of women, they may have been particularly inclined to describe his passing in this way. Throughout the day and evening, he had been snoring loudly as he slept, but in his final moments, he groaned hoarsely and writhed in pain. Nangaku was sixty-eight.

The day before Kishimoto Nangaku died—that is, on October 19—Kitami Jikai came by to see him, arriving just after Nangaku's wife, Hideko, had stepped out on some errands. Jikai was the head priest at the Kohōan, which was located at the foot of Mt. Kinugasa. He said he had been passing by, and wanted to drop in to express his concern. He was wearing a short black robe over his kimono and had a white silk band draped around his neck. Pleats of purple cloth were peeking out from beneath the hems of his robes. It appeared as though he was on his way home from a memorial service somewhere.

A maid Jikai recognized by sight met him at the entryway. He peppered her with questions as he proceeded to make his way straight into the house. "How're things? How's he doing?" he asked. Behind him was a short acolyte, who couldn't have been more than twelve or thirteen years old. The boy shuffled hurriedly after the priest.

The Kishimoto household was among the benefactors of the Kohōan. Since Nangaku was an honorary representative of the temple's patrons, it was not at all unusual for Jikai to barge into the inner recesses of his home in such a familiar, unceremonious way. Nevertheless, it discomfited Sasai Nansō, the most senior of the disciples, who was moistening his master's lips with a strip of dampened cotton when he arrived. The doctor had already given up and left, and now here was the priest of the family temple. Nansō considered it a bad omen, and the dour expression he wore made his feelings evident to everyone. Still, when the maid withdrew to fetch tea and sweets, Jikai breezed past the artist's disciples, seemingly oblivious to their consternation, and headed straight for the patient's bedside. Peering into Nangaku's sleeping face, he repeated his questions: "How're things? How're you doing?"

Nangaku had been lying like a toppled, decayed tree, a silk quilt pulled up to his chin, but Jikai's voice was so loud that he could feel it reverberate off the low ceiling and beat against his ears. With a slight flutter of his lids, he half-opened his eyes and, in a voice wracked with pain, said, "Is that you, Reverend?"

His disciples were startled. Since morning, Nansō had repeatedly called out his master's name but to no reply. Now, Nangaku opened his parched lips ever so slightly and told the priest in a raspy voice, "I knew I could count on you to come."

"I hate performing this duty," Jikai replied. Lowering his stout shoulders and leaning closer into Nangaku's face, he added haughtily, "You're the one person I never wanted to call on for this purpose."

Only then did the priest seem to register the presence of Nansō and the three other disciples. Glancing about at them arranged in the large, ten-tatami-mat room, he chuckled. Then he abruptly called out to the young acolyte. "Hey, Jinen! Hey!"

Moments earlier, the boy had stepped out onto the veranda overlooking the garden and was just then gazing intently at a stone lantern entwined with ivy in its autumn colors. Hearing his name, his shoulders stiffened. He turned toward the priest and peered into the room. He was a disturbingly odd-looking boy, his shaven head emphasizing the enormity of his crown, and his protruding forehead and deep-set eyes making his face appear small and narrow.

"Come over here!" Jikai called again, motioning with his hand.

The young acolyte stepped forward quietly, taking care to avoid the cloth trim of the tatami. He shuffled his feet, sliding them over the mats.

"His name's Jinen," Jikai told Nangaku. "He just went through his ordination rites yesterday. He's good at keeping the garden tidy, too. When you get better, you must come to the temple to relax."

Could this be the reason Jikai had dropped by? Whenever a novice is ordained, it is customary for Zen temples to announce the event to the representatives of their patrons. The priest appeared to be introducing the boy he had chosen as his assistant. Watching the boy in profile, the disciple Nansō thought he had certainly picked a rather glum-looking lad.

After a few moments, Jikai got up and began retracing his steps away from the sickbed. Before the priest had reached the veranda, Nangaku abruptly stirred again. "Look after Sato, Reverend," he said in a hoarse whisper. "She belongs at the temple."

No sooner had he uttered these words than Nangaku closed his eyes and was overtaken by a violent fit of coughing. Nansō quickly returned to his side and resumed moistening his master's lips with the dampened cloth.

The priest glanced back to survey the scene. Bowing deeply, he saw that Nangaku's complexion was already a pale greenish shade. "Take care of yourself," he called. Patting his acolyte once on the head, he quickly withdrew from the Kishimoto house. His visit had lasted no more than four or five minutes.

Nangaku did not say another word until the following day. At times he snored loudly or gasped painfully, and at other times he was quiet, as though his breathing had abruptly stopped. When he was on the verge of taking his final breath, he parted his lips ever so slightly. Because it appeared he wanted to say something, his disciples leaned in and listened closely. What they heard was "Sato."

Nangaku's disciples all glanced over nervously toward Hideko. Sitting at the head of her husband's bed, she was sobbing, her face pressed into the sleeve of her kimono. It appeared she had not heard.

This "Sato" who consumed Nangaku's last thoughts was Kirihara Satoko, whom he had taken from her job at a small restaurant in Kiya-machi and set up on the second floor of a flower shop in Demachi, Kamigyō Ward. In his final years, the artist had visited her so often that even his disciples and the priest Jikai knew all about their relationship. And while she was now thirty-two and no longer a young woman, Satoko was the type favored by men—petite and buxom, with an hourglass figure and delicate features. Why, then, would Nangaku think it necessary to ask the priest to look after her?

When Kishimoto Nangaku was in good health, he had traveled as far as China and Europe for his work. Yet when it came to creating those master-pieces on which he lavished his greatest care, it was his custom to borrow the guest quarters at the Kohōan and work there. The artist was drawn to the area around the temple because of the groves of deciduous trees that skirted the base of Mt. Kinugasa. He used the Kohōan's guestroom as his atelier in his later years. In fact, ten years before his death, he had even spent an entire summer in residence at the temple doing nothing at all. He had brought Satoko to live with him during that time.

Nangaku had painted wild geese on the four-panel *fusuma* doors in the corridor running from the cedar entryway of the head priest's residence to the main hall, and on the doors of the inner sanctum and the two chambers adjoining it to the left and right. Strolling the premises with Satoko, he would gesture to them and say, "These are the geese I painted."

The panels of the *fusuma* had been painted in ink and gold dust. The setting was an ancient pine with enormous roots stretching its great branches out over a pond. Each of the needle-like leaves had been drawn in exquisite detail. A flock of wild geese, some perching, some flapping their wings, was pictured settling in the lower branches. As one bird was about to fly off, its white-feathered belly flashing in the evening sky, another nestled motion-lessly on a branch, appearing as if it were part of a knot on the trunk of the pine. There were goslings. And there were chicks with their mouths open to receive food from their mothers. Although every one of these countless birds had been painted in monochrome ink, no two of them were alike. One could almost hear the sound of the brush through which the artist had focused his passion, rendering each with the greatest care. The geese seemed to be alive.

Nangaku had poured his heart and soul into these panels, completing them in the spring two years before that summer he spent with Satoko at the Kohōan. Indeed, they were so brilliantly executed that the artist himself could not hold back his pride. Intoxicated with drink, he gently stroked the nape of

Satoko's neck and smiled. "After I'm dead and gone," he told her, "this place will come to be known as 'The Temple of the Wild Geese,' and the number of famous places in western Kyoto will increase by one."

"Yes, you can almost hear their cries!" Satoko, who was enraptured, whispered ecstatically. Standing in the dusky light of the main hall, Nangaku beamed and caressed her neck.

Was it because Nangaku had been unable to forget the events of that summer that he had entrusted Satoko to the care of the priest?

In fact, the three of them had often passed the time together drinking in the temple's guest quarters. Although Jikai was ten years younger than Nangaku, his face and body suggested he was of equal virility. Their similar personalities meant he also got along well with Satoko.

"Can't you please remove the hair from your ears, Reverend?" a drunken Satoko had once asked, squinting at him through heavy eyelids. Jikai had laughed and studied his two companions, but a flash of sexual desire had settled in his eyes. Knowing full well that the priest was attracted to her, Satoko often remarked to Nangaku, "Jikai's eyes are frightening."

Indeed, Jikai and Nangaku shared identical tastes. When it came to women and drink, they were in total agreement. Perhaps for this reason, Nangaku always seemed dissatisfied that Jikai had never married. The Kohōan held special status as a branch temple within the Tōzenji sect; and because it was physically separate from the grounds of the main temple, keeping a wife would not have attracted undue attention. In any case, it was an open secret that all the branch temples—even those located on the main temple's grounds—kept a woman in the head priest's residence. Nangaku had told Jikai to his face that a priest with sexual urges had no reason to maintain his bachelorhood. But Jikai had just laughed and ignored him. When Nangaku pressed him on the matter, he replied, "To cut off one's hair is to sever the roots of attachment. That is the meaning of a Zen priest's tonsure."

·

When it came time to observe the Buddhist rites on the seventh day after Nangaku's death, Kirihara Satoko once again walked through the gate of the Kohōan. She was wearing mourning robes and a brownish agate rosary on one of her slender white arms. The sky was overcast, and there was a slight breeze. The peak of Mt. Kinugasa, overgrown with small pines, was covered in a thick mist. The leaves were sparse on the deciduous trees in the groves around the gentle base of the mountain. Japanese maples, brilliant in their autumn foliage, were clustered between open spaces where bare patches of the mountain's reddish soil peeked through.

An iron chain was attached to the wicket located at the side of the temple gate. The slapping of Satoko's sandals against her feet and the metallic creaking of the chain as she entered the precincts broke the peaceful silence of the surroundings. The young acolyte Jinen came out to greet her. It was the first time Satoko had encountered the boy, with his large head and deep-set eyes. He was dressed in a lined robe of solid blue that was a little long for him. As he knelt on the wooden floor against the backdrop of the polished, soot-blackened pillars of the temple's living quarters, his appearance and manner seemed disagreeably adult-like. Satoko felt a little unsure of herself.

"Could you please tell the Reverend that a caller has arrived from Demachi?" she said from the steppingstone at the entryway.

"Yes," he replied, and immediately returned to the living quarters.

Presently, Satoko heard the sound of hurried footsteps coming from the hallway. Then Jikai appeared, dressed in a lined white robe tied with a stiff obi. "Please, come in. Come in," the priest said, and a look of nostalgia rose in Satoko's face.

Satoko's buxom figure moved as briskly as ever, and—was it Jikai's imagination?—her pale face seemed luminescent. Seeing her this way, Jikai clucked with delight. He led her into the guestroom, where Nangaku's funeral had been conducted. It was a quiet space that looked out onto the small landscaped hill and pond in the garden. For Satoko, it was a place filled with memories. She placed her palms on the tatami floor, her eyes moist with tears. "It's been so long," she cried.

It had been out of the question for Satoko to attend Nangaku's funeral. She told the priest how she had been at home on the second floor of the florist's in Demachi when she learned of Nangaku's death. How she had known the date of the funeral, but had mourned his passing alone. "I'd like to offer a prayer right away," she said. "And Reverend," she added fawningly, "could you show me his paintings of the wild geese?"

Satoko was shown into the main hall, where the memorial tablet for Nangaku instantly caught her eyes:

**Shūgakuin nantō ikken koji**

It was specially decorated and set atop an altar cloth that had been spread out on the ordination platform. Satoko found it hard to breath. In recognition of his devoted service to the temple, Jikai had included the honorific title *"koji"* in Nangaku's *kaimyō*, his posthumous Buddhist name. Seeing it there, Satoko pondered how Nangaku's entire being was now reduced to a thin, rectangular wooden tablet less than a foot high.

She placed some incense in the censer, and the ten-mat inner sanctum soon filled with white smoke. As the smoke began to flicker above the tatami, the geese Nangaku had painted on the sliding doors appeared to move within the haze. They were so beautiful. Seeing them again, it occurred to Satoko that Nangaku had surely achieved Buddhahood.

The two geese at the center of the sliding doors that opened onto the chamber left of the inner sanctum were puffing out the white down of their bellies. One of them was pressed into a hollow of the pine and nuzzling the side of the other with its beak. Satoko kept staring at their image. Jikai, who had been standing behind her the whole time, finally broke the silence: "Let's go in over there and have a drink."

He was in a state of excitement. For the first time ever, Satoko was about to step into the dusky six-mat room that served as his private quarters. The acolyte Jinen was already inside, kneeling and setting out cushions for them to sit on. The priest motioned toward the boy with his jaw and said, "He's my substitute wife. His name's Jinen. He recently completed his ordination rites."

Bowing, Jinen dropped his head slightly and glanced toward Satoko. His deep-set eyes were gleaming, but he looked down immediately as though embarrassed. He quickly left the room.

"I was surprised when I first saw him at the entrance," Satoko remarked. "He strikes me as a rather strange boy. How old is he?"

"Thirteen."

"Really? Does he go to school?"

"He goes to the middle school at Daitokuji."

"Is he your successor?"

Jikai regarded Satoko's face but did not respond. He stood up and went to open a small sliding panel beneath one of the altars. Inside were several magnum-size bottles of sake. Jikai took out the *Sawanotsuru* and said, "Let's open this one today." A child-like smile spread across his cheeks and he clapped his hands. "Heat this up for us, all right?" he asked when Jinen reappeared.

The boy withdrew into the hallway clutching the large bottle. After a short while, he returned carrying a tray loaded with cups and flasks filled with the prepared drink. The acolyte's odd appearance belied the fact that he was actually a diligent child, Satoko thought. The first time she saw him, she felt his face was somehow disagreeable. Now that she was becoming more accustomed to seeing him, however, she began to find the boy curiously touching.

"He works very hard. You've found a good acolyte," she told Jikai, her tongue quickly loosened by the sake.

Because Satoko had not had occasion to drink for some time, the alcohol quickly went to her head. But even after night fell, she still felt relaxed and at ease. When she stayed with Nangaku at the Kohōan, they had often stayed up all night drinking with the priest.

"I had a last request from Nangaku," Jikai finally told her, a glittering light settling in the large pupils of his dark eyes. "He asked me to look after you. He knew very well how much I liked you. Won't you come here and live with me?"

Jikai moved closer, exposing his knees beneath his white robe. He seemed to be waiting intently for her answer, but Satoko remained silent. This silence gave Jikai his opening. He kicked his cushion aside and seized her from behind, passing his hands under her arms and pinning her to the floor. As the priest began to press his lips to her, an earlier premonition that this day would come flashed in Satoko's mind. She closed her eyes but did not resist. The priest quickly pulled open her robes and pressed his powerful body up against her. Satoko's eyes fluttered open.

A shadow suddenly darted across the shoji directly in her line of vision. Startled, Satoko instinctively pushed the priest away. It must be Jinen, she thought. But the shadow's significance quickly faded from her consciousness. As her body was once again overwhelmed by the priest's strength, Satoko's mind drifted away.

Short of breath from exertion, Jikai began to repeat his request for Satoko to join him at the temple. "You'll come here, won't you? Won't you?" he panted again and again. Her hair disheveled and her face pressed to the tatami, Satoko shook her head each time, but soon even that much resistance seemed too much trouble.

The following day, Satoko agreed to live in the residence of the Kohōan. More accurately speaking, she could not return home because of what had happened with Jikai. The rites of the seventh day following Kishimoto Nangaku's death had become the day of Kirihara Satoko's initiation.

eld her body that she caught a glimpse of that shadow on the shoji? Thinking ack on it, it was eerily like a threat. Most likely, the shadow had been Jinen, e boy-priest with the large head. Because she had been intoxicated, Satoko uickly let the thought slip through her mind. Forced down onto the hard tami by the vigorous Jikai, she had lost herself in the sound of the breeze imming her back. What had that shadow been? Only much later would she ome to understand.

There were a number of reasons why Satoko accepted her role
law wife. First, there were financial considerations. After Nanga
needed a way to support herself. Satoko had received nothing fr¢
moto household, not even a hanging scroll for use in the tea
Nangaku's wife, Hideko, was not a woman to show such kindn
course, there was no solatium, or separation money. In fact, as tl
out, it was hardly surprising that Satoko was left with nothing at ;
it seems, had pursued a decadent lifestyle, and he left behind a ¡
pile of debts. After his death, unpaid bills came in from totally
places. It was all Hideko could do to hold onto the house in M
Satoko considered getting a job, but given her age and experienc
be hard-pressed to find anything outside of waitressing. Just
of a woman over thirty having to endure such hardship was ¡
distasteful. And if she were to return to her former job at the re;
knew she would be a laughingstock to her fellow workers.

The Kohōan, then, was not such an unattractive alternative.
designated a special status within the Tōzenji sect by the main te
many patrons. As the wife of Jikai, she would never have to worry
her next meal was coming from. Meanwhile, Jikai was fond of d
serving as his companion suited Satoko. Because of their long ass
knew his personality very well. Jikai's features had an earthiness i
to a Zen priest; and his laughter lent his face a childlike quality.
she liked about him.

On top of this, Satoko preferred the Kohōan to any other tem
To wake up and go to sleep every day in view of the peaceful, gei
of Mt. Kinugasa was an attractive prospect; and she was fond ¢
garden, which was surrounded by sweet persimmon, silverberr
Best of all, Nangaku's wild geese were there in the temple's main

Having been with Nangaku a decade, she was just as d
Kohōan as he had been. It occurred to Satoko that the artist ha
any payment for his paintings of the geese. Perhaps he had inte
temple to manage his posthumous affairs. If that had indeed b
then she understood why Nangaku should want the Kohōan to
permanent home.

"It was Nangaku's last request," Jikai had said.

When the priest approached Satoko with these words, he
instantly stiffened. But she soon found her initial sadness ov¢
feeling of burgeoning ecstasy. Hadn't it been at the exact moment

# II

A lone chinquapin stood in a thin stand of trees that stretched from the bamboo grove behind the Kohōan to the foot of Mt. Kinugasa. Its top was flat, as if its tip had been snapped off, and its trunk was so thick it would take two people to wrap their arms around it. With no leaves or branches, the chinquapin looked less like a tree than a great black pole jutting into the air. At some point, a solitary kite had taken to roosting atop it. Perched there, the kite resembled a stuffed bird set against the backdrop of the white sky.

From time to time, this kite would circle above the residence and main hall of the Kohōan. Tracing out a spiral, the bird would gently soar higher and higher. Occasionally, it would roost on the roof of the living quarters, on one of the end tiles embossed with the face of a demon. Lording it over the garden, where fine white gravel had been spread, the kite's glittering eyes would dart about as it surveyed the pond and its surroundings.

"It's terrible, Reverend, look! That horrid kite is sitting on that tree again!" Standing on tiptoe, Satoko called out to Jikai from the edge of the corridor at the rear of the head priest's residence.

"It has its eye on the carp, the damn nuisance."

Satoko turned to him, her puffy eyes staring wide.

"When no one is looking, it'll swoop down the minute a carp sticks its head above water."

"A kite can catch such big carp? How can it fly off with them?"

"Kites are clever. They stab at the fish with their beaks, then grab and lift with their talons. Once they've carried the fish to sufficient height, they drop it. The carp dies when it hits the ground. Only then does the bird take it back to its nest. Pretty remarkable."

"That's horrible!" Satoko cried. "You should stretch a screen over the pond!"

Because she sounded like a child, Jikai dismissed her. Making a face as if to say, 'Don't be stupid,' he withdrew into the room.

In truth, Satoko was bored. There was nothing for her to do. Almost every day, Jikai was busy visiting parishioners or presenting himself at the main temple, while she was stuck having to pass the time in the gloomy recesses of the residence. At first, life at the Kohōan was fascinating, and Satoko had explored every corner of the place: the sooty kitchen of the living quarters, the assistant priest's room, the storage closets. Everything had seemed so novel. But now that these things were familiar to her, the atmosphere of the temple, with its floors elevated on wooden piles, struck her as very different from that of her small room on the second floor of the flower shop. She found the place cold and forbidding.

Satoko's room at the Kohōan was located at the back of the priest's residence. *Fusuma* doors separated the six-mat space from Jikai's room, and four shoji panels led out to the corridor on the south side. Satoko had placed a wooden-framed *kotatsu* in the middle of the room and covered it with a futon she had brought from Demachi. She would often sit at the *kotatsu*, her legs hidden beneath the red, floral-patterned silk. Whenever Jikai had free time, he would go and cozy up next to her there.

The priest had a much stronger sexual appetite than Nangaku. Satoko assumed this was due to an enormous buildup of urges stemming from his days of ascetic training and continuing through all his years as a bachelor. And although he made demands on her morning, noon and night, Satoko felt no resentment or disgust toward him. Comparing her lovers, she recalled how Nangaku would take pleasure in merely stroking or gazing upon her hips and narrow waist. Rarely did he engage her in intercourse, as Jikai always did. After sleeping with Jikai, Satoko realized that Nangaku had never satisfied her. When she came to the temple, she became a woman.

Not once since arriving at the Kohōan had she and Jikai ever had so much as an argument. The only thing that unsettled her was the acolyte Jinen. Simply speaking, Satoko just did not like the boy. His big head and small body made him look strange, deformed. And although he was unaffected and simple and listened obediently to what he was told, Satoko couldn't stand the dark expression he wore whenever he looked at her.

"Where did you find that boy, Reverend?" Satoko once asked Jikai while they were lying in bed together.

"Jinen?" he replied. "He's the son of a temple carpenter in Wakasa, in western Fukui Prefecture. I heard about him when there was some construction work at the main temple. The priest at the Seianji in Wakasa Hongō brought the boy here. I asked for him specifically because I'd heard he was good at his studies. He's smart. He's got a big brain."

Indeed, Satoko thought to herself, if Jinen's brain extended from his protruding forehead all the way to the back of his skull, which jutted out behind him, then it must be big and the boy must be smart. "So he's doing well in middle school?"

"He got the award for top student. I've got high expectations for him. Even when he was a student in his hometown, he received a commendation and a scholarship from the old feudal lord of the Fukui domain. He got the top prize in elementary school, as well. A lot of the branch temples have trouble with smart-alecky kids, but this boy is going to be somebody—so treat him nicely." With that, Jikai fell asleep and was soon snoring loudly. It had become the priest's habit, once he had sated his desire, to sleep—and snore—for about an hour or so.

Satoko was left to ponder the story on her own. *So Jinen was the son of a carpenter? And he had been separated from his mother at the age of ten to serve as an acolyte here?* Satoko knew nothing of the circumstances of the carpenter's family, but she couldn't help wondering how they could have sent such a small child to a place like this. Thinking back, she could not recall a single day when the recesses of Jinen's deep-set eyes had not been filled to overflowing with sadness. Satoko thought that she would never be capable of sending her own child away from home.

Jinen was in fact lonely at the Kohōan. His room, which was located just off the entrance to the living quarters, was a small nine-by-six foot cell with a wooden floor on which a single tatami mat had been laid. Jinen kept a wicker basket at the foot of the tatami and spread a black cotton futon over the mat to sleep. The room's single window consisted of a lattice grille that opened out in one direction only. It was too high for Jinen to reach and allowed only three hours of sunlight a day. Although the room faced east, the eaves of the roof of the main hall blocked the sun's rays. The young acolyte would copy out the *Kannon Sutra* in the dim, lattice-striped light that managed to filter in.

According to his daily routine, Jinen would get up at five every morning, wash his face, perform his religious services and prepare rice. When he was finished, he would spread a mat in the kitchen of the living quarters and eat. At eight-thirty, he would leave the temple, taking the mountain path until it opened out at Kuramaguchi. Walking along Senbon Avenue, he would make his way to Murasakino Middle School, located just east of Daitokuji Temple in Kita Ōji.

Jinen's school had originally been the Han'nyarin, which was operated by a consortium of Zen temples for the purpose of training apprentice priests. The Han'nyarin was converted to a middle school in compliance with Ministry of Education regulations and was obligated as such to conduct military exercises and drills. For this reason, students had to wear gaiters over their uniforms when they attended. As the school had once been the Han'nyarin, however, its calendar and course of study were adapted to suit the young priests-in-training, who had numerous temple responsibilities. Classes ended after the morning session.

After finishing school, Jinen would set off at once for Mt. Kinugasa, arriving at one. First, he would have lunch. Then, from two, he would perform chores around the temple. His duties included chopping wood and cleaning. He also had to weed the garden and pump out the latrine when it was full. His chores would end at sunset, and he would return to the residence at six. Then he would prepare dinner. Dinner would be over at eight. After that, he would practice copying sutras. He would retire at ten.

Observing Jinen's lifestyle, Satoko was struck by how rigorous Zen training could be. In a normal family, parents would still have coddled a child his age. She thought it must be hard for him to keep such a strict schedule without a break. There must have been days when he was sick with fever or suffered a headache and simply didn't want to do anything, but she never heard Jinen complain. It made her wonder if some children were immune to illness. Satoko felt a growing curiosity for this odd boy who so silently met the demands of his daily routine. *Could he actually be grateful to live such a life?*

The family of the temple carpenter was almost certainly poverty-stricken. If a boy used to being wrapped in warm quilts and fawned over by his parents were sent to a place like this, he would never have been able to work as hard as Jinen. Whenever these thoughts occurred to Satoko, she wanted to ask him about the family that had raised him and whether he felt fortunate to be living at the temple now.

.

It was early March. Winter was ending, but the winds were still cold. Satoko slipped on a pair of wooden clogs and stepped out into the garden at the back of the residence. Jikai was out visiting a patron of the temple, and Jinen was on the far side of the pond weeding the garden under some maple trees on the landscaped hill.

In truth, Jinen wasn't "weeding" exactly because no tall grass had yet to appear amid the cyptomeria moss. Even so, Jikai was very particular when it came to temple chores. Because it was early March, the moss appeared brownish and withered for the most part, but some of it was beginning to take on a bluish-green color. Small clumps of grass about the size of a pinkie finger had sprouted here and there among the dark brown roots of the maples to which the moss clung. If these clumps weren't removed, the grass would take over and ruin the moss. Jikai had assigned Jinen the task of eradicating this grass during the spring. In recent days, Jinen had begun weeding as soon as he returned from school.

Because these small clumps of grass had broken through the winter soil, their roots were very strong. Jinen's little fingers were not strong enough to pull them up, so he used a small blade made of bamboo. He would thrust the blade into the surface of the ground, hold the grass with his thumb and pluck the clumps out one by one. He put the grass in a thick board box about the size of a mandarin orange crate.

Jinen was utterly absorbed in his work. The water flowing down from Mt. Kinugasa burbled and splashed into the pond. He did not notice Satoko slipping on her clogs and climbing the stone steps of the landscaped hill.

"Jinen!" Satoko called out from the front of the teahouse a short distance away. "Why don't you take a break? The Reverend's not here." She took out the two rice crackers she had slipped into the sleeve of her kimono and set them on the veranda of the teahouse. "Come on over!"

Jinen stared at Satoko with fearful eyes. His expression bothered her. She had expected him to be happy and to join her immediately.

"Hurry up . . . Aren't you coming?"

Jinen continued to squat, his hand resting on the edge of the box holding

the uprooted grass. His work trousers were torn at the knees, exposing the
worn, lined robe of cotton he wore beneath them. Satoko noticed that his
face was slightly swollen. His eyes were puffy and bloodshot, as if he had been
crying. Suspecting that to be the case, Satoko observed him more closely and,
sure enough, both eyes were smeared with the dirt from his hands.

"Your name is Sutekichi, isn't it?" Satoko thought she might draw him out
this way.

"Yes."

"Are your mother and father well?"

"Yes."

"Do they write you?"

"Yes."

"Come on over here. Look, I've got some rice crackers."

The teahouse was a single six-mat room in the traditional Sukiya style. It
had been built on top of the hill as an embellishment. The door was rarely
opened. Drops of rain and dew had stained the doorsill and the boards of
the veranda. Because the veranda was dusty, Satoko blew on it before she sat
down.

Jinen rose slowly and made his way over. As he sat down beside her, Satoko
caught a whiff of his sweaty head and felt her stomach turn. Jinen must have
been hungry, because as soon as she gave him the rice crackers, he shoveled
them into his mouth. The boy had white teeth and he made a smacking sound
as he ate.

"Do you think about your mom a lot?" Satoko blushed as soon as she said
this, realizing how irresponsible the question was. This child was supposed
to forget about his parents and single-mindedly pursue his priestly training.
Ashamed of herself for not having been more considerate, Satoko allowed the
boy to continue munching on his crackers while she told him some of her
own story.

"I have a father, too, Jinen. He manufactures a medicine patch called
*Mugiwara Poultice*. He's an old man now. But he still works hard, making his
medicine." Thinking Jinen's face had brightened ever so slightly, she continued.
"My mom is dead, but I have a stepmother. I was sent out as a servant when I
was little. I've gone through a lot of hard times, but now here I am, with the
Reverend looking after me. I guess everybody has to experience hard times
when they're young, the same as you."

Jinen listened intently, his tired eyes blinking repeatedly.

"You're going to be a priest, aren't you, Jinen? I envy you. Once you leave school, you'll start training at a Zen monastery. Then you'll become a priest, right? That's what the Reverend tells me. You're lucky. I was born a girl, so there was never much chance for me. No matter how hard a girl tries, the only road open to her is to rely on the help of others."

Seeing Satoko's expression turn melancholy, Jinen quickly spoke up. "Ma'am? How does your father make *Mugiwara Poultice*?"

"The patch?" Satoko laughed. "Well, you spread pine resin on a thin strip of hinoki wood, lay five pieces of barley straw across the wood, then pile another strip on top. It's sort of like when you wrap pounded rice cakes in oak leaves. And that's it. That's the poultice."

Jinen laughed, too. Was this the first time she had seen him do so? Now that Satoko had brought up her own family, however, she felt unusually sad and reflective. It seemed strange to her that she should have mentioned her father, Isaburō. He still lived in Kyoto, in Hachijō, but she had never thought much about him before.

Satoko had been sent to work at a restaurant in Gojōzaka when she was thirteen, and you could count on the fingers of one hand the number of times she had been back to Hachijō since. Her father had been a modest manufacturer of the poultice patch she had told Jinen about. He would cut thin strips of bamboo bark or hinoki wood into squares, and then boil a mixture of pine resin and black powder in a pot on top of a clay stove. Once the mixture had become a pasty, sticky liquid, he would apply it to the bamboo or hinoki squares with a brush. He then lined up sticks of barley straw, which had been cut to the length of disposable chopsticks, and placed them on top of the mixture. When the tallow dried, he would stack another square smeared with the pine resin on top. The ends of the straw would stick out on both sides. He wrapped these in Japanese paper and affixed a label on which the following had been printed by woodblock:

*Kirihara Saitendo Pharmaceuticals*
*Made With Care*
*MUGIWARA POULTICE*
*Good for contusions, aches and pains, rheumatism*

Back then the price was three sen. The product was similar to the poultice patches now sold under the brand names *Kishinkō* or *Tokuhon*, but apparently *Mugiwara Poultice* was not cheap. Isaburō would sell the patches himself. He would place them in a basket and ride his bike around the towns of Toba, Fushimi and Kuze in southern Kyoto. He would scold Satoko whenever she came near his workplace and the kettle he used to boil the pine-resin mixture. During the period between her mother's death and the arrival of her step-mother, Tatsu, Satoko had been lonely and cried constantly. Whenever her father went out to peddle his wares, he would lock Satoko inside their tene-ment row house. Because the eaves were so low, she would have to wait in the dark until he returned.

"Jinen?" Satoko said after a while. "The more hardships you endure, the better things will turn out in the end, so please be patient. One day, you'll be an important priest."

Satoko tried to get up from the teahouse veranda, but the loose strap of one of her clogs caught on the steppingstone and she lost her balance. Her upper body swayed and her kimono opened at the knees, exposing her red undergarment. Muttering, Satoko righted herself just as she was about to fall over and with one hand quickly straightened the overlapping folds of her kimono. Feeling the breeze on her thighs, she instinctively glanced over at Jinen. She could not miss the glittering light that flashed like a kite across his clear eyes.

*The little brat!* she thought angrily. *I'm sure he saw us that time, too!*

But this was merely her intuition, so she said nothing. Descending the stone steps of the garden hill, Satoko glanced back. "Hurry up, now. Finish your weeding and come inside. The Reverend had to perform a memorial service today. They'll invite him for drinks, so he'll come home drunk. Come in early and rest in your room."

But Jinen had already left the teahouse. She spied his large head under the branches of the maple trees as the boy hurried toward the other side of the pond.

# III

Although his relations with Satoko continued as usual, Jikai began to suffer a decline in his appearance and behavior sometime around the start of summer. Just as the rainy season was ending, his complexion—usually flushed and shiny as a result of his drinking—grew dull and sallow, and dark, sagging circles began to appear under his eyes. Jikai had always taken pride in his ears, which were much larger than average, and in the strong, full line of his jaw. Now, the luster had gone from both cheeks. He was fifty-eight and on the verge of old age. Over the course of the past year, spots had begun to appear on his cheeks and the backs of his hands. And while none of this was really any matter of concern, it must have come as a blow to someone who had taken such satisfaction in his robust good looks.

"Is everything all right, Reverend?"

"There's nothing wrong with me. Nothing at all!" Jikai would scoff at Satoko's womanly misgivings. "You're just draining the life out of me."

It was true that since Satoko had arrived, Jikai had been focusing on her with the energy of a young man in his twenties. Still, it was unusual for a person's complexion to change so much in less than a year. When he stepped into the bath, the paleness of his skin surprised even himself. For all that, Jikai didn't seem to have any problems with his organs or his appetite, and he refused to take the changes in his appearance seriously. "I'm fifty-eight, after all," he would say.

While he recognized the decline in his appearance, Jikai remained oblivious to the changes in his behavior. Only Satoko and Jinen were aware of his increasingly short temper and irritableness. These days, whenever Jikai drank, there was nothing cheerful or lively about him. No longer did he strip down to his loincloth and dance like he would in the old days. On top of this, he was drinking more than ever, and if anyone noted that he was drunk, he would become sullen and morose.

*The Reverend's changed*, Satoko thought. As Jikai's partner, she was sensitive to his gradual transformation, but she found it impossible to pinpoint its cause. The temple was not doing poorly. While Jinen was off at school, Jikai was always busy meeting guests. He worked diligently visiting patrons and conducting services at the main temple. It was true that when he returned home, he was often on edge, as if he had met with a difficult or strange encounter. But often nothing untoward had happened. It seemed Jikai's short temper only showed in his behavior toward Satoko and, of course, toward Jinen.

Jikai had started sleeping late after Satoko moved to the Kohōan, so the responsibility for morning prayers fell solely to Jinen. The priest's residence was connected to the main hall where the Shakyamuni Buddha was enshrined by a passageway. The guest quarters were located in between the two buildings. Despite the distance, Jinen's chanting and the reverberations of the prayer bell could be heard in Satoko's room at just after five each morning. Jinen would chant the sutra to the statue of the Shakyamuni Buddha for about twenty minutes. Satoko knew his prayers were coming to an end when the sounds of the bell and the wooden gong gradually became slow and gentle. From there, Jinen would pick up a handbell and make his way down the corridor chanting the *Heart Sutra*. A metal clapper was attached to the handbell with a cord. Because he would strike it sharply, it rang out more powerfully than the bowl-shaped prayer bell in the main hall. The boy made no sound as he walked along the corridor, but Satoko could always tell where he was by the sound of the bell. As he reached the living quarters, still chanting the *Heart Sutra*, he would stop before the statue of the guardian deity Idaten. The sutra offered to Idaten, whose shrine stood next to the entryway inside a space barely two tatami mats in size, took about fifteen minutes to complete. There was no wooden gong there, and because the shrine had been set in an alcove whose base was exactly Jinen's height, he recited the sutra standing up. From this spot, his voice could be heard even more clearly in Satoko's room. When the recitation of the sutra before Idaten was finished, Jinen would remove his prayer robes and surplice and, wearing only his kimono, begin preparing breakfast. Audible, too, were the sounds of the boy setting the water to boil and washing the rice.

It was Jikai's habit to sleep through all of it, and Satoko preferred it that way. Occasionally, if the chanting awoke him, he would reach out and begin to caress her. Satoko understood that Jinen's morning routine was part of his training—that it was the responsibility of an acolyte—so it bothered her that the priest overseeing him should be making love to her while he performed his duties. Nonetheless, Satoko always did as Jikai urged. She never resisted. She simply kept these things in her heart and dared not speak of them.

Just before dawn during a stretch of humid days at the start of July, Jikai awoke earlier than usual to find the Kohōan silent. Quickly leaving Satoko's side, he rushed out of the room and down the corridor. Still half-asleep, Satoko lay in bed confused. Not because Jikai had gotten up unusually early, but because she could not hear Jinen chanting the morning sutras. Listening intently, she heard the sound of Jikai's footsteps come to a halt outside the small room beside the entrance to the living quarters. Then the priest's angry voice came echoing down the hall. Now wide-awake, Satoko tried to take in everything that was said. A few minutes later, Jikai returned.

"That idiot overslept and didn't go to the main hall! I found him fast asleep!" Jikai spat out his words, then flipped back the yellow linen futon and climbed back into bed beside Satoko.

"He's probably exhausted. He has military training every day at school."

"Military training?" he shouted. "What are you talking about?"

"It's true. Just recently, I read in the paper that they've assigned a soldier to teach in every middle school. The students have to carry rifles on their shoulders, and they have to undergo military training."

"What a load of nonsense!" By this point, Jikai was shouting so loud it hurt Satoko's ears. "What do they think they're doing, having Zen acolytes playing soldier? It's outrageous!"

"You can shout all you want, but it's a regulation. There's nothing you can do about it."

Jikai's expression softened slightly. "It's a regulation? Who'd make such a ridiculous rule? What good is it to have Zen acolytes running around with rifles?"

"How would I know? And I don't know who decided it, but the students are all happily carrying their rifles."

"So what are you saying?"

"I'm saying that Jinen's exhausted by his training. He can't help being sleepy."

"That may be, but an apprentice can't oversleep!"

Jikai's eyes were wild with fury. To Satoko, it felt as if she were the one being scolded. She also thought the priest shouldn't be so hard on Jinen. The boy had only overslept one day. And he was surely worn-out. Such a big, heavy head on such a small body, barely four feet tall. There was no way he could perform his religious duties, his chores and his schoolwork without an extremely strong constitution. Satoko was subconsciously protective of the boy.

"Oh, well, never mind. Starting tomorrow, I'll tie a rope to him so I can pull on it to get him up."

Jikai clicked his tongue, and glanced amorously at Satoko out of the corners of his eyes. Moving closer, he groped for the cords that fastened her undergarment to her warm body. It was not uncommon for him to want her in the morning. As his eyes grew narrower, emphasizing his crow's feet, he pulled open the front of her robe with his stubby, hairy fingers and began to fondle her breasts.

.

That evening at around nine-thirty, when he had finished copying sutras for the day, Jinen came and knelt on the veranda outside the head priest's residence. "Here it is, Reverend," he said, his voice weak and miserable.

After a moment, he peeked his head silently through the partly opened shoji. Satoko, who had been sitting with her knees drawn up, fanning herself in the heat, was startled and hastily rearranged the skirt of her kimono.

"What is it?" Jikai finally said, turning toward the shoji.

"Here it is." Jinen thrust the end of a white hemp rope through the opening in the sliding doors.

"Yes, yes, very good." Jikai took the end of the rope and pulled it till it reached the edge of his futon. "Do you understand? You have to tie the end of the rope to your wrist. You got it?"

Standing with the moonlight from the garden at his back, Jinen cast a dwarf-like shadow on the shoji.

"You got it?" Jikai asked again.

"Yes," the shadow replied and disappeared to the sound of shuffling foot-steps.

Jinen dragged the rope along the corridor, stretching it from the priest's residence to a spot near his pillow in his own small room. Slowly and deliberately, he made a loop in the end of the rope and slipped it over his wrist, which was still discolored from last winter's chilblains. Wearily, he dropped down onto the single tatami mat to sleep. There were mosquitoes swarming in his room, their noisy buzzing resembling the reverberations of the prayer bell in the main hall. They were always there. Jinen did not have mosquito netting.

Jikai had devised the hemp rope to work as a substitute alarm clock, and the next morning he awoke remarkably early—at five o'clock sharp—to tug on it. Twice or three times he pulled, hard enough so that the rope cleared the floor along the length of the corridor to the opposite end of the living quarters. After a short while, Jikai could feel something pulling from the opposite end. Just as planned, Jinen was reeling in the rope. In this way, the old priest knew for sure that the boy was out of bed. The instant his end of the rope slid out of sight, Jikai smiled.

This method of preventing Jinen from oversleeping struck Satoko as terribly cruel. In contrast, Jikai's new habit of awaking early—and immediately engaging her in sex—did not bother her at all. Her body always seemed to be ready for him. When morning came, her lower half would gradually heat up, the sensation moving up her body until her chest burned uncomfortably. There were even times when she would take the lead and initiate intercourse herself. Each morning, the sounds of Jinen ringing the prayer bell, walking along the corridor and chanting before the statue of Idaten would accompany their lovemaking in the priest's quarters. It was customary for the recitation of the sutra to Idaten to finish at around six with the *Shariraimon*, and the lines gradually became committed to Satoko's memory:

*We worship you with single-minded devotion, Shakyamuni Tathagata, who embodies the ten thousand virtues. The remains of your original body are the Buddha nature, the eternal dharma, a towering shrine for the whole world. We bow in reverence before you. The Buddha appears in bodily form; we are one with the Buddha, the Buddha is one with us; all living things are in accord with the Buddha, and by the power of the Buddha's grace and mercy we may cast off illusion, know enlightenment . . .*

Satoko's body had grown stronger since she arrived at the Kohōan. She had even gained weight. Her delicate skin regained its youthful luster, and when she undressed she could see that her torso had lost a little of its hourglass shape. The muscles of her lower stomach had lost their definition and were beginning to soften. People said that she looked just like her mother, Rie, in the days when she would fan the fire in her husband's workshop while Isaburō prepared his *Mugiwara Poultice*. Rie, who had been robust and healthy, died of cholera when Satoko was six years old. She died in a quarantine hospital, lying in a bed with rusty metal fittings. Satoko, however, recalled her mother as she was when still in good health—buxom and good-looking. Satoko had definitely inherited her mother's genes.

Despite his increasingly sallow complexion, Jikai never went a day without making love to Satoko. He was capable of this in part because Satoko was a ready partner but, perhaps more importantly, because he felt immeasurable attraction for her and took tireless pleasure in exploring her body.

"For ten years, Nangaku always wanted you near him. Now I understand why, Sato," he told her, his voice husky with excitement. "You're my blessing, my true love."

He exploited every possible sexual technique to satisfy her powerful, burning urges. As soon as she was satisfied, she would fall asleep and awake an hour or so later, completely recovered as if nothing had happened.

.

The end of the rainy season meant the approach of O-Bon, when Jikai was expected to visit all of his patrons to offer prayers for the dead before the family altar. Every month, he paid calls on the especially devout to mark the anniversary of the death of a family member. But for O-Bon, it was customary for every family to open the doors of their Buddhist altars and wait for the services of a priest from the local temple. The recitation of the sutras would be scheduled only for August 15 and 16. Laity would call back the spirits of family members and past ancestors by removing their memorial tablets from the family altar and placing them in the tokonoma alcove, or on a shelf. Cucumbers, yams, tomatoes, dumplings, sweets, fruits and other items would be placed on lotus leaves and presented as offerings before them. Worship of the spirits would continue for seven days until Jizō Bon, which is celebrated in Kyoto on August 23 and 24. For small branch temples that did not receive a lot of financial support from the main temple, O-Bon was the busiest season for revenues.

The Kohōan had fifty-eight patrons. Most of them lived in either central Kyoto or in the vicinity of the cloth-making district of Nishijin. Jikai did not go around to visit all fifty-eight households himself. He arbitrarily designated the status of each one, dividing them into first, second and third classes. He would send Jinen around to the third-class households. Jinen was still copying out the *Kannon Sutra*, but he had already memorized the scriptures needed to perform the services for O-Bon. By now, Jikai had taught him the lines of all the sutras through oral recitation.

The main sutras and charms used for the parishioners were the *Heart Sutra*, the *Dharani of the Great Compassionate Heart*, the *Dharani to Eliminate Disasters and Promote Fortune*, the *Dharani of the Victorious Buddha Crown*, and the twenty-fifth chapter of the *Lotus Sutra*, which is known as the *Universal Gate of the Bodhisattva Kanzeon*, or *Kannon Sutra*. Because most services consisted of these scriptures and charms, Jinen was now required to copy out the *Kannon Sutra*.

One day in early July, Jikai called Jinen to his quarters.

"O-Bon is coming, and I'd like you to go perform some of the services like you did last year. Your white surplice must be spotless. Have you cleaned it?"

"Yes."

"How much of the *Kannon Sutra* have you finished copying?"

"I've done as far as the lines, 'The Bodhisattva Inexhaustible Mind said to the Buddha, "I ask you, World-honored One, possessor of all wonderful qualities, why is that son of the Buddha named Kanzeon Bosatsu?"

"Bring your copybook here." Jikai did not doubt Jinen; he just wanted to see how he was going about his work.

"Yes." Bowing his head to the tatami, Jinen stood and, pivoting on his right foot, executed an about-face—a move he had learned as part of his military training at school.

Soon, he returned to Jikai's room and handed over his copybook, which consisted of rough Japanese paper bound by a paper cord. Jinen had written on the cover: *Lotus Sutra. Chapter 25: The Universal Gate of the Bodhisattva Kanzeon. Copied by Jinen, servant of the Kohōan Temple.*

"Uh, hmmm . . ." Flipping through the copybook, Jikai flared the nostrils of his freckled nose, something he did whenever he was feeling self-satisfied. *Niji Mujinni Bosatsu—The Bodhisattva Inexhaustible Mind.* Jinen had written out the scripture carefully, letter by letter, using block characters in black ink. "Good, good," Jikai said, and made an expression to indicate he was in a mildly good mood.

Then he changed the subject.

"Is it true that you have to do military training at school?"

"Yes."

"What sort of things do you have to do? Tell me." Jikai's eyes were twinkling.

Jinen remained expressionless, only his deep-set eyes moved as he answered. "Everyone has to carry a Murata rifle. We're learning how to clean and fire a gun."

"Does a soldier come to school?"

"Yes. There's a special drill sergeant. He has three gold stripes on the shoulder of his uniform."

"Is he a teacher at the school?"

"Yes. He's like one of the teachers."

"And you have to carry a rifle, too?"

Jinen fell silent for a moment.

Jikai had asked because no matter what the training was called, he could not envision Jinen, who was just over four-feet tall, shouldering the same kind of rifle soldiers did.

"Well . . . I don't actually carry a Murata rifle."

Jikai's face relaxed.

"But I do have to carry a cavalryman's rifle."

"A cavalryman's rifle?" Jikai exclaimed.

"Yes. It's the kind cavalrymen carry on their backs. It's a little shorter than the other rifles. Still, it comes up above my shoulder." Jinen gestured at the shoulder of his work shirt. But he stared ahead, expressionless, avoiding eye contact with the priest.

Satoko, listening to their conversation from the side, was unable to gauge exactly what Jinen was thinking in the depths of his heart. He answered his master's questions but appeared to be thinking about something else. His coldness, his lack of affect, these were things Satoko had sensed in Jinen from the very beginning.

Jikai had spread open the front of his robes, exposing his knees so that he could sit on his haunches. But back toward his crotch, his swarthy testicles could also be seen dangling from his loose loincloth. Satoko tried to call it to his attention.

"Reverend! Reverend! Come over here!" Then, ignoring the boy, "You're exposing yourself! Jinen can see you!"

When Jikai finally understood, he quickly muttered, "Oh, I see," and pulled the front skirts of his robe together.

Even then, Jinen's expression did not change. Only the whites of his deep-set eyes flashed for the briefest moment.

*What a strong-willed child*, Satoko thought as she retied the priest's loose obi. *What a strange child. I don't understand what he's thinking at all.* And yet, the copy of the *Kannon Sutra* lying at Jikai's feet struck Satoko as remarkably accomplished.

It was from about this time that Satoko began to grow afraid of Jinen. Because Jikai was the boy's master, no matter how taciturn Jinen remained, the two of them were bound to one another by common circumstance. However, she could not fathom the hidden meaning of Jinen's silence. Whenever Jikai and Jinen were talking together, she felt all the more alienated. She wasn't jealous. Rather, she felt there was something the boy was hiding from her— something he would never reveal. At the same time, there was something in his look that suggested he was keeping a watch on all that she did.

.

During an especially hot night just before O-Bon, Satoko left the shoji doors leading into Jikai's room open. It was so hot, it was hard to sleep and she lay in bed wearing only a chemise. Jikai had been out all day. He had visited some patrons and then gone to the Genkōji, a sister temple of the Kohōan, to play Go with the head priest. When he finally came home just after one in the morning, he was very drunk. As always, Satoko put a bleached cotton undergarment around him and then had him put on short summer pajamas. He didn't even bother trying to tie the cords of his pajamas and was soon fondling the shoulder strap of Satoko's nightdress. Thinking it too hot to sleep anyway, Satoko removed her slip and lay there naked, as Jikai preferred her. As always, her body felt feverish and she was soaked in sweat. Satoko tried to stifle her cries, but as Jikai worked his lips below her waist, she reflexively cried out and thrashed her legs about the bed. Jikai, spurred by the effects of the alcohol, was more insistent than usual. As he pushed himself onto her, Satoko caught a glimpse of a dark shadow scurrying behind him. She had left the shoji open. The corridor had outer glass doors, and the light of the moon was shining on the surface of the pond in the garden. The reflected moonlight illuminated everything right up to the innumerable crossbeams of the eaves. She thought she heard a voice.

"Reverend?"

The voice was definitely the voice of the shadow in the corridor.

"Reverend? Did you call?"

Jikai instinctively released his hold on Satoko. "What is it?" he said, pulling together the front of his pajamas and stepping out into the hallway.

It was Jinen. "Didn't you call me? You pulled on the rope."

"You're still half-asleep. I didn't call you. I didn't call," Jikai said. "Now go on back to sleep!"

Satoko held her breath. Her legs must have caught on the rope and pulled it while she writhed in bed. "He saw us for sure. He's seen us again."

Satoko remembered the deep-set eyes in Jinen's enormous head, and at once the lower half of her body, which should have been burning hot, went slack and cold, as though all her strength had been drained away.

Jikai closed the shoji and in the darkness he called for her again.

# IV

Hasunuma Yoshinori, who taught at the Daitokuji middle school that Jinen attended in Murasakino, turned up at the Kohōan on July 12. It was an awkwardly timed visit. Jikai had caught a cold and was asleep when he arrived, and Jinen was forced to greet the visitor at the entryway. Upon seeing his teacher, the young acolyte blanched, yet he had no choice but to announce his arrival. Back in the priest's quarters, Jikai was lying under his futon in a feverish sweat, wrapped in a thick robe. Informed of his guest, he raised his drawn, unshaven face and said, "Bring him here."

Presently, Hasunuma appeared. He was a tall lanky man, about forty years of age. He had on a surplice of purple silk over his black robe. His hands touched the threshold as he bowed politely.

"I was asleep. What brings you here? Please, come in." Jikai had tried to assume a robust voice but was immediately overtaken by a fit of coughing.

Closing the doors that separated Jikai's room from her own, Satoko moved to the priest's bedside. After bowing low to Hasunuma, she began to leisurely study the visitor's face. She had sensed that he had come to talk about Jinen.

Hasunuma Yoshinori took a moment to sip his tea and then spoke deliberately. His voice was deep and he had a Tokyo accent. "It's about Jinen. I'm concerned about his poor attendance over the past term. He's missed twenty-five days. The school affairs section always takes absences into consideration when calculating grades for conduct, especially when there are no written excuses. Skipping twenty-five days, well . . . that's close to one-third of the entire school term. If he was absent because of temple duties and services with you, then we'd like you to start informing us of that in writing."

Jikai's and Satoko's eyes widened in surprise. Coughing violently, the priest said, "What are you telling us? That Jinen has been absent without permission? That's preposterous. He leaves the temple every day."

Satoko nodded broadly in agreement.

"So you're telling me that Jinen, on his own . . ." Hasunuma's expression changed.

"If he's been absent, then he did it on his own. What a complete waste of money, paying all that tuition!" Jikai's voice grew louder. "Sato, tell him to get over here now!"

Satoko was upset. She wondered if calling Jinen before his teacher was really for the best. She knew Jikai would scold the boy severely, and because she worried that his fever might worsen as a result, she considered trying to stop him. But when the priest was angry, he didn't listen to anyone.

"The stupid idiot! Hurry up and tell him to get over here!"

Satoko reluctantly stepped out to fetch the boy. Because he wasn't in his room, she walked along the corridor that skirted the main hall calling out his name, but he was nowhere to be seen. Slipping on her garden clogs, she went back toward the teahouse on the landscaped hill. She found him squatting among the cypress moss under the maple trees. He had brought out the box he used for disposing of weeds and was innocently pulling up the grass.

"Jinen!" Satoko called out. "The Reverend wants to talk to you."

"Yes, all right," he answered in a subdued voice and came to meet her.

"You skipped school without telling anyone, didn't you?" Satoko said as gently as she could. "The teacher came here to scold you."

"I hate military training!" he shot back. "It wears me out to carry a rifle." He looked at her pleadingly, his sunken eyes red and swollen. He had been crying again.

"You don't like the training?"

"No. Once I start carrying the rifle, I get really tired."

Jinen's expression became increasingly pathetic, and Satoko found herself feeling sorry for the boy. *Making such a small child carry a rifle . . . maybe they can't go against orders, but the school is behaving outrageously.* "Well, that may be," she finally said, "but the teacher is here and the Reverend is really angry. You'd better be getting over there."

"Okay," he said and flung his small bamboo blade down into the moss with such force that it pierced the ground. Vibrating there, the blade issued a humming twang that made it seem almost alive.

Satoko accompanied Jinen back to the priest's quarters, where Jikai and Hasunuma could be heard laughing and enjoying themselves. The moment Satoko and Jinen appeared, however, the two men fell quiet.

"Jinen." The priest was sitting up, his futon folded back behind him to provide support. "Why are you skipping school? Do you hate it that much? Monthly tuition costs me a lot. Explain yourself!"

After glancing awkwardly at Satoko, Hasunuma settled his gaze on Jinen. The boy was motionless except for a slight movement of the eyes. His face was stained with tears and grass.

"I don't like military training, Reverend. I feel like dying whenever they have military training."

"What do you mean by that?" Jikai stumbled over his words, his gaze also drifting unconsciously toward Satoko.

Hasunuma interjected. "You may not like it, but it's part of the curriculum now. The Ministry of Education requires it as part of middle school regulations. We can't do anything about it. Starting in the second year of middle school, all students have to learn to use a rifle as part of their military training. It's what we've been ordered to do."

It was unclear whether Hasunuma was directing his argument toward Jinen or Jikai, but he continued. "Military training counts for one course, and if you don't complete that course, you can't graduate. The comments of the drill sergeant are critical in deciding which students are promoted to the next grade."

Jinen turned his downcast face toward Jikai, and pleaded, "Reverend, please ask them to excuse me from having to carry a rifle. The rifle comes up past my shoulder, and I can't carry it very easily."

"Ah-hah," Hasunuma murmured to himself. "Just as I thought. That's the reason, isn't it?"

He turned to face Jikai. "I often watch the second-year students training in the schoolyard from my window, and I know very well that Jinen is much smaller than the others. He's always lined up at the very end. When the students march in formation and everyone shifts to face right or left, Jinen is the only one who has to move at double time to keep up. Whenever I see that, I feel sorry for him. It's easy for the tall ones on the far right to keep up regardless of which direction they are commanded to go, but Jinen is off on the far

left, and he can only stay even with the line by running. It's even harder for
him when he has to shoulder a rifle. Nonetheless, he is going to have to put up
with it for the time being. After all, he'll grow bigger soon enough, right?"

Hasunuma turned again to face Jinen and said simply, "As a middle school
student, you have to complete the entire course of study."

Satoko, who had been following the conversation carefully, felt that she
understood Jinen's dislike of military training. His body was not big enough
to handle a rifle the same way the other students could. The middle school
curriculum assumed a standard height for all students when they created
their manuals, but Jinen was only as tall as a third-grader in primary school.

"We understand, we understand," Jikai said in a booming voice. "Jinen,
starting tomorrow you have to work at your training. It would be a waste
of tuition if you couldn't finish middle school. If you don't finish, you can't
become a priest. Understand? So be strong and stop skipping school! Got it?!"
Overcome by a chill, Jikai excused himself and reclined back in bed.

Jinen sat there crying in a corner of the corridor. Hasunuma regarded
him coldly, his expression conveying his annoyance at having to deal with a
troublesome student. To sympathize with the boy was pointless. There was no
budget to create a special class for the sake of just one child.

"Until he gets taller, he'll just have to put up with it. I'd like to have him
at school," Hasunuma said. Bowing to Satoko and Jikai, he stood up. "I'm
sorry to have disturbed you when you are not well. So long as there are no
problems with attendance, I expect his grades to be excellent. Jinen is a flaw-
less student. Please encourage him not to skip class."

Hasunuma aimed to mollify the situation with this final bland exhorta-
tion, but after the teacher left the room, Jikai's fever went up. Nothing more
was said to Jinen.

After seeing Hasunuma out, Satoko made her way back along the corridor
toward the rear of the main hall. The section of the hall that housed the altar of
the inner sanctum jutted out toward the back, creating a storage space beneath
it in which the banners used at the service for departed spirits, the platform for
the Jizō Bon and various other items were heaped in a jumble. Stepping into
the shadow cast by this rear section of the hall, Satoko glanced nonchalantly
toward the garden and was stopped cold.

Jinen was standing stock-still on the island in the middle of the pond.
Satoko had come around the back way thinking she might find him weeding
on the hill beside the teahouse. But there he was, staring intently at the
surface of the water. The burbling sounds had evidently drowned out Sato-

ko's approaching footsteps, because Jinen seemed oblivious to her presence. Pale green leaves of water chestnut floated on the pond, and the plant's spiky fruit could be seen bobbing here and there. Satoko wondered what Jinen was looking at. Was it the carp? All at once, the boy raised his arm above his head and hurled something into the pond. Jinen's enormous head trembled violently as he stared fixedly on the point of impact. Satoko squatted down in the corridor and looked on from afar. Then she saw it, and a cry nearly escaped her lips. A large gray carp was thrashing about in the water, a small bamboo blade protruding from its back. The blade plowed through the leaves of the water chestnut, sending the whirligig beetles flying. The fish was more than a foot long, and blood oozed from its wound, flowing in lines that looked like red woolen thread floating on the surface.

Satoko was on the verge of shouting at the boy, but she stopped herself. *What a frightening child*, she thought. *There's no telling what he'll do.*

She stealthily moved through the corridor along the side of the main hall and returned to the head priest's residence. Jikai had pushed aside the damp towel that had been placed on his perspiring forehead and was now snoring.

Satoko never told Jikai about what she had witnessed. She decided that Jinen had simply directed at the carp all the pent-up rage he felt for the teacher who had exposed his truancy.

Jinen was completely alone at the Kohōan. Even if he wanted to, there was no one to whom he could vent his frustrations. If he raised his voice, Jikai would scold him. He could only face the wall and fade away. His single solace was to cry under the maple trees below the landscaped hill. Satoko's heart ached for the boy. She truly felt sorry for him and again found herself trying to imagine what his life had been like back when he was still called Sutekichi.

All that Satoko knew was that he was the son of a temple carpenter in Wakasa. To rid herself of her fear of the boy, she wanted to learn everything there was to know about him. Whenever she had the opportunity, she would ask Jikai about Jinen's home in the country. The priest, however, did not seem to know very much. To him, Jinen was just a small boy with a big head.

How did the woman who gave birth to this child feel when she sent him off to the temple, Satoko wondered. She wanted to see his mother's face. More than that, she wanted to know what Jinen was like when he still lived at home. Was he sullen and withdrawn then, too? Did he make that devious expression? Did he look at people with that upward glance as he did at the Kohōan? Satoko became obsessed with finding out about Jinen's past.

Just after O-Bon, when the first autumn breezes were beginning to blow, a letter arrived at the temple bringing news that was better than anything she could have wished for. It was sent by Kida Mokudō, who was head priest of the Seianji temple, which was located in the hamlet of Sokokura, in the village of Hongō, Ōi County, Fukui Prefecture. The letter was addressed to the Reverend Jikai, so Satoko could not open it herself. The priest told her about it.

"Sato, the priest from the Seianji is coming."

"Is he coming on business?" she asked.

"He has things to take care of at the main temple."

"Where will he be staying?"

"He'll stay up at the main temple," said Jikai, misunderstanding the point of her question. "There are branch temples affiliated with the Seianji on the grounds there, so you don't have to worry about anything."

"Reverend?" Satoko asked. "He's the priest who brought Jinen here, isn't he?"

"Yes, he's the one. It's been four years now. I'm sure he'll want to see him."

Jinen's father lived in the same village as the Seianji temple, and it was the Seianji priest who had recommended that the carpenter help refurbish the main temple of the Tōzenji. It was through that connection that Jinen had eventually been brought to the Kohōan.

"He's sure to visit here when he arrives," Jikai said. "He likes to drink. When he does drop by, you can drink with us."

Satoko waited impatiently for that day to arrive.

Three days later, Kida Mokudō made his appearance. Tucking the hems of his robes into his obi and pulling his yellow silk gauze skirt up to his knees, he entered the temple grounds with long strides, his hairy shins exposed. Satoko was surprised to see how much younger the priest was than she had imagined. He was just forty-four years old. She was told that he had left the Zen training monastery of the Kenninji temple fourteen years earlier to take over the Seianji in Wakasa. He was also the secretary of his village's record office. With his high-bridged nose and wide forehead, he had an intelligent-looking face. But it was these clean-cut features that made his overall countrified manner and appearance all the more conspicuous.

As soon as Mokudō stepped into the entrance hall, he did not try to disguise his feeling of excitement when he saw the disciple Jinen, who had come out to meet him.

"Sute, Sute, how big you've grown!"

Jinen had placed his hands on the wooden floor and, with his usual absence of expression, turned his gaze up toward Mokudō's tanned face. "Oh," he said with an air of surprise, "it's the reverend from the village . . ." The boy's expression revealed no hint of how he felt on being addressed as Sutekichi.

Mokudō could see that Sutekichi—now "Jinen"—had endured a great deal of hardship and grown into a young man during his time at the temple. He also saw that he had developed remarkable reserve.

"Your mother and father are well, Sute, so don't worry about them," the priest said. Then, standing just inside the door and carefully eyeing the interior, he reached into his mendicant's pouch and quickly pulled out an envelope and a square object wrapped in paper.

"The package is from your mother and the letter is from your father, Kanji," he said. "And this," the priest whispered into Jinen's ear, which looked like a small shiitake mushroom sprouting from his head, "this is just a whim of mine . . . some money for you. One yen."

Mokudō raised his pouch with a jingle and pulled out two silver fifty-sen coins. Rubbing them together between his thumb and forefinger, he placed them in Jinen's hand as the boy knelt there impassively.

"Now, then, could you tell the Reverend that I've arrived?"

Satoko and Jikai beamed with delight at the arrival of their rare guest. Jikai came out to meet him in the corridor that ran from the entryway back to the priest's quarters. He was grinning like a child, excited to have a drinking companion come to visit.

Mokudō bowed three times upon entering Jikai's room. He placed his hands on the floor and bowed so low that his head almost touched the tatami. Observing the formalities of a Zen temple, Mokudō's actions acknowledged the superior status of Jikai. As the Kohōan priest had studied under the venerable Kigakutsu Dokuseki at the Zen training monastery of the main temple, it was natural for a young priest from the countryside to believe he had reached the rank of a master.

Jinen set out the New Zealand spinach with ground sesame and the tofu broth he had prepared. Jikai and Mokudō began drinking, and Satoko joined them, keeping the priests supplied with food and drink.

As the alcohol began to take effect and Satoko began to fret that her eyes were flushed from drinking, she finally broached the topic of Jinen. "He's really grown up, hasn't he?" she asked the visitor.

"He certainly has. Thanks to you, missus, he's well behaved. He's become

a fine young man. I could hardly believe my eyes when I saw him." Mokudō
bowed his head several times to indicate his gratitude.

"He completed the ordination ceremony last fall," Jikai told him.

"Is that right?"

"He's performed funerals and prayers for the dead at O-Bon. He can even
perform memorial services, and he's excellent at memorizing sutras." Jikai's
voice suddenly dropped a note. "Still, it's not clear if he'll be able to graduate
from middle school."

"Why is that?" Mokudō's expression became one of concern.

"He hates military training. He skips school on days when training is
scheduled. He's got a troublesome disposition."

Mokudō didn't seem to understand. His face darkened as Satoko explained it
for him.

"He's causing you trouble, isn't he?"

Satoko could sense that his thoughts had drifted elsewhere. *Something
happened to the boy back in his home village,* she thought. *That's why he is so
quiet all the time. Something made him sullen.*

"Reverend Mokudō, if you don't mind, would you please tell us about
Jinen when he was little? We really ought to hear about him from you. If we
don't learn about his background, we may have problems when he gets older."

Mokudō drained his sake cup and lowered his voice. "He's a peculiar boy,"
he said. "You see, he was abandoned in the Amidadō."

Satoko paled as she saw a smile cross Jikai's face. *Had he known all along?*
"Is that true? Did you know about that, Reverend?"

"Me?" Jikai said, reaching for the flask of sake. His tone indicated that he
found the whole story bothersome. "He was abandoned. That's why he was
named *Sute*kichi—*sute*, abandoned. Get it? Sato? Is there something wrong?"

# V

"The Amidadō is in Kojikidani, on the western end of the hamlet of Sokokura. Beggars use it as a shelter during the winter. A large wooden statue of Amida is enshrined there, and worshippers leave offerings of food in front of it. The beggars are hungry, and so they gather there . . ."

Although Mokudō kept glancing worriedly in the direction of Jinen's room, his voice grew louder as he got caught up in the story.

"Among the beggars was a young woman—about twenty-two, twenty-three years old. Her name was Okiku. Every autumn, she would come collect the pounded rice cakes that had been left as offerings. Well, one time, this young woman turned up pregnant. It snowed heavily that year, and she ended up giving birth in the shrine. People in the village made a big fuss about it, bringing in quilts and boiling water. She gave birth to a boy."

Satoko listened intently, her face a pale white.

"No one knew who the father was. It might have been some young man from the village, or it could have been one of the widowers, but no one would come forward. It was a real problem. Because Okiku was a beggar, she would have to go somewhere else in the spring to beg. People began to wonder who would look after the baby when, by chance, Mr. Kaku stopped by on his way home from a worksite. 'Very well then, leave it to me,' he immediately informed his wife. 'We'll just have to look after him.'"

Jikai smiled, pretending to show interest in the story; but he was drinking heavily and every now and then would cast a worried eye on the sake flask. Satoko, for her part, was eager to hear more. "So what happened then?" she pressed.

"What do you think happened? Mr. Kaku already had four children. And when he brought the infant home, it made for two babies in his house at the same time. His wife told him that it made no difference how many children they had, she didn't want to raise a beggar's child."

"So what did he do?"

"Well, Mr. Kaku is very manly, so he managed to persuade her. The problem, you see, was that during the winter Okiku had slept in a clutter of dirty quilts in the Amidadō, keeping the baby's head pressed up against her the whole time. Maybe she did that because it was cold. In any case, there was no reason for her to let go of him, because he hadn't been weaned yet. But because she held him like that while she slept, his head became misshapen."

"They call it a mallet head, right?" Satoko asked.

"Mallet head? In our village, you know, the kids called it a 'battleship head.' They really bullied him. He did well at school and was a good kid . . . At some point, though, he took a dislike to his name—Sutekichi—and kept asking his father to change it."

Satoko began to feel she could finally understand the boy. Although her face had grown paler as the story unraveled, she felt a sense of satisfaction at finally being able to hear it.

"He was abandoned, so the name's good enough for him," cut in Jikai, who had become more and more drunk as the story progressed. "There's nothing wrong with it, is there Mokudō?" He looked directly at Satoko as he spoke, and she felt her chest go tight.

"Tell me, Reverend Mokudō," Satoko said, lowering her voice, "does the boy think of Mrs. Kaku as his real mother?"

"He does think of her that way," he said. "She raised him as if he were one of her own. The hardest thing for her to deal with was that his head was so big and his body so small . . . but he was the cleverest kid in the village."

"Is that so?" Satoko wondered aloud. She had heard the phrase "orphans of the storm" before, but Jinen, it turned out, was the real thing. She recalled the time on the veranda of the teahouse when she had told him of the days when her father had sold his *Mugiwara Poultice*. She remembered that Jinen had merely listened and looked on in silence. The hardships Satoko had endured were a dime a dozen. She had had both a father and a mother. Jinen had neither.

"Did the beggar, Okiku, ever come back after that?"

The priest of the Seianji wiped the corners of his mouth with the back of his hand and continued. "I never saw her after she left. I heard that Jinen's mother had scolded Okiku. Said that if she was going to raise Jinen the same as her own kids, Okiku couldn't come back to the village for rice cakes. After that, Okiku didn't show herself anymore. She never came back to beg. Not in the spring and not in the summer. She was only a beggar, but Sutekichi was her only child. Don't you think it's kind of sad?"

Large teardrops were falling from Satoko's eyes.

At that moment, a small bell could be heard ringing down the corridor. The hour had come for Jinen to perform the evening prayers to Idaten.

That night, instead of reaching out for Satoko's body as usual, Jikai fell asleep right away. Satoko, however, was restless. She couldn't get the story of Jinen's birth and childhood out of her head. It had shattered all her preconceptions about the boy. His enormous head, his protruding brow, the way he rolled back his eyes, exposing their whites—these things were naturally repellent, but now they possessed a sorrow that endeared him to her. Satoko quietly removed herself from Jikai's side and stepped out of the priest's quarters. She was curious to see what Jinen was doing in his little room. He was probably already asleep, she thought, but if he were still up, she wanted to try to talk with him. Moving stealthily along the corridor, she stood outside his door. A light was on, and Satoko peeked inside. Jinen was sitting on the tatami mat. He was facing his small desk, copying a sutra.

"Jinen? Are you still up?" She moved to his side.

Startled, Jinen turned. Seeing her standing over him, he quickly set his writing brush down and stared up into her face.

"Why are you looking at me like that?" She settled herself down next to him. "Jinen?"

Satoko felt a sweet affection for the boy welling up inside her breast. Unable to control her feelings, she abruptly embraced him, reaching her arms under his own and around his back. "Jinen, I feel so sorry for you. I heard all about you tonight," she gently sobbed.

Jinen shifted his head above her plump white breasts and remained fixed there. His eyes were moist with tears. Satoko quietly cradled him on her lap. Then his face rubbed against her body. It smelled of perspiration and Satoko found herself overtaken by a violent passion. She pressed the boy's face to her breasts. "I'll give you anything," she told him. "I'll give you all I have."

At that moment, Jinen's whole body suddenly gathered strength and he pushed Satoko down against the floor. The wind had picked up outside the lattice window and the leaves in the garden trees began to rustle loudly.

.

Jikai's cold worsened. He finally emerged from bed ten days after the Reverend Mokudō returned home to the Seianji. The first anniversary of the death of Nangaku—October 20—arrived soon after, just as the maples in the garden and on the mountainside were beginning to display their gorgeous autumn colors.

Nangaku's wife, Kishimoto Hideko, accompanied the disciple Nansō to the Kohōan that day, and the two paid a quiet visit to the main hall. Instructing Satoko not to show herself, Jikai brought out Nangaku's tablet from the memorial hall and placed it on a brocade mat on top of the ordination platform. He burned incense and chanted a sutra. Despite his recent recovery from illness, he was interrupted every now and then by a fit of coughing. To Nansō and Hideko, the priest's face seemed drawn and tired compared to a year earlier. He had taken pains to shave, but there was no disguising how ill he looked.

Jikai sat on a large, dark red cushion in the sanctum. Jinen sat on the small assistant's cushion, nodding his head in time with each strike of the large wooden gong, which was carved with fish. Just as Jikai finished chanting the memorial service, the sun broke through the clouds and shone on the white gravel of the garden. The interior of the main hall brightened.

Memories of his master flooded over Nansō as he and Hideko strolled through the hall, gazing leisurely at the four-panel *fusuma* leading off to the chambers adjoining the inner sanctum. "Every time I see them, the geese seem to be alive," he said. Then he stopped and turned to Jikai. "Reverend, how long did Master Nangaku stay here?"

"Well, let's see . . ." Jikai tilted his head and switched the small bell he was carrying from one hand to the other. "He was here for ten years, I suppose," he answered nonchalantly.

"Ten years . . . was it that long?"

"He borrowed this place for ten years?" Hideko cut in.

"He always said how good the Kohōan was for him. All he ever talked about was what a great place it was."

Hideko had been five years younger than Nangaku, so she was still only in her early sixties. Jikai gazed upon her profile, taking in her oval face and broad nose. It seemed that her round cheeks had somehow become even fuller than they were when Nangaku was alive. "You haven't changed a bit," he told her.

Hideko pulled a handkerchief from the sleeve of her funeral kimono and restlessly dabbed at her forehead. She had once been a woman of the Gion district. The carefree Nangaku would go about looking for women at random—a waitress, a geisha. He would bring them back to his house, then break up with them soon after. He chose all his women at second-class establishments. Hideko had been a geisha at the Toyokawa in Higashi Shinchi in Yasakashita. She stayed with Nangaku until the end. Because Jikai had known the Hideko of old, seeing her this way now made him think they had certainly gone back a long time.

"You haven't changed a bit either, Reverend," Hideko replied. "It's nice that you're in good health."

Nansō and Hideko left the main hall and made their way toward the Kohōan's graveyard, which was located just beneath Mt. Kinugasa. Jinen walked ahead to show them the way. He was carrying a bucket and some incense, and smoke trailed behind him. Seeing the diminutive Jinen and his battleship head, Nansō thought back to the day before his master's death. In his mind, he could still see the suffering in Nangaku's face as he had called out the name "Sato."

Evergreen ferns with silvery white undersides grew in profusion under the small pines that lined the edge of the graveyard, and damp leaves covered the ground. With the party's approach, a jay went darting into the sky. Nansō and Hideko listened to the clear resonance of Jinen's voice reciting the service at the graveside. Nangaku's headstone had been set in place on the day of his interment. It was a tall, natural rock, with greenish-blue moss already forming in the spaces where the characters of his name had been carved into the stone:

**Shūgakuin nantō ikken koji.**

Hideko murmured a *nembutsu* prayer—"*Namu Amida Butsu, Namu Amida Butsu*"—as she poured water from the bucket over the top of the stone.

When the service was finished, Kishimoto Hideko walked back toward the temple, weaving her way among the gravestones, with their wooden memorial tablets standing erect. As she walked, she turned to Jinen and asked, "Jinen, does the Reverend have a wife?"

The boy said nothing. He simply shook his mallet head. The way he fixed his deep-set eyes upon her, however, startled Hideko. She felt it was a sign of reproach. The rest of the way to the Kohōan, she followed Jinen in total silence.

"What an odd young priest," she remarked to Nansō after they returned to Maruta-machi. The unpleasantness she felt over his lack of response had stayed with her all the way home. "I really dislike that weird boy."

Nansō, listening in silence, thought that while Hideko's censure of the boy was in part a veiled criticism of Jikai, the real target of her criticism was in fact Satoko, who had remained hidden away in the priest's quarters.

.

Hisama Heikichi's home stood just to the east of Imadegawa Senbon in Kamigyō Ward. Heikichi was a patron of the Kohōan, and Jikai, according to his own classification system, had assigned him to second-class status. On November 7, the third anniversary of the death of Heikichi's father, a messenger from the Hisama household arrived at the temple and requested a memorial service. After the messenger's departure, Jikai called for Jinen.

"You'll need to go to the Hisama's for a service. I have to go to the Genkōji."

Jinen nodded without a word.

"To do the memorial service, you'll need to read the *Dharani of the Great Compassionate Heart*, the *Offerings to the Spirits of the Dead*, and the *Kannon Sutra*. You can end with the *Dharani to Avoid Calamities and Ensure Fortune*."

Jikai led Jinen to the main hall. He pulled out the registry of deceased patrons from a drawer in the assistant priest's desk. Shuffling through the pages, he looked up the posthumous name of Hisama Heitarō, who had died two years earlier. A thick bound volume decorated with gold dust, the registry was organized according to date of death. Each *kaimyō*, or posthumous name, was given a particular designation—*koji* for patrons who had done merito-rious service or who had made a gift to the temple; *shinji* for male believers; and *shinnyo* for female believers. Licking his fingers, Jikai flipped through the pages.

"Ah, here. Here it is . . . This one. You have to memorize this well," said Jikai. He pointed to the name:

**Hōkō chisan koji.**

"Got it? Try reading the name."

"Hō-kō-chi-san-ko-ji," Jinen said mechanically. He continued mumbling the name repeatedly under his breath.

Jinen left just after two o'clock. From the Kohōan, he passed through the woods behind the Tōjiin temple and then walked along the perimeter of the Tōa Cinema film set until he came out into Hakubai-chō. Cutting across Kitano Tenjin, he walked along Kamishichiken and soon arrived at Senbon Imadegawa. Jinen was short, but he walked relatively fast. It seemed that his quick gait was an attempt to compensate for his feelings of inferiority. Jinen could walk from Mt. Kinugasa to Senbon in only thirty minutes, less time than it would take an adult. With his short, quick steps, black robe and protruding forehead, it was no wonder he attracted the attention of the neighborhood residents.

"What a sight! See that odd-looking little priest walking along there?" passersby would exclaim to one another.

Jinen was used to being stared at on the street. During O-Bon, he would have to perform services for as many as ten patrons a day. If he had allowed the stares to bother him, he would have never been able to set out each morning to visit even a single household. On the days he attended school in Murasakino, he was even more conspicuous by the gaiters he was forced to wear with his stiff-collared robe. Still, the sight of the tiny middle-school student had already become familiar to the people along that route. On this day's outing to Senbon, Jinen walked along without glancing left or right. The stares of derision he felt upon him just made him walk all the faster.

The Hisamas sold painting supplies wholesale. Their shop faced the city tramline on Imadegawa Avenue, and their residence was located in back. When Hisama Heikichi saw the acolyte rather than the priest come through the shop doors, he wondered what had happened. Hisama knew that Jikai divided his parishioners into classes. Did Jinen's arrival mean that the family had fallen from top rank? With a look that expressed his dissatisfaction, Heikichi called out to Jinen, halting him as he made his way through the shop and toward the family altar.

"Where's the Reverend Jikai?"

"He's at home in bed."

Saying nothing more, Jinen disappeared into the interior. After a short while, his voice could be heard chanting the prayers. To reach the altar, Jinen had to pass by the pale, recumbent figure of Heikichi's older brother, Heizaburō. Heizaburō was dying of tuberculosis. Lying in an interior room with little exposure to sunlight, the patient listened to Jinen's recitation with his eyes closed.

Heikichi followed in shortly after Jinen. He had wrapped up an offering and some sweets, placed them on a tray, then sat down and waited. When it came time to recite the *Kannon Sutra*, Jinen reached into the breast pocket of his kimono and took out his copybook. Because he had to read the passages, the service took an inordinately long time. Even though Heikichi thought the boy was careful and courteous in his delivery, he did not feel the same gratitude toward him he would have felt had Jikai been giving the service. His wife was out running errands, and Heikichi had to watch over not only his dying brother, but the shop as well. He began to feel irritable and impatient.

When at last Jinen finished his chanting, he tapped on the bell and turned around. In the interior room, the patient stirred slightly, drawing his attention. According to gossip he had heard from Jikai, Heizaburō had already twice coughed up blood and the doctors had given up hope of recovery. The patient began to snore loudly. Jinen could hear the raspy, strangling noise of air passing through his throat.

"He's been unconscious like that for three days now," Heikichi said with weary resignation, his hands resting on his knees.

Jinen gazed upon the figure of Heizaburō lying amid the paint cans stored in the room. He was thin, in his forties and had a light grey quilt pulled over him, his despairing face directed toward the ceiling. Then, suddenly, as if he'd just remembered something, Jinen said, "The Reverend told me that he wanted to undertake ascetic training."

"The Reverend Jikai?"

Thinking it a strange thing for Jinen to say, Heikichi wondered if he had heard correctly. Heikichi was a devout believer, and he had learned from his late father that Jikai was an exceptionally accomplished priest, even within the Tōzenji sect. The Kohōan had a special designation that put it in the upper tier of branch temples. It did not attract tourists like the Kinkakuji or Ginkakuji, but it stood alongside the Ryōanji and the Tōjiin at the foot of Mt. Kinugasa, and its history was long. Musō Kokushi had founded the temple, and its high status was a source of pride. What could it mean that the priest of such a temple would want to undertake ascetic training?

"So he wants to study, huh?" Heikichi did not know how else to interpret Jinen's words. "What are you going to do, then?"

"I'd like to leave middle school as soon as I can and enter a Zen training monastery."

"Really? A training monastery is a pretty severe place. Even when it's cold, you have to wander around begging for money or sit outside in meditation. Whenever I see a priest adhering to these disciplines, I feel sorry for him. It's hard training to be a priest, isn't it?"

Heikichi thought that if a priest underwent the rigors of ascetic training, wandering and begging, he would attain enlightenment and become a head priest. As Jikai was already a head priest, what kind of hardships would he have to endure if he undertook such training now? It was hard for Heikichi to fathom. "When you get back, give my regards to the Reverend," he said.

Heikichi accompanied Jinen back through the shop at the front of the residence. Just as the boy was stepping across the threshold and into the street where the tramline ran, Heikichi suddenly called him back. Bending at the waist, he whispered in the boy's ear, "My brother will soon pass away. When he dies, we'll have to have another funeral. Please ask the Reverend to conduct the service for us."

Jinen fixed his expressionless eyes on the asphalt of the road and said nothing. From behind him could be heard the sound of a pushcart vendor selling roasted sweet potatoes. The vendor elongated the syllables as he called out the name of his product—"*Yakiii–imooo.*" Jinen cocked his head in the direction of the voice and set off trailing after the cart.

On the near side of the intersection between Imadegawa and Senbon avenues was a cutlery shop, Kikukawa Hardware. Inside the shop sat the owner's wife, who was about thirty. When the large-headed novice suddenly emerged from behind the sweet potato cart, she was startled. Jinen had stopped directly in front of the store, standing and staring at the array of knives, sickles, and scissors, their blades glinting under the setting sun.

"Ahh . . . welcome," the shopkeeper said. She assumed Jinen was a customer from the temple, and her practiced eyes informed her he was looking to buy something.

Pointing to a pocketknife, Jinen said in a small voice, "This one."

"All right, then," she said. She imagined him using the blade to sharpen his pencils. "That'll be twenty-three sen."

Jinen's demeanor remained meekly obedient but his eyes flashed ever so slightly. He thrust his hand into his pilgrim's pouch and quickly pulled out a silver fifty-sen coin. It was part of the money he had received from the head priest of the Seianji.

.

As night approached, Satoko went out into the corridor that ran behind the main hall to take in the mountain scenery. Jikai had just left to play Go at the Genkōji, and she found herself mulling over the events of that afternoon. Just after Jinen had departed for Imadegawa, Jikai had returned to his quarters and stripped Satoko naked. His desire was understandable because he had been sick for so long, and her body had quickly responded. Sweating more than usual, Jikai finished quickly. He allowed Satoko to put her kimono back on and then changed into his best white robes, as if preparing to go out. Satoko usually took his robes and things from the drawers for him, but this time Jikai briskly pulled them out himself.

"What's the occasion, is there a blue moon tonight?" she joked. But as she gazed into her hand mirror, rearranging her tousled hair, the question started to nag at her. *Why, this one time only, would Jikai take his clothes from the drawer and dress himself?* Her puzzlement, however, was easily resolved. Jikai had been rough with her in bed. When she pleaded with him, as she always did when his lovemaking became too aggressive, he relaxed his grip and handled her less forcefully. His dressing on his own was probably a gesture of consideration to Satoko, who was exhausted. At least, that's how she interpreted it.

From the rear corridor of the main hall, Satoko gazed up at the late autumn scenery of Mt. Kinugasa. She truly loved this view of the mountain. It was at this very spot that Kishimoto Nangaku would tickle her ears while describing the mountain's beauty.

It was said that no matter how much time came to pass, black pines would never grow on the thickly wooded mountainside. And, indeed, only small pines with reddish trunks dotted the slope all the way up to its rounded summit. At the base of the mountain was a covering of evergreens, as well as a sparse stand of deciduous trees, their delicate branches bare of leaves. Soon, the fog would come rolling down.

Satoko stared up at the lone chinquapin at the mountain's base and saw a kite perched atop it. Could it be the same kite from before? Satoko got the feeling that when she and Nangaku were at that same spot ten years earlier, a kite just like it had been perched there, looking over the temple garden. As Satoko watched, the bird flew off and spiraled languidly up into the sky. Then it quickly returned to its perch atop the chinquapin, and sat there perfectly still.

Satoko heard the sound of someone approaching from the entrance hall. It sounded like Jinen's shuffling footsteps, but she kept her gaze fixed toward the mountain. Jinen had changed into patched black trousers and a work shirt that had once belonged to the Reverend Jikai. The priest had worn the garment as an undershirt when he was a novice, and it was now re-sewn together like patchwork. The pattern of lines formed by the stitches made it look like one of those jackets worn for judo practice.

"You're back early," Satoko said. "I was just watching that kite."

"Kite?" Jinen looked toward the mountain. "Ma'am, do you know what that kite is doing?"

"What's it doing? It's just sitting there, not doing anything." Satoko took a sidelong glance at Jinen. He was being oddly talkative. "But since you asked," she said, "just what is it doing?"

Jinen chuckled softly. "That kite? It stores things up there."

Satoko found it an odd thing to say. "What do you mean it stores things?"

"There's a big hole in the top of the tree. It looks like a dark urn. The other day, on my way to school, I climbed up and peeked inside."

"You climbed that tree?"

Satoko was actually more shocked to learn of the urn-like hole at the top of the tree. She felt tempted to plug her ears and stop listening, but Jinen continued on innocently.

"When I climbed up there to have a look, I found this big hole at the top—just like an urn. The bottom of it is completely dark. I stared inside and could make out some things moving inside. Lots of snakes and fish and mice squirming around. The snakes were red and white. The kite had only half-killed them before dumping them there."

*So perched motionless atop the withered chinquapin, the kite was staring down the hole at its captured prey. The bird had filled the hollow of the tree with dying mice and fish. Half-dead snakes were wriggling among them.* Satoko squeezed her eyes shut and cried, "Stop it! You're scaring me. It sounds horrible. Stop it!"

Her voice threaded its way through the autumn leaves and limbs of the trees and echoed off the mountainside. When she finally collected herself, she realized that Jinen was gone. She could just see his head moving about the garden before it disappeared behind the landscaped hill.

Whenever he went to the Genkōji, where his host served him sake, Jikai always stayed out late. Alone, Satoko shut herself up in her room that night but couldn't clear her mind of Jinen's story. Visions of snakes writhing in the hole atop the tree kept flashing in her mind. It made her so sick that she had to spit out her food during dinner, but then the sight of it back in her bowl made her feel even queasier. *What a disgusting thing for Jinen to tell me about,* she thought.

Satoko tried to read the paper and then a magazine, but she could not escape the image of the kite. She wondered if Jinen had told her the story to bully her. *Had the events of that evening in his room somehow affected his mind?* Thinking it over, Satoko deeply regretted her actions. She had behaved insanely. What she had done was not proper at all. She made a silent vow to never do it again.

Even though it was past midnight, Satoko could not sleep. At a moment like this, she needed the Reverend to be with her. She felt so alone. The wind had picked up during the evening. The back door began to rattle. Because Mt. Kinugasa was small, the groves behind the Kohōan were in the direct path of the wind, and the trees swayed and bent.

One o'clock. Two o'clock. Satoko heard the chime for three, but Jikai still failed to return.

Kitami Jikai disappeared from the Kohōan that day. Satoko had been the last person at the temple to see him. After their lovemaking that afternoon, she simply watched from behind as he pulled his things from the drawers and prepared to leave.

# VI

November 8 was an eventful day in and around the Kohōan. Jikai was still missing, and Satoko was in an ill humor. She had a terrible headache and took all of her anger out on Jinen. No matter how late Jikai had stayed out before, he inevitably turned up. It didn't matter whether he was calling on a parishioner or going out for drinks, he always returned by two. And whenever he planned to stay overnight somewhere, he would tell Satoko in advance. For that reason, she was certain that Jikai's failure to return meant that the unthinkable had happened. If there had been an accident, the head priest at the Genkōji would surely have sent word. And even if the hard-drinking priest had suffered a stroke on the way home, then surely the hospital or a passerby would have reported it. Yet by noon the next day, she had heard no word from anyone.

"Jinen. What did the Reverend say to you when he left?" Satoko asked the boy harshly.

"I don't know. He called me to the main hall and talked to me about the training monastery."

"When was that?"

"Just before I went to Mr. Hisama's place to do the memorial service."

"And after he spoke about the monastery, did he say anything else?"

"He said that, in order to become a priest, I'd have to undergo ascetic training by shutting myself away to fast and meditate. He said that I should persevere until they let me become a priest."

What a peculiar thing for Jikai to talk about, Satoko thought, recalling the stories he had once told her in bed about the life of a priest in training.

"That's all he said?"

"He looked up Hisama's posthumous name for me."

"And after that?"

"He told me to recite the *Dharani of the Great Compassionate Heart* and the *Prayer for the Spirits of the Dead*. Then he told me it was all right for me to read the *Kannon Sutra* from my copybook. I left at two and don't know what happened after that."

Jinen turned to face Satoko, his eyes shining beneath his protruding forehead. His look made her cringe. Yesterday, after Jinen had left, Jikai had made her undress and have sex. She had the feeling that Jinen had seen them. *Don't be foolish*, she told herself. *He couldn't possibly have seen anything. The boy went off to Imadegawa to perform the memorial service, didn't he? While he was out, it was just the two of us here. No one could have known.*

Jinen was still glaring at Satoko as if he could read her thoughts.

"I'm sorry, but could you go and check with the priest at the Genkōji for me? Ask him what the Reverend said to him when they finished playing Go."

"Okay," Jinen said, blanching slightly.

Just as the boy seemed ready to leave, the chain on the wicket rattled and footsteps could be heard approaching. Hisama Heikichi was standing just outside the entryway when Jinen came out to greet the visitor. The boy knelt before Heikichi on the wooden floorboards.

"Is the Reverend in?" Heikichi asked.

"He's out," Jinen answered.

"Where—Ah, well, thank you for yesterday," Heikichi faltered, bowing his head. "As expected, my brother passed away. This morning. A peaceful death. We would like to have the funeral tomorrow afternoon. Please ask the Reverend for me."

Heikichi was a little uncomfortable leaving such a message with an acolyte. But he seemed to be preoccupied with matters at home and hurriedly made to leave. Then, abruptly, he turned back. "Tell the Reverend that we'd like a nice service, but not the most expensive one. Second-class will do." Bowing his head once more, Heikichi set off on his way.

Jinen watched him until he heard the chain on the wicket drop down with the thud of a heavy weight. He went straight back to the priest's quarters.

"Mr. Hisama said that his brother died," he reported to Satoko. "He said it happened this morning. He's asking that the funeral be held tomorrow."

The corners of Satoko's fierce-looking eyes twitched. "And what did you tell him, Jinen?"

"Nothing. Mr. Hisama just said that when the Reverend gets back, I should say that he wants to have a second-class service."

Jikai's whereabouts were unknown. Satoko had been concerned that Jinen might have told Hisama Heikichi about the situation, but seeing the boy appear so calm, she felt reassured.

"Is that right? In any case, there's a funeral to be held, so go to the priest at the Genkōji and explain what's going on." Satoko was able to stay somewhat calm because she figured that Jikai was simply asleep somewhere and would return home soon.

"All right, then. I'm going now."

Wearing a sober face, Jinen left the Kohōan, taking short, quick steps toward the tea fields of the Tōjiin temple. Satoko watched him until he was out of sight.

·

Each Zen temple has associate branches known as *hōrui*, whose affiliation is such that they may be called sister temples. There were twelve Tōzenji *hōrui* in the eastern temple precincts of Karasuma Kamidachiuri, where the main temple offices were located. These twelve included the Keishun, the Shunkō, the Gyokuhō, the Genshō, the Rinsen, the Kōmyō, the Fukō, the Gazan, and so on. Each of these had its own head priest, and together they managed the business affairs of the main temple and attended to functions such as funerals, confessionals, and memorial services for the 17th, 25th, 50th and 100th anniversaries of a death. Apart from these *hōrui*, there were also associate temples located outside the precincts of the Tōzenji. They included the Jukaku, the Rokuonji, the Sōkaku, and the Jigenji. The Kohōan belonged to this particular group of branch temples. At the time, it was prohibited to inherit a temple, and there were regulations governing succession when a head priest resigned or retired. First, the associate temples would convene a council. Then, the administrator of the main temple, the chief abbot and the senior priests would discuss the matter and afterwards report on the outcome. The *hōrui* with which the Kohōan was affiliated included the Genkōji, the Zuikōin, the Myōhōji, and the Myōchiin.

Among these only the Genkōji was not located in the mountains, but was tucked away in a residential neighborhood situated along a river to the east of

Onmae Avenue in Shimotachiuri. A yellow, roofed earthen wall surrounded the main hall and the detached residence.

The head priest of the Genkōji was Uda Sesshū. He was the same age as Jikai and had also undertaken his ascetic training at the Tōzenji monastery. Sesshū and the Kohōan priest were close associates, and because they both liked to drink, they could often be seen coming and going together. Whenever Jikai had some free time, he would walk from Mt. Kinugasa to Shimotachiuri Onmae to play Go.

Just past twelve on the afternoon of November 8, the Kohōan acolyte Jinen entered the gate of the Genkōji. Following the steppingstones set amid the sasanqua trees, he cut across the garden to reach the entrance of the residence hall. The novice Tokuzen greeted him at the entryway and then momentarily stepped back inside. Sesshū was out on the veranda shaving his head in the sunshine. Kneeling before him, Tokuzen announced, "It's Jinen from the Kohōan. He's asking if the Reverend Jikai is here."

"Jikai? Here?" Sesshū removed his hand, wet with shaving soap, from the back of his partially shaved head. "That's strange."

Jikai hadn't been by the Genkōji. Sesshū had invited him over to play Go, but the priest had never shown up.

"Jinen's here?" he asked.

"Yes."

"Show him in."

Stepping astride his bucket, Sesshū made his way back inside with only half the back of his head shaved. Coming quickly around through the main entrance, Jinen met him at the threshold of the priest's room and knelt before him.

"When did Reverend Jikai leave?" asked Sesshū.

"Yesterday."

"About what time?"

"The missus said it was about two-thirty."

"Well, he didn't come here."

Sesshū appeared slightly perplexed by the extremely tense, pale look of the boy's face. He knew that Jinen's frightful expression was the effect of his unusual features. His forehead jutted out much further than was normal. And his eyes were so deeply set in his face. Even so, the look in his eyes seemed somehow different today.

"Satoko doesn't know where he went?"

"That's right. She said he told her he was coming here to see you. I was sent to fetch him."

This was troubling. Jikai had not come by the Genkōji. Sesshū had no idea where he might have gone. "This is really peculiar," he said, his bafflement obvious in his face.

"Mr. Hisama's brother died this morning at his house in Imadegawa," Jinen continued. "He came to the temple to request a funeral service. He said that Reverend Jikai had promised him he would do it. We have to make preparations."

"A funeral?"

"Yes."

"Mr. Hisama? Is he a patron?"

"He has a wholesale paint shop east of Imadegawa Senbon."

"Ah, yes. His status allows him to request services from Jikai. I went with Jikai for a memorial service at his house once." Sesshū vaguely called to mind the Hisama shop and Heikichi's face.

This was a serious problem. The funeral would have to be conducted in the absence of the head priest because he had failed to return home. Sesshū knew very well that if the main temple heard about this, there would be a serious reprimand coming from the head administrator, Etsuzankutsu.

"Jinen?"

"Yes?"

Sesshū looked down upon the back of Jinen's lowered head. "Don't mention this to anyone. And tell Satoko to keep quiet about it, as well. Do you understand? Because we are affiliated with the Kohōan, we can take care of the funeral, all right? Now hurry along and get your main hall decorated."

Jinen bowed so low that his forehead almost touched the floorboards.

Sesshū then called in the acolyte Tokuzen and asked him to take a message to several of the associate temples. Tokuzen had already graduated from middle school and was about to begin training at the monastery. Told of Sesshū's conversation with Jinen, he understood exactly what was happening. He accompanied Jinen to the main gate, where they each went their separate ways.

"What a mess!" Tokuzen said before setting off in great strides toward the Kitano shrine. "Jikai has drunk himself into a stupor somewhere. What recklessness."

It was almost four o'clock by the time Jinen returned to the Kohōan. Seeing that Jikai was not with him, Satoko reproached the boy. "You've come back alone?"

"Yes. He never went to see the priest at the Genkōji."

"What?" Satoko's temples began to throb. "He wouldn't do such a ridiculous thing! The Reverend took his white robe from the dresser himself, put it on and said he was going to play Go."

Jinen gazed up silently at Satoko.

"So what did Sesshū say?" she asked.

"He said the Reverend hasn't been there recently."

Satoko was mortified. Jikai had often come home late telling her he had been at the Genkōji. That he had been invited to have drinks there. Had he been lying all along?

"If that's true, then where did the Reverend go?" Satoko asked in desperation. "What do you think, Jinen?"

"I don't know. I have to get ready for the Hisama funeral now. The Reverend Sesshū said that a group of priests from the associate temples would perform the service so the main temple won't find out what's happened."

Satoko's face turned even paler. She understood the kind intentions of Reverend Sesshū. But since the funeral would be a second-rank ceremony and the assistant priests from the Kohōan's sister temples would come to help, once they were here, there would be no way to cover up Jikai's absence.

His head bowed, Jinen left the distracted Satoko and made his way to the main hall. Because he worked so hard, Jinen often made up for the negligence of the hard-drinking Jikai. Watching the boy walk calmly toward the main hall to prepare for the funeral, Satoko felt so grateful to him. Of course, as Sesshū had implied, when a priest shirks his duties to his patrons and goes about playing, he is certain to be severely reprimanded by the main temple. Even though she was fretful and worried, she could not manage the temple responsibilities on her own. She had never touched a single utensil in the main hall, and she hadn't the slightest idea of how to prepare for a funeral.

She had no option but to put her hands together in supplication and place her trust in Jinen. *Please do your best,* she prayed.

Upon returning to the head priest's quarters, she again became irritable. She was deeply preoccupied with the question of where Jikai had gone if he had not gone to the Genkōji.

A full year had passed since Satoko arrived at the Kohōan the previous fall. At first, Jikai had made love to her every night. And often not just at night;

their lovemaking had taken place regardless of time of day. Yet throughout that time, he continued to visit the main temple as well as his patrons and the associate temples. Whenever he left, Jikai would tell Satoko that he had various things to do. And whenever he went to a memorial service, he always returned bearing gifts—offerings or sweets he had slipped into his pouch or his sleeves. There had been no reason to doubt his whereabouts.

Apparently, however, on the one or two occasions he had gone out after his recent illness, Jikai had gone somewhere he kept secret even from Satoko. Jealousy surged in her breast. *Was he keeping another woman?*

It seemed the most likely explanation. Jikai may have had a chance meeting with a woman from his past. Perhaps the embers of an old flame had blazed up inside him and he had gone to this woman's house. Imagining this, it made sense to Satoko that, on the day he left, Jikai had put on his white robes himself.

Her doubts, however, disappeared in a flash. None of that could be true and Satoko knew it. Jikai was the type of man who had refused to take a wife, even though Nangaku had repeatedly advised him to do so. He loves me, she thought. In bringing Satoko to the temple, Jikai had found contentment. Her body told her that.

Two messengers from the Hisama household arrived at five. Jinen met them at the entrance. "We know that Mr. Hisama has already asked the Reverend," they said, "but could we hold the wake in the main hall tonight? Our house is so small, and the back rooms are full of paint."

"If the Reverend promised, then it's all right. Please go ahead," Jinen told them.

"Thank you very much. So if it's all right, we'll plan on it." Heikichi's messengers returned home straight away.

Jinen placed a white cloth on the ordination platform in the inner sanctum of the main hall, then laid out a three-corner brocade cloth on which he set a pure white porcelain censer he had brought out from the back of the inner sanctum. The ceremony had to be performed with a tray set, candleholders and an assistant's desk all made of unvarnished wood. The funeral director would go to Hisama's house, where his employees would do the bulk of the work. They would place the body inside the coffin, wrap the coffin in a white cloth, place a wreath of gold and silver artificial flowers on top and carry it to the temple. Once the body was in the temple, it was customary for the funeral director to withdraw.

From there, the burden of labor fell to Jinen. It wouldn't do to invite the ridicule of the sister temples, nor to allow the Hisama family to think the service shabby. From time to time, whenever he conducted a funeral, Jikai had instructed Jinen on the proper procedures to follow. Jinen arranged the implements he would use just as Reverend Jikai had taught him. Opening the *fusuma* doors leading into the chamber to the left of the sanctum, he spread a white mat over the tatami. The cloth was laid out so that it would cover the top of the threshold, as well. He left the chamber to the right of the sanctum as it was. He would have the Hisamas' relatives sit in the room to the left, and have visitors offering incense line up in the corridor that ran along the front of the main hall. This was in keeping with the way Jikai always did things. Jinen brought out straw mats from the storage space and spread them out on the broad veranda. Just as he had aligned the mats with the edge of the veranda and was about to unroll them, Satoko entered the chamber to the right of the sanctum.

"Jinen? Tokuzen from the Genkōji has come to help." Sesshū knew Jinen would be extremely busy and had sent him to ensure everything was ready in time.

"Oh? Thank you," Jinen replied. He unrolled the mats to the far end of the veranda and then walked back across them to smooth out the wrinkles. As he made his way back toward Satoko's direction, he saw Tokuzen standing there talking with her.

"Have you heard anything from the Reverend Jikai yet?" There was a gleam in Tokuzen's eyes.

Bothered by Tokuzen's attitude, Satoko thought, *How do you expect me to know?* "We haven't heard anything," she said.

"Is that right?" he continued. "I wonder where he went?" Tokuzen had been forced on occasion to be a drinking companion to the priest, so he knew all about him.

"Tokuzen? When was the last time the Reverend went to the Genkōji?" Satoko asked.

"As far as I know, he hasn't come around for a long time."

Her suspicions confirmed, Satoko couldn't help wondering again where Jikai had been going. *He kept it secret from me all along, so he must have another woman somewhere!* Satoko's body knew very well that Jikai was not the kind of man who would stay away all night if there weren't another woman involved.

Before returning to the head priest's quarters, Satoko asked Tokuzen to help Jinen with the preparations in the main hall. "We're counting on you, Tokuzen, so please do your best."

Back in Jikai's room, Satoko went through all the drawers and shelves and began pulling out letters addressed to the priest that might offer some clue to his whereabouts. She pored over every letter, looking for anything that might reveal Jikai's secrets. She found nothing of significance.

*Reverend? Where have you gone? Where did you go, leaving me by myself?* Satoko plopped her rounded bottom on the tatami with a thud. Covering her eyes, she lay face down on the red futon and for a long time did nothing.

                                    •

The coffin bearing Hisama Heizaburō arrived at the Kohōan at half-past seven. After it was removed from the hearse, Heikichi and three of his cousins—Inokichi, Sakuzō and Denzaburō, all of whom worked as painters—hoisted the coffin on their shoulders. They opened the small gate leading into the temple and carried the coffin from the main entrance through the garden to the front of the main hall. There, they set it down temporarily on the veranda, where Jinen and Tokuzen were waiting in their robes. The men removed their sandals, stepped out onto the white gravel of the garden in their white tabi and then carried the coffin up the steps at the front of the building and into the inner sanctum. The coffin holding the body of Heizaburō, who had also worked as a painter, was placed horizontally on top of a bier over which Jinen had draped a red three-cornered cloth. After murmuring the *nembutsu* prayer—*Namu Amida Butsu*—three times, Heikichi briskly bowed his head to Jinen and said, "I leave him to your care."

Jinen looked up at Heikichi and in a calm voice asked, "How many people will be attending the wake?"

"The four of us here—me and my cousins," he replied. "Our other relatives arrive by train from the country tomorrow, so there will be a crowd then. But the wake will be just the four of us."

Jinen bowed his head.

Sesshū hurried over from the Genkōji and performed the recitation of the sutras for the wake. He had changed into his purple robes in the guest-room and had Tokuzen serve as his assistant. Jinen led the chanting for the service. The four members of the Hisama family sat quietly in the room to the left of the sanctum while the recitation took place, but when the Reverend Sesshū stepped down from the chair on which he had been sitting, they began to whisper among themselves. Soon after, they entered the sanctum to offer incense. As the incense began to burn, the smoke trailed out like fog over to the panel doors of the upper chamber. The geese Nangaku had drawn appeared to begin to flap their wings. Sesshū gazed at the drawings on the door for a while, then, with a wink, signaled to Tokuzen and withdrew from the hall. Jinen followed after them.

"Now, Jinen, you and Tokuzen can handle the wake, can't you?"

"Yes," Jinen said, bowing his head deeply. "I prepared the guestroom by spreading out futon for anyone who wants to stay over."

"Very good. A wake is supposed to last all night, but the members of the family won't make it all the way through. They'll have to take turns staying up."

"Yes."

"So, Tokuzen, you'll stay over at the Kohōan, as well?"

Tokuzen bowed his head.

"In that case, I'll go back now." With that, Sesshū turned to enter the corridor that wound back to the head priest's residence.

Satoko was in her room. She had drifted off with her head pressed to the futon over the *kotatsu*. When she heard footsteps, however, she straightened up and looked around.

"Hasn't he come back yet?" Sesshū asked.

Catching sight of his large ruddy face through the opening in the shoji doors, Satoko was startled. "I checked," she said, "but I couldn't find his black everyday robes or his black surplice. He must have taken them when he left."

Sesshū cocked his head. "He certainly took some odd things."

"The books that were here are gone, too," she told him, pointing to the top of the shelves.

"The books?" Sesshū took a moment to think. "It looks like he set out to do some ascetic training. He probably lent the books to someone at some point and you never noticed. It's nothing to worry about. He'll likely come back tomorrow morning as if nothing happened. He doesn't know about the Hisama funeral, so he's probably off somewhere, sleeping without a care."

Sesshū started back down the hall, but halfway he stopped, backed up and peeked in on her again. He peered down at Satoko's puffy face from the corner of his eyes and said, "You must have worn Jikai out."

"Don't say that, Reverend," Satoko said. She could hear Sesshū chuckle as he disappeared down the corridor and blushed at the thought of what Jikai must have told him during his visits to the Genkōji.

The wake proceeded under Jinen's direction. The four members of the Hisama family waited in the chamber to the left of the sanctum. Tokuzen finished chanting sutras at eleven. Jinen arranged four sets of futon in the eight-mat guestroom and planned to have members of the Hisama family take turns resting there. Tokuzen retired to a four-and-a-half-mat room that abutted the living quarters. Jinen said to Heikichi and his cousins, "The Reverend Jikai told me many times that the incense at a wake must never be allowed to go out. I'll watch it carefully. You have things to do tomorrow, so please rest."

"Thank you," said Inokichi.

Inokichi, Sakuzō and Denzaburō had worked all day, and Jinen could see in their faces that they wanted to sleep. Jinen thought it was understandable considering the nature of their work. Slowly surveying the four men, he asked, "Could you please take turns staying awake?"

"Yes, we can take turns."

"All right, then, please do so."

Jinen was sitting in the center of the sanctum. He began reciting the *Kannon Sutra* from his copybook. Jikai had taught him that he should not raise his voice when chanting a sutra for a wake, but should recite it quietly and slowly. The reading had to continue until dawn. Jinen brought the prayer bell over from the accompanist's desk and placed it beside his cushion in the middle of the room. Heikichi was sitting in a formal posture, but was soon leaning against one of the panel doors and beginning to nod off. It was after midnight. By the time Jinen finished reading the sutra for the third time, Heikichi was fast asleep.

"Excuse me, Heikichi?" Jinen woke him suddenly. "You'll catch cold. Your replacement is up. Please come with me to the study and rest."

It must have been about two in the morning. A carp could be heard splashing in the rear garden as Heikichi sleepily trudged along behind Jinen. When they reached the guestroom, however, Heikichi thought he glanced three figures bulging beneath the futon. Had someone gotten up to replace him? He didn't think much more about it, however, for as soon as he lay down, he was overcome with fatigue and began to drift off to sleep.

*I had to look after him for so long, but in the end he died, anyway. Ah, I had to nurse him for such a long time . . .* Heikichi imagined for a moment that he was in the dark backroom of his house in Imadegawa, that he was sleeping next to his elder brother and that his brother's chamber pot was still there set off to the side. But the tall ceiling of the guestroom gave Heikichi a greater feeling of repose than he could have experienced in his cramped house, with its wholesale paint shop. *Heizaburō died peacefully, and now he sleeps peacefully at the Kohōan.*

Jinen left the room and went out into the corridor of the main hall to light incense. Heikichi could hear the faint shuffling of his footsteps. In the priest's quarters, Satoko was still dozing. Jikai had not returned.

*Reverend? Where did you go, Reverend? You've gone off somewhere leaving me alone!* Lying on the futon, Satoko repeated these words over and over as if in a delirium. Eventually, sleep washed over her like a wave.

Night deepened at the Kohōan, and then gradually the dawn broke.

The funeral was conducted under the leadership of Reverend Sesshū of the Genkōji. Priests from the Zuikō, the Myōhō, and the Myōchiin stood in attendance in the inner sanctum. They lined up, their drums and the crimson tassels of their bells dangling. In accordance with custom, Jinen acted as assistant. The acolytes Tokuzen, Daisen, Jishō, Ekishū, and Kisan, who had come from the associate temples, lined up across from the priests and softly chanted sutras. Heizaburō's posthumous name was **Kōshun chidō koji**. Sesshū occupied the chair where Jikai was supposed to sit. In his natural gravelly voice, he led Heizaburō over to the next world. The recitation of scriptures, which began at one, finished at three. Twenty-eight relatives of the Hisama clan were gathered in the chambers on either side of the sanctum. Each time one of them thanked Heikichi, Inokichi, Sakuzō and Denzaburō for their trouble in attending the wake, the cousins beamed back from well-rested faces. They had worked diligently, but early in the morning, when it came time to select who would dig the grave at the Hisama plot, an energized Inokichi told Heikichi, "I slept really well last night. Let me do it."

"I'd be grateful if you would do that for me," he replied. And with Heikichi's consent, Inokichi and Denzaburō went out to the foot of the mountain to undertake the work.

When the priests finished reciting the sutras, they withdrew to the guest-room for a while. Four different pallbearers were chosen to take the coffin to the gravesite—Heizaburō's uncles, Sukezō and Kishichi, who had come in from Heizaburō's hometown in the mountain region of Fukuchiyama, and his two younger brothers, Kumatarō and Kōta. Jinen brought tea to the priests in the guestroom. He went back to the main hall to make sure that preparations for moving the coffin had been completed, and then led the priests out once again. The priests' robes—red, purple, yellow, orange—formed a line on the white gravel of the garden, providing a vivid spectacle of color for the mourners. As the coffin, still wrapped in white cloth, was carried out through the Chinese-style gate, the heavy clouds in the sky parted slightly and sunlight filtered through.

*Chin, Pon, Jaran. Chin, Pon, Jaran.* Handbells, drums, and prayer bells rang out in accompaniment to the chanting of Reverend Sesshū, who led the procession. The coffin followed the attendant priests as they made their way toward Mt. Kinugasa. Following behind the coffin were twenty-two relatives, each fingering a rosary.

The graveside service ended at four. Heizaburō was laid to rest at the foot of the mountain beside a grove of black bamboo that was overgrown with young pine. Using a hoe they had borrowed from the temple, Denzaburō and Heikichi had covered the coffin over with black soil, and a mound of dirt equal in volume to the coffin topped it. The unvarnished tray that Jinen had prepared earlier was placed atop the mound of earth. The tray held a bowl of dried bean curd broth and a bowl of rice piled high in the shape of a dome. Chopsticks had been inserted into the rice so that they stood straight up in the likeness of a memorial tablet.

A breeze with the scent of wild mushrooms wafted down the side of the mountain, creating ripples on the surface of the broth.

# VII

The Hisama family left the Kohōan at around six o'clock. The wreathes, the artificial flowers, the bamboo-work incense stands, and other items left over from the funeral were strewn about the side of the main hall. Inside the temple, too, things were far from back to order.

Although everyone thought he would return while the funeral was in progress, Jikai was still nowhere to be seen. The priests of the sister temples who had gathered at the Kohōan were forced to discuss remedial measures.

Shōan, the senior priest of the Myōchiin, Chikuhō, the new head priest of the Zuikōin, Reverend Kaiō of the Myōhōji, and Sesshū of the Genkōji met in a room off the back of the guestroom. Chikuhō began the discussion.

"What a strange story," he told Sesshū. "Jikai left here saying he was going to play Go with you. Isn't it odd that he never showed up? It makes me think he may be keeping another woman somewhere."

"He didn't come to my temple," Sesshū responded. "In fact, he hasn't visited for a long time. I also started to suspect that maybe it was a woman. But knowing Jikai, if there had been another woman, it's likely he would have told me about her. I already asked Satoko about it, but she said she didn't think that was the case. So I wonder if he was in an accident or something."

"If there'd been an accident, someone would have come to tell us," said Chikuhō.

"It's really odd. No one has come to the temple to report anything. When you look at the facts, it seems reasonable to conclude that he went into hiding somewhere, don't you think?" said Kaiō.

"And yet," said Sesshū, lowering his voice, "Satoko mentioned that Jikai had taken some books he used while in training . . ."

"He took books with him? What a peculiar thing to do! Did he pack his robes and bowl, as well?"

"So it seems," said Sesshū.

Shōan was blinking rapidly. "At this point in his life, he wouldn't become a mendicant and undergo ascetic training. Call the acolyte . . . what's-his-name . . . and ask him what Jikai said."

Sesshū glanced around. Not hearing Jinen's footsteps outside, he stood up with a grunt and went out into the corridor. The interior of the Kohōan, which had been a whirl of activity only moments earlier, was suddenly calm, like an ebbing tide. Because the floors were dusty, Sesshū worried that his white tabi would get soiled as he walked across the rough-grained boards. Springing along on tiptoe, he made his way to the residence.

"Jinen?" he called out, but there was no sign of the boy. "That's odd," he muttered to himself. "Is he in the main hall?"

Because he was the only acolyte at the Kohōan, Jinen would naturally have a heavy load of responsibilities. Imagining that he might still be in the main hall cleaning up, Sesshū turned back, moving along the corridor to the chamber to the left of the sanctum. Glancing out into the rear garden, he was startled to see smoke rising at the side of the pond. Looking more closely, he spied Jinen, his blue-lined kimono tucked into a sash he must have put on especially for that purpose. The boy was busily burning something.

"Jinen!" Sesshū called out in a loud voice.

Jinen showed no reaction but continued topping the fire with green bamboo, star anise and other scraps of wood. With each new addition, the flames would rise, while white smoke billowed and seethed from the embers. It appeared that Jinen was burning trash from the funeral.

*He really works hard!* thought Sesshū. Even so, he had to call him to the meeting for questioning or there would be no conclusion to the inquiry. He called out again, "Jinen!"

Jinen dropped the bamboo pole he was holding and it fell with a thud. Startled, he stared toward Sesshū in blank surprise.

"Come over here!"

"Yes." Thrusting his large head forward, Jinen made his way hurriedly to a spot just below the back corridor. He looked up at Sesshū, his protruding forehead covered in sweat.

"Enough cleaning up," Sesshū spoke gently. "I want you to come with me to the guestroom for a few minutes."

"Okay," he said, and meekly stepped up into the corridor. Looking back, he appeared to be concerned about the fire. White smoke was still rising, and the raw smell of star anise hung over the garden. The smell was so pungent it seemed to penetrate Sesshū's nostrils.

Jinen was brought to the room off the guest quarters, where the four priests stared as if confronted with his deformed shape for the first time. Shōan began the questioning.

"Did the Reverend Jikai say anything to you? Not just on the seventh, but before that, as well?"

Jinen rolled his eyes back into his head. "Yes, the Reverend talked to me on the seventh about the Zen training monastery."

"The training monastery?"

"He told me about ascetic training. About *tangazume,* when a postulant has to sit alone in a room for five days, facing a wall."

"Yes, we talk about that sort of thing. Did he say anything else?"

"He also told me about *niwazume,* where a priest has to remain in bowing posture for two days to beg admission to a temple."

"We know all about *niwazume.* Did he say anything about where he was going?"

"The Reverend once said that he wanted to leave the temple and go on a trip."

"He talked about a trip? When was that?"

"Once when he talked to me about ascetic training, he muttered something about it."

"He said he wanted to leave?"

"Yes."

All four priests concentrated their focus on Jinen's deep-set eyes, the whites of which remained exposed.

Shōan, the senior priest of the Myōchiin, sighed. "This is a real problem. Do you think Jikai has run off, like the administrator of the Tōfukuji?"

Sesshū's eyes widened. "I think I know what happened!"

"What is it?" Kaiō looked at Sesshū in surprise.

Sesshū, speaking in a hushed voice, said, "It may be that Satoko was too strong-willed for him. I'm sure that's why he ran off."

The other priests looked skeptical, but it wasn't entirely impossible.

"If you think that's what happened, Sesshū, then shouldn't we call Satoko in?"

Sesshū went to fetch Satoko from the priest's lodgings. Arriving at the guest's quarters, she sat down before the group. She kept her pale face lowered and had a distracted look in her eyes.

"The Reverend was acting normal," she began, "up until the early afternoon of the seventh. Then a messenger from the Hisama house showed up asking for a memorial service to mark the anniversary of the father's death. The Reverend told Jinen to go perform the service. Because the Reverend had always done it himself, I thought it was a little odd. Then he came back to his room and, shortly after, said that he was going to the Genkōji to play Go. That's what he said. When I responded, 'Is that right?' he opened the drawer and took out his white robes all by himself. Then he changed and left."

"And the books?"

"I didn't notice it at the time, but later I had a look at the shelves and found that some volumes were missing."

"Hmm." Shōan cast a sharp glance toward a spot directly in front of Satoko's plump knees. "Did he say anything to you about ascetic training?"

"Training? What do you mean?"

"Did he ever mention anything about going to a training monastery?"

"The Reverend?"

"Yes, the Reverend. Did he talk to you about wanting to go on a trip?"

"This is the first I've heard of such a thing."

Satoko's expression indicated that she had no idea what was going on. Her full, pale lips were parted as she looked in confusion at the elderly priest.

"Jinen!" Shōan said. "Your fire is really blazing. It's dangerous. Go tend to it."

Jinen, who had been sitting in a corner of the room, quietly stood up and shuffled out to the corridor. The fire in the garden was burning so brightly that it cast a red tint on the paper of the shoji.

"Missus," Shōan continued, "it's possible that the Reverend left on a trip to undergo ascetic training."

"What?" Satoko sidled around to face him.

"Let's wait and see," he continued. "If we don't hear from him, then we'll know he left on a trip. Sometimes all of us priests feel that . . . Well, we're bothered by various things—the temple budget or tiresome administrative duties—and we don't want to do them anymore. Maybe that's what happened to Jikai. Don't you think so?"

With this last comment, all the other priests nodded in agreement. It appeared the group had reached its conclusion.

Because their temples were associated with the Kohōan, however, the priests could not remain silent about Jikai's sudden disappearance. Even though they agreed that he had probably left for ascetic training, they would have to inform the police just to be safe. They could not rule out the possibility that Jikai had collapsed somewhere. Then again, he was only fifty-eight, and healthier than the average person. It hardly seemed likely that the priest had met a humiliating end at the side of the road. On second thought, they decided, perhaps it was best to wait just a little more before informing the authorities.

The four priests left a little after seven, having already sent their assistants home carrying the gifts received from the Hisama family. By then, the fire Jinen had built was already extinguished, and the Kohōan faced the prospect of another evening without its master.

.

Satoko was the first to become convinced that Jikai had indeed gone on a far-off journey. She tried recalling how he had behaved just before leaving the temple that afternoon. He had made her undress, but that was not unusual. Still, there was something somehow different about the way he had handled her. What made her feel that way? At the time, she attributed his roughness to the fact that he had just recovered from illness. Upon reflection, however, that conclusion had been misguided. He had pushed her down violently. Normally, he would have kissed Satoko—her breasts and sides, her legs and arms—until she could no longer stand it. For some reason, however, he selfishly skipped foreplay that day. If he had been lying about going to the Genkōji, then what was he thinking to have treated her so roughly like that? Hadn't he already made the decision to leave the temple by that time? If he hadn't, then there would have been no reason to lie about going to the Genkōji to play Go.

*I've been made a fool of, haven't I?* As soon as the thought occurred to her, another question flashed across her mind. Why, she wondered, did Jikai have to betray her? *It's Jinen. Jinen told him about that night!*

*But what is it I have done exactly? When I first saw him in his little room copying the sutra, I had no intention of doing anything. But after hearing his story from the priest of the Seianji, I couldn't help finding the boy indescribably sweet. He was so unbearably pitiful. That night, I embraced him, having lost myself in feelings of pity and sorrow. I told him to keep quiet, to say nothing of it to Jikai. But had he told the Reverend, anyway?*

If she wanted to believe that Jikai truly loved her, then Satoko had no choice but to assume that he had betrayed her because of what she had done with Jinen. As these thoughts raced through Satoko's mind, an image of the boy—his protruding forehead, his deep-set eyes and all that was expressionless about him—loomed before her like an impenetrable wall. She was beside herself.

She left the priest's residence and ran over to the acolyte's living quarters. She had to confirm her suspicion. How could she stand to be treated this way by such a child?

"Jinen!"

He was crouched in a corner of the three-mat room, apparently asleep.

"Get up!" Satoko yelled. The light of the moon streamed in through the lattice window and cast a striped pattern on the disheveled skirts of her robes. Nevertheless, the area where Jinen remained huddled was so dark she couldn't see him. "You told the Reverend what I did!"

He finally stirred. Satoko could just make out his large head in the dim light and heard the sound of him smoothing out his black futon.

"Say something! Don't just sit there in silence! Tell me!" Her body was trembling. *If he doesn't tell me,* she thought, *I'll never find out where the Reverend went.* "Tell me!" she shouted.

But Jinen said nothing.

Was he half-asleep? Satoko leaned forward, trying to catch sight of his face. Then, from the corner, his voice came abruptly. "I never said anything about what happened. I could never tell anymore."

Satoko squatted to the floor. Was the boy lying? She peered into the corner of the room and heard Jinen sniffling. She listened intently, her eyes focusing on the spot where he sat doubled-over. He was crying.

"I never said anything. How could I tell anyone about that?" His sniffles grew louder.

Satoko rushed over to Jinen and embraced his shoulders and shaved head, taking in the smell of his perspiration.

"You didn't tell, did you? You didn't tell, did you?" As she repeated these words, Satoko became inexpressibly agitated. Her throat was terribly dry. Although she was relieved, deep in her heart, she wanted now more than ever to savor the cruel pleasure of having Jinen tell Jikai their secret. But then, the more she thought about it, the less any of it seemed to matter. She felt a powerful impulse to take Jinen into her arms again.

"Jinen, you're a good boy. You didn't tell, did you? You didn't tell." With all her strength, Satoko hugged Jinen's fleshy body and shaven head.

"We'll be forced to leave this temple, Jinen. If the Reverend doesn't come back, we'll be discarded. There won't be any use for us here."

Jinen stopped crying. Heaving against her breast, he listened as Satoko continued her lament.

"That's what happened, isn't it? The Reverend's gone on a trip, hasn't he? He's left us and gone far away. That's right, isn't it? Jinen, did you know? About the Reverend talking about the monastery? He told me that it isn't proper for a Zen priest to have desires, that as soon as he has desires, he's finished as a priest. Whenever I felt desires, I abandoned them, just like the Reverend told me to do. Even though we don't have desires anymore . . . The Reverend left. He abandoned his temple and went away. Even though we didn't have any desires . . ."

Great tears fell from Satoko's eyes onto Jinen's misshapen head.

·

As the representative of the Kohōan's associate temples, Kodera Shōan, the senior priest of the Myōchiin, had a report drawn up regarding Kitami Jikai's disappearance for the Mannenzan Tōzenji sect's office of administrative affairs. Seventeen days after the disappearance, the office of administrative affairs informed the council on religious affairs of the report's findings. There had been serious doubts as to whether Jikai had really left the temple with the intention of undertaking ascetic training. If he had, then surely there would have been word of his entering a training monastery somewhere. Priests who went on pilgrimages these days faced very different conditions than priests who did so in the Edo Period. They were not limited to travel on foot and begging at the gates of the monasteries at Mt. Kokei or Ibuka. Modern pilgrims could travel by steam train and buy boxed lunches at the station. Even if Jikai had gone very far, say to a monastery in Gifu Prefecture, it was surely reasonable to expect him to send a postcard at the very least. In the report, which was signed by all the priests of the temples associated with the Kohōan, Tera-saki Giō, the head priest of the Shunkōin and chief administrator for religious affairs, expressed his opinion in this way:

> *He was a priest who became slovenly because of his drinking. Jikai did not attend the regular services in honor of the Emperor held on the first and fifteenth of each month. It is likely that he collapsed in a stupor some-where and died . . .*

·

The suspicions voiced by Giō were not unreasonable. The priests of the branch temples discussed the Kohōan problem repeatedly, though without resolu-tion. At a loss, the council finally decided to leave the matter to the judgment of the chief abbot. If patrons learned that a priest who had renounced worldly concerns had fled the temple, then the news would hit the papers and all the priests would become laughingstocks, just as they had become after the abbot of the Tōfukuji fled.

That being the case, Jikai's disappearance didn't just pose a problem for the Kohōan, it was a potential source of embarrassment for all the temples.

Kigakutsu Sugimoto Dokuseki was chief abbot of the Tōzenji at the time. When Terasaki Giō, the head priest of the Shunkōin, relayed to him the outcome of the council's deliberations, the chief abbot laughed softly. Kiga-kutsu was ninety. Working his toothless mouth in a constant chewing motion, he looked into the worried face of the junior priest and said, "So Jikai ran away from his temple? That's no big deal, is it? He's still wearing the robes of a mendicant priest. Let it go. Let it go."

Giō bowed numerous times, left the abbot's quarters and reported on the meeting to the council.

Perhaps the reason why the papers never reported the disappearance of Kitami Jikai, head priest of the Kohōan, was due to the councils' respect for Abbot Kigakutsu's judgment on the matter.

# VIII

It had happened on the evening of November 7, two nights before the Hisama funeral.

At around nine o'clock, Jinen walked through the corridor from the entrance of the living quarters to the back of the main hall. He opened the door to the storage space located beneath the rear section of the inner sanctum. Feeling around with his hand, he took out the pocketknife and the bamboo blade that he had stashed away on a shelf there. A strong wind coming down the mountain shook and rattled the door several times, and Jinen hastily latched the door behind him. He tried peering up through the floorboards. The temple floors were a little higher off the ground than those of an ordinary house, and the wind would get trapped in the space beneath it, sending dust swirling about. Placing his large head up against the underside of the floorboards, Jinen fixed his gaze outside. Just beyond the perimeter of the hall, the white gravel appeared as a line drawn across the garden. For several minutes, he squatted there motionless. Then he slowly made his way back up to the corridor. Nothing stirred except the heavy winds.

Jinen returned from the main hall to the living quarters and his own small room. It was storming outside. The dark gray sky could be glimpsed faintly beyond the lattice window. Jinen sat down on the tatami mat. He was holding the bamboo blade and the knife in his hand. After a while, he got up quietly, went out to the entrance hall and disappeared into the darkness of the front garden.

At just past one in the morning, the clatter of a chain could be heard. Someone had opened the wicket beside the main gate. It was Jikai. He was extremely drunk. As he passed through the gate, the hem of his outer robe had brushed up against the stone weight on the iron chain, setting the chain rattling.

Jikai stumbled along the flagstones set in the gravel path to a spot under a crepe myrtle, where butterbur was sprouting. That's when it happened. A shadow resembling a black dog sprung at his feet. In an instant, Jikai felt a terrible pain below his ribs.

A small bamboo blade had been thrust into his left side and firmly yanked with an upward motion, gouging a large hole near his heart. As a finishing blow, he had been stabbed forcefully in the stomach with a small knife. Blood spurted out. With several staggering steps, Jikai grabbed at the crepe myrtle, but his hands slipped on the smooth bark, and he weakly clutched at the air. His groans dying in his throat, the priest fell straight to the ground.

Jikai's body landed atop the butterbur leaves. As soon as it stopped twitching, the black shadow raised it up and pulled it through an inner gate standing between the front garden and the main hall. The wicket gate had not been latched, so it opened smoothly. The shadow was Jinen. Dragging Jikai's body behind him, he slipped beneath the floor of the hall.

There was a portable clay stove inside the crawlspace. On top of it was a screen grill used for toasting rice cakes. Strewn here and there were the bones of the carp that Jinen had speared with the bamboo blade and eaten when hungry. Because Jinen was short, he walked briskly around the crawlspace. He dragged Jikai's body into a dark area beneath the rear section of the inner sanctum and grabbed a mat to cover it.

Placing his ear to Jikai's chest, he listened carefully. After a moment, he nodded, then stood and made his way back to the front garden. He began pulling up the leaves of the butterbur under the crepe myrtle in the dark shadows before him. He worked for about an hour, his hands stained black from the grime of the leaves. Jinen made several trips hauling the leaves to a spot in the crawlspace.

The wind had begun to blow more fiercely. Jinen stepped up from the rear garden to the back of the main hall. He shuffled through the corridor and returned to his room. A light rain fell deep into the night.

The following day, November 8, Jinen got up before dawn and went out to the front garden. Some butterbur leaves remained scattered here and there. The rain had washed the blood away from the butterbur and the gravel, but Jinen swept the area clean anyway.

Hisama Heikichi, Inokichi and the others delivered Heizaburō's coffin at about seven-thirty that evening. Jinen had them set the coffin on the platform in the inner sanctum of the main hall and was waiting for Sesshū of the Genkōji to come and recite the sutras. Sesshū arrived at the main hall. With Jinen leading the chanting, he finished the service for the wake and went home soon after.

At eleven that evening, Tokuzen came to the main hall and read sutras under the watch of Inokichi, Denzaburō, Heikichi and Sakuzō, who were in the chamber to the left. When the reading was finished, Jinen asked the men if they wouldn't mind taking turns staying awake.

"Yes, we can take turns."

"All right, then, please do so," he had told them.

Sakuzō, Denzaburō and Inokichi retired to the guestroom, where four sets of bedding had been laid out.

Jinen sat on the cushion at the center of the sanctum. He pulled out his copybook of the *Kannon Sutra* from the assistant's desk and began to read slowly. When he reached the end, he turned back to the beginning and recited it again. Each time he finished, he would do the same. By two o'clock, Heikichi had fallen asleep in the lower chamber.

"Excuse me, Mr. Hisama? Why don't you go and rest?"

The sleeve of Jinen's robe rubbed against Heikichi's cheek. It smelled of burnt incense. Heikichi opened his eyes slightly.

"It's time to switch. Tomorrow's going to be another hard, busy day, so rest a little."

Heikichi felt tremendous exhaustion and drowsiness flood over him. "All right, then, I'll rest," he mumbled. Jinen led him by the hand to the guestroom. There were four futon there. In the dim light, Heikichi lay down on the one directly before him.

After making sure Heikichi was asleep, Jinen returned to the main hall.

He extinguished the flames of the large candles. Then he began to slowly pass his hand over the coffin. He roughly grabbed some incense, dropped it into the censer and began to recite from the *Kannon Sutra*:

*Call the name Kannon Bosatsu and your bonds will be broken and you*
*will be free. Suppose, in a place filled with all the evil-hearted bandits of*
*the thousand-million-fold world, there is a merchant leader who is guiding*
*a band of merchants carrying valuable treasures over a steep and*
*dangerous road, and that one man shouts out these words: 'Good men, be*
*not afraid! . . .'*

&bull;

While he was chanting, Jinen walked beneath a large tablet hanging on a pillar
and made his way to a corner shrine containing memorial tablets. He reached
in and pulled out a T-shaped hammer used for both driving in and pulling
out nails.

Continuing to chant, Jinen pulled away the white cloth covering
Heizaburō's coffin and began to pry open the lid. A loud, creaking noise broke
the silence.

*If you recite his name, you shall surely be saved from these robbers, and if*
*upon hearing that, the merchants all cry out together, Namu Kannon*
*Bosatsu, then they will immediately be saved because they recited his name.*

To gain leverage, Jinen slipped the hammer into a slight opening in the coffin
and pressed against it with all his strength. The creaking noise culminated in
a sharp *pop!* and the lid rose up of its own accord, as if alive, pulling out the
nails on all four sides. In the depths of the box, Jinen could see Heizaburō's
bearded face. Only one of his eyes was closed, and his stiff cheeks were discolored like garden stones splotched with purple. Jinen carefully measured by
eye the space between Heizaburō's face and the lid of the coffin. A work jacket,
a kimono and some of the painting tools Heizaburō had used when he was
alive had been placed in the coffin for his journey to the next world. Jinen
took the tools and the kimono out and stacked them in a corner.

He immediately replaced the white cloth over the coffin. Grasping the
large, bowl-shaped prayer bell next to the assistant's desk, he gathered all his
strength and lowered it onto the tatami. With quick steps, he hurriedly rolled
the bell on its side through the chamber on the left and out to the rear entrance.
Leaving the bell in the corridor, he stepped down to the storage space under
the floor. Jikai's corpse lay rigid under the mat. Jinen dragged it out and pulled

it up over the steps into the corridor. Then he lifted the stiff body and lowered Jikai's buttocks into the bell's hollow. With a slight springing motion, the body shifted and quickly settled inside the bell. Jinen rolled the bell back from the lower chamber into the sanctum. Inside, Jikai's body looked like a carp in a bowl. Jinen rolled the bell over next to the coffin and removed the white cloth. Gathering all his strength, Jinen lifted the corpse until its stiff head caught on the edge of the coffin. Then, again mustering all his might, Jinen shifted the body over the rim until it slipped inside completely. The two corpses ended up in opposing directions. Jikai's face was pressed up against Heizaburō's dirty, hairy legs, and his own slightly splayed legs ended up on either side of his former patron's chest, such that Heizaburō's face was sandwiched between the priest's feet. Jinen pulled out the jacket Heizaburō had worn in his work as a painter and used it to cover Jikai's back. Then he closed the lid, pounded the nails back in and wrapped the white cloth around the coffin, thus restoring it to its original appearance.

Jinen relit the large candles, settled himself on his cushion and resumed chanting:

*Contemplate the power of Kannon, and the executioner's sword will be broken to bits! If you are imprisoned and your hands and feet bound by fetters and chains, contemplate the power of Kannon . . .*

.

A sidelong glance at the panel doors had caused Jinen to abruptly stop in the middle of the recitation. His eyes flashed in the flickering light of the candles. The wild geese on the *fusuma* panels appeared to be moving. With each flicker of the flames, the geese cried out to him.

Continuing with the sutra, Jinen stood up and went back to the storage space to dispose of the mat and Heizaburō's belongings. He slowly returned to the main hall. Resuming his position on the cushion in the center of the sanctum, he started chanting once more. By that time, the tops of the pine trees on Mt. Kinugasa were beginning to reflect the light of dawn.

The funeral service was conducted on the afternoon of November 9 with twenty-six members of the Hisama family present. The priests of the associate temples were arranged in two lines, while Sesshū led the spirit of the deceased into the next world. Two uncles who had come from Heizaburō's hometown in Fukuchiyama and Heizaburō's two younger brothers, Kumatarō and Kōta, carried the coffin to the graveside. Of the four pallbearers from the previous day, Inokichi and Denzaburō had volunteered to dig the grave, while the other two, Heikichi and Sakuzō, were kept busy with other tasks.

"Man, Heizaburō is really heavy!" muttered Kumatarō, a charcoal maker who worked in Tanba. If one of the four men failed to pull his weight, the load of the coffin would be too much for the other three. Still, Kumatarō's husky voice was drowned out in the flow of the chanting of the four assistant priests and the five acolytes accompanying them. The Chinese-style gate had been opened in advance. The coffin passed over the white gravel, followed by Sesshū and the procession of priests in red, purple, yellow, and orange surplices and robes. Jinen, the assistant, was holding a large red umbrella over Sesshū's head and watching from behind as Kumatarō, Kōta and the others strained under the weight of the coffin. At last, they entered the graveyard at the base of Mt. Kinugasa.

The grave had already been prepared when they got there. Eight men lowered the coffin into the earth, and within minutes it had been covered with black soil.

Jinen returned to the temple and prepared a fire immediately. He burned the green bamboo and artificial flowers left over from the ceremony. He also burned the mat, the butterbur leaves, Heizaburō's belongings and the books he had collected from Jikai's shelves.

These items had to be burned completely. Jinen got the fire blazing hot and watched closely until the flames consumed everything. As he did so, he recalled the harsh days and months he had endured since arriving at the Kohōan. Jinen had always been alone—whether here in Kyoto or back in his home village—and there was nowhere to go to soothe his lonely heart. What hopes and dreams could there be for him? He attended middle school, but it instilled in him only a hatred of military training. He always felt so humiliated going through the streets of Kyoto, struggling under his rifle and tottering along behind everyone else. With things as they were, what dreams could life at the temple afford him? In his mind, Jinen could imagine only one.

Whenever he had a break in his harsh routine, Jinen fantasized about committing a murder and disposing of the body by stealing it into a coffin during a funeral. This had always been nothing more than a fantasy—one requiring skillful timing and the exploitation of the resources of the temple, which he had grown accustomed to despite his many hardships. The fantasy was never directly tied to any murderous feelings he might have felt toward

Jikai. But everything changed that evening he was violated by Satoko. He was shocked and overcome by a volatile mix of inexpressible hatred and affection for the priest's wife. His feeling of sweet intoxication quickly gave way to the realization of how violently he hated Jikai. He hated the priest who was capable of waking him up by pulling on the hemp rope so hard that his hand went numb. And wasn't the Reverend's lascivious behavior reminiscent of the snakes Jinen spied squirming at the bottom of the kite's nest—the insane behavior of Jikai and Satoko in bed together that he had witnessed?

In the end, Jinen managed to hide that Jikai away from the world once and for all.

One morning ten days after the Hisama funeral, Jinen made his way to the main hall and entered the sanctum. Gazing upon Nangaku's geese, a grotesque light flashed in his eyes. He was standing in front of a painting of chicks. They were nesting in the shade of pine needles with their mother, who was feeding them. Jinen violently thrust his fingers around the image of the mother bird and tore it out. It left a hole in just that area of the panel, exposing a layer of paper and the wooden frame beneath.

Jinen left the Kohōan the next day, the thirteenth day after Jikai's disappearance.

"I'm going on a trip. To where the Reverend went," Jinen told Satoko two or three days before he left, but she hadn't taken him seriously. She was thus genuinely surprised on the morning following his disappearance when she awoke to find him gone.

"Jinen! Jinen!" she went about calling loudly. But Jinen was nowhere to be found. His tatami mat was still laid out on the wooden floor of his little room. By the door sat the wicker basket and Jinen's worn-out, neatly folded futon.

Arriving at the main hall, Satoko realized she was alone. She stared at Nangaku's paintings in the sanctum. The ten years since that moment when she had gazed upon them while Nangaku caressed her ear rushed past and disappeared.

"The Kohōan will become known as 'The Temple of the Wild Geese,' and the number of famous places in western Kyoto will increase by one."

These words, which Nangaku murmured to her from time to time, still echoed vibrantly in her ears. Just then, glancing at the bottom half of the fourth panel, Satoko noticed the spot where one of the geese had been ripped away. *Who could have done such a thing?*

It occurred to her immediately that it had been Jinen. The missing image was of a mother goose, her white down puffed out around her—a beautiful painting of a mother feeding her crying chicks, which were still covered in downy feathers.

Satoko blanched. She recalled that whenever he entered the sanctum, Jinen would stare at that one area of the panel. She felt sad that he would be compelled to tear out the image. All at once, however, Satoko was gripped by a strange suspicion that Jinen's act of vandalism and Jikai's disappearance were related. A shudder of fear raced down her back.

Satoko called to mind that late, lonely night of the seventh when the wind was blowing hard and Jikai had failed to return home. She hadn't been able to sleep then because of an indescribable fear. Jinen had gone to the Hisama household in Imadegawa to perform a memorial service that day, she recalled, and he must have seen that Heizaburō was in his death throes. And yet he didn't say a word about it after he returned. They learned of Heizaburō's death on the eighth. So why hadn't Jinen mentioned the dying brother? Satoko wondered if Jinen hadn't done something terrible? But what terrible thing could he have done? Satoko could never give voice to the suspicion growing in her heart. She trembled. Then she shook her head to clear it of her terrifying suspicions.

Kirihara Satoko returned to her family home a month later. During the second month after her departure, a new head priest was appointed to the Kohōan. No one ever learned the whereabouts of the former priest Kitami Jikai or of his acolyte Jinen. The rumors that circulated about them and Satoko, who was also known to reside at the temple, eventually died away.

The *fusuma* paintings of wild geese by the artist Nangaku remain to this day in the main hall of the Kohōan in western Kyoto. With the passing of the years, these large panels, which had been sprinkled with gold dust, darkened until they arrived at their current dusty, reddish hue. The flock of wild geese perching in the branches of the ancient pine, however, is still wonderfully alive.

The spot in the painting where the mother bird had been ripped away was never repaired, but was left as it was in its damaged state.

# BAMBOO DOLLS OF ECHIZEN

# I

Deep in the Nanjō highlands, in the ancient province of Echizen, modern-day Fukui Prefecture, there was a tiny hamlet called Takekami. Consisting of just seventeen households tucked within a steep valley of the mountains, the place was hidden away and nearly forgotten. That its name ever crossed the lips of even neighboring villagers was due solely to the fame of its bamboo.

Takekami was a hamlet of bamboo craftsmen, and every variety of the plant was grown there—*madake, hachiku, mōsōdake, medake, Hakonedake, Iyodake.* Even rare varietals such as black bamboo were cultivated because they were necessary to the local craft. The households of Takekami were located along both sides of a hollow. Bamboo groves, spaced about a hundred meters apart, surrounded the dwellings and enveloped them in silent obscurity.

All of the properties were dark and gloomy, in part because of the proximity of the groves, but also because the hamlet was entirely in the shadow of the Nanjō range, which rises precipitously from the city of Takefu to form a sheer bluff that faces the Sea of Japan and towers over a tributary of the Hinogawa River. Each household consisted of a main building with a thatched roof and a work shed whose cedar shingles were held in place with stones. These roofs were sharply gabled due to heavy snow in the region, and at no time during the year did they ever completely dry. Mushrooms sprouted in the nooks and crannies of the village road, which was always damp and smelling of mildew.

The hamlet's first settlers were not bamboo craftsmen. They used bamboo to pipe water from a valley stream, the Takekami River, to rice paddies that had been terraced along the hollow's slopes. All of the paddies were small, some no larger than a single tatami mat. The villagers also tended fields of sugarcane, dry-paddy rice, cabbage and barley higher up the mountain. These fields were more difficult to irrigate, and hauling compost up the long, winding paths was extremely hard labor. In the winter, it was customary for the villagers to venture into the snow-covered mountains to make charcoal.

Eventually the residents of Takekami began to cultivate and sell bamboo for profit. Wholesale merchants from Takefu or Fukui City would buy the raw material, which would then be fashioned into laundry poles and fishing rods. This became a steady source of cash income for the villagers, who otherwise barely managed to eke out a living.

Around the beginning of the Taishō Period, a man named Ujiie Kizaemon, who had once served as village head, pioneered the art of bamboo crafts in the hamlet. From childhood, Kizaemon had been skilled with his hands. He would cut bamboo from a grove behind his house and use it to make various items, including open-weave baskets, colanders, tea whisks, and ribs for umbrellas and fans. Wholesalers who sold sundry goods around Sabae and Takefu heard about Kizaemon and started coming to Takekami specifically to buy his wares.

If the villagers had continued to sell the bamboo wholesale, then over time they would have depleted the groves on their narrow strip of land. Not only was it was more profitable to make and sell bamboo crafts, it was also better for conserving the groves. Thus, the practice won favor, and the villagers began coming to Kizaemon's shed to learn the trade. At one point, it is said, fully two-thirds of the villagers labored as bamboo craftsmen.

Because the hamlet had been built at the foot of a steep mountainside, the original settlers had planted the groves as protection against avalanches. It was only after the bamboo became a secondary source of income that Takekami became known to neighboring towns. Each spring, at the time of the snowmelt, the settlers' descendants could be seen crossing the high Nanjō range on their way to the lowland towns to sell their wares, their backs loaded with open-weave baskets, colanders, pot mats, flower vases and other items crafted during the winter.

Takekami's first master bamboo craftsman, Ujiie Kizaemon, was a widower who lived together with his only son, Kisuke. The boy's mother had died when he was just three years old, and Kisuke had no memory of her. Kizaemon raised his son lovingly, tending to him as carefully as he tended to the rare black bamboo.

Kizaemon was very small in stature—just over four feet tall—and built like a child. Even his face was small and childlike. His head, however, was disproportionately large. Because it protruded in the back and because Kizaemon kept his hair closely cropped, it resembled the prickly shell of a chestnut. Overall, Kizaemon had the air of a religious novice. But his small, deep-set eyes, which shone with a penetrating light, lent him the expression of a craftsman. His son was his spitting image.

Kisuke was teased because of his small size, but because his father was so well respected no one in the hamlet openly ridiculed him. By the time he was a little boy, however, a branch school had been built in the neighboring village of Hirose and Kisuke was obliged to attend. The children there taunted him, and the boy began spending more and more time at home learning the art of bamboo crafts. No one would ridicule him, Kisuke told himself, once he became a master like his father.

Kizaemon, too, had taken up bamboo crafts because of his small size. The villagers had constructed a charcoal kiln seven miles into the interior of the mountains and would shoulder straw bundles of charcoal up and down the steep slopes in winter. Because Kizaemon lacked the physical strength to make the trek, he would instead spend the winter holed up in his work shed. Seated atop an old cushion with cotton stuffing poking out, he would fashion exquisite birdcages as well as practical items such as tea whisks, bud vases, writing brush holders and lunch boxes.

In his draft physical, Kizaemon had been classified Rank 3, which meant he was fit for military service but deferred from active duty. The year following the exam, he went to Kyoto, where he met with several bamboo craftsmen and dealers who taught him the trade. When he returned home, he skillfully copied their work and created his own designs, which he shared with his fellow villagers. The villagers of Takekami were industrious. Soon they began clearing land to cultivate specific varietals in order to ensure an abundant supply of raw materials. In this way, Kizaemon was responsible for the increase in the number of bamboo groves around the hamlet. In return, Kiza-emon seemed to live for the bamboo. His fingers were small and slender like a child's, but when they touched a piece of bamboo they moved assuredly, as if possessed.

In the late autumn of 1922, death claimed Takekami's first master crafts-man; Kizaemon was sixty-eight years old. He had been turning the lathe in his workshop under the damp roof of cedar-bark shingles just before he passed. The lathe was a handmade tool necessary to bamboo work. Kizaemon would wrap a strip of leather around a spindle made of oak and thread this through a crosspiece. Then he would attach a three-pronged awl that looked like the teeth of a mouse to the tip of the spindle. Moving the crosspiece up and down would cause the spindle to turn. It was a convenient tool for drilling holes in hard bamboo. Kizaemon had been making a birdcage when he collapsed.

Thinking it odd that the workshop had gone so quiet, Kisuke had rushed into the shed to find his father prone on the floor, his face drained of color and his eyes glazed. A neighbor named Yohei happened to be passing by. He helped Kisuke carry Kizaemon back to the main house, where they laid him on a futon. Old age and long hours of sitting in the workshop had weakened his body. Lying there limp atop the well-worn futon, its stuffing bursting the seams, he looked like an emaciated crow. Seeing him like this, Kisuke under-stood that his father did not have long to live. He sent word to the villagers. By the time the men and women of all the other sixteen households arrived, Kizaemon was on the verge of death. Just before he drew his final breath, he called to his son in a voice racked with pain. "Kisuke, Kisuke, open the door to the veranda."

Kisuke obediently ran to the large door and undid the latches. Outside, the small, narrow garden was bathed in the weak glow of the late autumn sun. Withered azaleas covered the garden's landscaped hill. Beyond the hill, the tops of a line of *madake* bamboo, their leaves just beginning to turn yellow, could be seen swaying gently in the breeze.

"Kisuke," Kizaemon called again in a weak voice. "Remember, cut the *ma-dake* in November. Understand?" Then, with a loud, strangling noise rising from his throat, he died.

All of Kizaemon's neighbors had been standing by, silently taking in his final moments. There was not one who did not shed tears over the loss of this benefactor, the man who introduced the art of bamboo crafts to the hamlet of Takekami. Yet only Kisuke could comprehend the significance of his father's dying words.

Usually when the wholesale merchants came to purchase raw bamboo, most of the villagers would ask them to return after the spring harvest. If the bamboo were cut in spring, the roots would rot over the summer and fertilize the new crop. Because this helped reduce costs, most grove owners harvested in spring and summer. Not Kizaemon. He harvested at the end of autumn, even though the roots would continue to live through the cold months and sap the soil of fertilizer, which would eventually have to be replaced. The practice incurred losses, but Kizaemon was a meticulous craftsman. He taught his son that the best bamboo for craftwork was harvested in the winter.

Kizaemon placed the bamboo he harvested in winter in the *tsushi* loft under the rafters of his house's triangular roof. There, the sooty smoke of the hearth would dry it out and turn it a reddish-black, doubling the strength of the bamboo in the process. There was nothing better from which to make birdcages, flower vases or confectionery trays. Kizaemon placed more importance on his workmanship than on his groves.

Kisuke was touched by the single-mindedness of his father. Even in the very moment of death, he thought of his bamboo crafts. Having reminded his son of the importance of the late autumn harvest, he could rest in peace. Looking into his father's lifeless face, Kisuke wept bitterly—not from sorrow—but at the memory of a trip they had taken to Kyoto and Osaka together to walk among the bamboo groves there.

"Your father put his heart and soul into his bamboo, Kisuke," the neighbor Yohei said, his wrinkled old face wet with tears. "You're going to have to work hard so he won't outdo you, you understand?

"From now on, your father won't be here for you. He's gone. His workshop is yours. And the tools he wouldn't let anyone touch while he was alive are yours. His lathe and vise, the blade he used as an awl and his triangular knife. They're all yours. Your father traveled all the way to Sanjō in Echigo to buy these tools. They belong to you now. So starting tomorrow, you do your best."

The wind was strong that day and the bamboo surrounding the house swayed violently. The noise of the rustling leaves sounded like a lamentation for the death of Kizaemon, who had given his life to bamboo craft making. It was late November in Ujiie Kisuke's twenty-first year.

·

Because there was no temple in the hamlet, Kizaemon's funeral took place at the Zuisenji temple in the village of Hirose, one valley over. The residents of Takekami had made this their permanent family temple, and everyone gathered there for the service. Because Kizaemon had done so much for their community, however, they wanted his grave in the hamlet so they could duly honor his spirit. At the suggestion of Yohei, who was then serving as village head, the craftsman's body was interred on a small, partially sunlit enclosure of level land between the bamboo groves that covered the hill behind his former home. In December, during a heavy snowfall, a stone marker was raised. It read simply:

**Ujiie Kizaemon, Master Bamboo Craftsman.**

Not long after the stone was erected, during a light storm of powdery snow, a stranger turned up at the door of Kisuke's workshop. It was just past noon. Kisuke had placed a brazier where his father used to sit and was hunched over beside it mindlessly turning the lathe to make a birdcage when the woman peeked inside. She was wearing loose work trousers over traditional robes and appeared to be about thirty years old. Bending over at the waist, she asked in a low voice, "Is anyone home?" From beneath the large wool shawl covering her head, she inspected Kisuke. "Is this the residence of Mr. Ujiie Kizaemon?"

Surprised, Kisuke put down his work and returned her gaze. He realized at once that she was not from the hamlet. There was an aura of the city about her; the collar of her red undershirt peeked through her clothes.

"Yes, this is Kizaemon's place," he answered stiffly but immediately sensed that he had seen this woman before. When she moved closer to the threshold, as if to get a better look of the dimly lit space, she blinked her narrow eyes and smiled. She was an attractive woman, with a plump sweet face and eyes like thin, fine threads. To Kisuke, she looked gentle, tender, but because he was bashful, he could barely speak.

"Would you be his son, by any chance?" the woman asked

"Yes," he answered, and a look of nostalgia washed over the woman's face.

"Your father was very kind to me. I heard he passed away and was hoping you would allow me to pay my respects at his grave. Could you tell me where it is?"

Kisuke was startled. Had his father shown this woman kindness? He thought he had seen her somewhere before—perhaps they had met once when he traveled with his father to Takefu or Sabae. But no matter how hard he tried, he could not place her. Gathering his courage, he said, "And you are?"

"Me?" the woman stammered. "I don't feel I'm worthy enough to tell you my name. Please tell me where I can find the grave."

Kisuke assumed she was the wife of a hardware store or toy shop owner in one of the nearby towns. He knew some of his father's clients had wives like this woman. When spring arrived, his father would call on the shops with which he had business. Sometimes he would be away from home for two or three days at a stretch. He had taken Kisuke with him on occasion, but because he had been so young at the time he scarcely remembered any of the details. No doubt this woman was someone his father had come to know through his business dealings.

Though it seemed odd that she would not give her name, Kisuke thought the least he could do was offer her some tea since she had come such a long way in the snow to visit his father's grave.

Although she insisted he needn't go to any trouble, she dutifully followed Kisuke over the snow-covered path to the main house. Once they were inside, Kisuke's expression changed. The woman had the scent of the mother he had never known, and he found himself drawn to her full breasts. After guiding her to the living room, he prepared some *bancha* tea, his hands trembling as he poured the hot water from the kettle. He was not used to serving guests, but the woman seemed kind-hearted. Sensing that she was no ordinary acquaintance of his father's, Kisuke found the courage to talk.

"Why won't you tell me your name?"

"Me?" she faltered and cast her eyes downward. "I'm Tamae, from Awara. You're Kisuke, aren't you?" Her eyes narrowed as if she too had found the nerve to speak. "Your father often mentioned you to me. I met you once, a long time ago. You were still a little boy. Your father was truly a good man. Whenever he came to Awara, he would always drop by."

Kisuke still had no idea who she was. He recalled going to Awara with his father; it was the only hot springs resort in Echizen. They had left Takekami, passed through Takefu, and arrived at Fukui City, where they boarded a coach headed for Mikuni, eventually arriving at the hot springs town. There were many inns there. Like the towns of Yamashiro and Katayamazu in the Kaga region of southern Ishikawa Prefecture, Awara had a rich history as a hot springs resort in Hokuriku. Kisuke had accompanied his father there on business, and they had stayed overnight. But apart from their room, which overlooked a sweeping garden, the only thing Kisuke remembered was rinsing off his father's back in the bathhouse's wooden tub. He had no memory of a woman there. Yet he felt certain that he had seen her face somewhere before.

"Do you remember me?" Tamae asked.

"No, I'm afraid I don't. When I was little, my father took me along to Awara, Kyoto and Osaka. But I can't recall any women on those trips. All I can remember are bamboo groves. The *mōsō* bamboo in Uji, the *madake* bamboo in Ogurusu in Kyoto . . . All I remember are those groves."

"I see." Tamae tossed Kisuke a flirtatious glance. "You remember the bamboo groves, but you don't remember anything about me at all. How disappointing . . ." She picked up the teacup with her slender, supple hands and sipped delicately as if afraid to spill a drop.

Kisuke's face grew hot, and he felt ill at ease. Never before had such a beautiful woman visited his dark, lonely house.

"Could you please show me to the grave now?" she suddenly asked.

"Of course."

Kisuke led her around to the *medake* grove at the back of the house.

"There's certainly a lot of bamboo here, isn't there?" the woman said in an admiring tone as she shuffled along after him in her straw boots.

Unlike *mōsō* bamboo, *medake* has slender leaves and narrow stalks. Kizaemon had planted the bamboo evenly so that the stalks resembled the teeth of a comb. Their joints, too, were perfectly aligned, creating the illusion of rows of white horizontal lines. It was as if the stalks were held together by a series of delicate threads.

"How lovely! The ground is so clean and tight. Not a leaf has fallen," the woman exclaimed.

Indeed, the snow seemed to have stopped once they entered the grove. From time to time, whatever had piled atop the leaves would fall with a plop upon the woman's shawl. On the way to the gravesite, she would glance at her boots now and then as if she were having trouble walking.

The grave was located between thickets of bamboo grass and a grove of *hachiku*. Kisuke stood by as the woman climbed the stone steps to the grave marker. She pulled prayer beads from the folds of her obi and pressed her hands together. Then she closed her eyes for a few minutes as if in prayer. Kisuke stared intently at her profile. Her full cheeks quivered, and tears streamed from the corners of her eyes.

**Hōchikuin seizan ichihō koji**

This was Kizaemon's posthumous Buddhist name, conferred on him by the priest of the family temple. The inscription—**Ujiie Kizaemon, Master Bamboo Craftsman**—was carved vertically on the front face of the marker, while the posthumous name was carved along the side. The woman muttered the name several times to herself. She chanted the *nembutsu*, the invocation to Buddha—"*Nanmandabu, Nanmandabu, Nanmandabu*"—then closed her eyes once more.

After a while, the woman politely thanked Kisuke for showing her to the gravesite and then started to make her way home.

Kisuke saw her off as far as the eaves of his workshop. Just as they parted, the snow began to come down much harder. The single road to the village turned and twisted along the valley; a large cedar along the way soared up into the sky like a needle, revealing its snow-covered tip. Kisuke watched the woman until her shawl-covered figure became indistinguishable under the giant tree, which was black mottled with white.

*Tamae. Tamae from Awara* . . . Kisuke muttered her name repeatedly to himself, but he could not remember having met her before. The smile she had left him with warmed his heart. He had sensed a kind of motherly nostalgia in her narrow eyes.

Kisuke returned at once to his workplace. He stirred up the brazier, where the fire was just about to go out. The image of the woman continued to linger in the room. Kisuke's feverish eyes glistened as he began to turn the lathe; it issued a faint, piercing squeak that reverberated off the ceiling of the lonely shed.

Outside, the wind had picked up and was blowing fiercely. Hearing a low rumbling in the mountains, Kisuke suddenly felt worried. Tamae was walking home over snow-covered roads in a blizzard.

# II

Kisuke suffered a complex because of his height. He had no doubt that his mother had been small, otherwise he might have inherited her genes and grown to a respectable size. In all ways, however, he resembled his father. He couldn't reach his fingertips to the arch of the doorway, and when sitting at his workplace he looked like a child. While Kizaemon had been alive, he hadn't been so self-conscious about his stature, but after he died Kisuke became increasingly vulnerable to feelings of inferiority.

After cutting bamboo in the groves, he would have to carry it along the village road back to his work shed. Because he was so short, the bamboo would drag along the ground, causing him great embarrassment. He had inherited his father's skills, and his craftsmanship was second to none; but when he passed the young women of the village, Kisuke would blush and break into a trot. The humiliation he had suffered in school had stayed with him, and he never forgot how the villagers would whisper derisively about his father's diminutive size. After his father's death, Kisuke felt that he had inherited the mocking laughter of the villagers. His sense of inferiority deepened, and he began to have increasingly dark thoughts.

Kisuke had also never been with a woman. Whenever he visited Takefu, Sabae or Fukui City, the merchants would greet him warmly and take him to dinner. On those occasions, he never looked directly into the faces of the women who came and waited on him. And he never drank a drop of liquor. Because he always kept his face downcast, he made everyone uncomfortable and spoiled many parties. Eventually, he would leave on his own and follow the dark mountain roads home. It wasn't that he disliked women. He enjoyed talking with them. But for some reason, he would tense up around them, embarrassed and confused.

Up until his twenty-first year, Kisuke had assumed that he wasn't alone in his feelings. His father, he thought, must have felt the same way. But the sudden visit of the woman from Awara changed everything. She had said his father had been so kind to her when he was alive, and Kisuke was startled to realize the possibilities of their relationship. *Did my father keep that woman?*

Kisuke half-believed and half-doubted this conclusion. Tamae didn't seem to be a bad woman. She had, after all, gone to the trouble of journeying over snow-covered roads to pay her respects at his father's grave. Certainly she would never have come such a distance had they not had some meaningful bond.

Tamae's physical appearance, however, forced Kisuke to reappraise his father in a new light. Was it possible that Tamae worked at a bar in Awara? Kisuke became convinced that when his father had stayed in town overnight, he had stayed with her.

Kisuke felt the urge to visit Awara and find out for himself. He wanted to visit Tamae and talk with her about his father and about the past. Even while at work, Kisuke could not stop obsessing over the circumstances surrounding their relationship. In the process, he recalled some distant memories.

The inn district of Awara was bustling and lively. The streets were lined with two-story buildings that had balustrades running along the outside corridors; they looked like the backdrop to a play. The inn where Kisuke and his father stayed was in the center of town. It had been one of the larger establishments. Kisuke remembered being met at the wide entryway by a large crowd of servants who pressed their hands to the floor in greeting. All the women wore a red sash and had their hair done up in a chignon. Their faces were covered in white makeup set off by crisply applied lipstick. As Kisuke passed through the hallway, he recalled, the women's pungent smell assaulted his nose.

Kisuke stayed one night at the inn with his father before returning to Takekami. He had no recollection of Tamae having been there. He had no memory of being shown any special kindness by any of the maids. His father must have met Tamae while in Awara for a gathering of bamboo craftsmen. He must have gotten to know Tamae at a different establishment. Kisuke wondered where.

Kisuke was powerfully attracted to Tamae's face, to the way she carried herself, and to her manner of speech. It seemed perfectly natural that his father must have been in love with her. But when the thought occurred to him, Kisuke experienced a twinge of jealousy.

Kisuke had no memory of his mother. He had been told that she collapsed in the middle of a bamboo grove. She had suffered a heart attack while carrying two buckets suspended from a pole hoisted across her shoulder. She died where she fell. Kisuke learned from his father that she had a naturally weak constitution, and that her health had diminished after giving birth. She had been unable to breastfeed, and Kisuke had been raised on rice gruel. When he heard the story of his mother's pathetic death in the bamboo grove, Kisuke felt overwhelmed by sadness because it reminded him that he would never experience the tender care of a mother.

Perhaps this is why Kisuke was so stiff and tongue-tied in the presence of women, even the younger girls of the hamlet. He had thought he inherited his shyness from his father, but the revelation that even Kizaemon could have relations with a woman as beautiful as Tamae shocked him. All his yearning came bursting to the surface.

*That's it! I should go to Awara, and I should get married. I'd be so fortunate to get a woman like Tamae to come live with me here. I'd work harder than anyone. I'll become the top master craftsman in Japan.*

These thoughts raced through Kisuke's mind as he sat in his workshop, silently turning his lathe.

Ujiie Kisuke visited the hot springs town of Awara in April of his twenty-second year, a full four months after Tamae had come to Takekami to visit his father's grave. Kisuke had not left the hamlet at all during that time because the snow was piled up so deep. The hamlet was located at such a high elevation that no one bothered to clear the roads in winter, and at a glance, it was hard to tell them apart from the valleys. Because the mountains were wild and rough, there was no mail delivery either. The hamlet itself had no electricity; it was utterly isolated.

In the coldest months, the residents of Takekami focused their efforts on the bamboo crafts they would sell in spring. Kisuke would fill the shelves of his shed in anticipation of the arrival of craft dealers from Kyoto and Osaka, who would come after the snowmelt to buy the best items. In addition to the colanders and open-weave baskets that all the villagers made, Kisuke also crafted high-quality goods, including special tea whisks and frames for fine fans. Kisuke worked more diligently than all of them.

On the morning of April 2, Kisuke made his way through the cedar forest, which was still patched with snow, and down the twisting mountain path. He carried on his back a large bundle with about thirty confectionery boxes. He was taking them to wholesalers in Takefu and Fukui City and looked forward to unburdening himself of them and to the money they would earn him.

Kisuke had spent the winter hidden away in his dark workshop, and his face looked dull and grimy against the bright mountain path. His eyes, however, were bright and cheerful in a reflection of the spring sun. He walked alone, having left the hamlet while it was still dark. It was his habit to leave earlier than the other villagers because he was slower on foot and because he disliked encountering women on the mountain paths.

Kisuke arrived in Takefu in the morning hours and then moved on to Fukui City. All of his business affairs were completed by three in the afternoon. From there, he made his way to Awara. He was brimming with excitement.

The streets of the hot springs resort were filled with passersby. Now that the snows had melted, visitors were flooding in from the neighboring towns. Men and women in padded kimonos and clogs jostled one another in the shooting galleries and souvenir shops. They made quite a racket.

Kisuke spotted a cheaply painted restaurant near a row of souvenir shops and stepped inside. Not only was he hungry, he thought he might ask the waitresses about Tamae, if they seemed young and good-natured. Three women greeted him as he entered. They all looked to be about eighteen or nineteen and wore splash-patterned kimonos with yellow muslin obis. Kisuke ordered a bowl of rice topped with scrambled eggs and took a seat at a table; its edge came up to his chin. Seeing this, the women exchanged peculiar glances and began to whisper among themselves. Eventually one of them—a short, round-faced, country girl—brought him tea.

Kisuke had to work up the nerve to speak to her. "There's someone I'd like to ask you about, and I was hoping you could help me out."

The young woman stared at him in blank surprise.

"I'm looking for a woman named Tamae. All I know is that she's from Awara, but I don't know where she lives."

"Tamae?" The woman glanced over at her companions and snickered. "You don't know her family name?"

"No, I don't. She told me only that her name is Tamae. She has a round face and white complexion."

"Oh, I know!" The woman's eyes widened. "She might be in Sanchō-machi." Once again, she looked back toward her companions and a vulgar grin spread from the corners of her mouth. "She's definitely in Sanchō-machi."

"Sanchō-machi . . . where would that be?"

"It's the red-light district," the young woman answered right away. "There are also bars over there. And a lot of women, too . . . She's probably there. If she's a geisha, however, then your woman, Tamae, won't likely be there."

*The pleasure quarters?* A chill ran up Kisuke's spine.

"It has to be Sanchō-machi for sure," the woman chirped, as if singing a song. "You should try going there for a visit. Your woman Tamae is likely there."

# III

The pleasure quarters of Awara consisted of a single narrow street lined with brothels. It wasn't an officially licensed district, and it wasn't all that large. Awara was originally a hot springs town, so it also had geisha. If a geisha was of the third or fourth rank, it was customary for her to leave her establishment and meet with clients at houses of assignation. Sanchō-machi, however, housed prostitutes plain and simple. It even looked like a red-light district. An equal number of single- and two-story houses hemmed in the narrow street, and their entryways were fitted with red and blue stained glass. Women would sit out front with their robes parted to reveal their powdered necks and call to the men who passed by.

By the time Kisuke reached Sanchō-machi, it was already dusk and the area was just coming to life. He hurriedly made his way to one of the buildings nearest the street's entrance and approached a young woman there. "Is there a Tamae on this street?" he asked.

The woman stared at Kisuke. She had thought he was a child, but her eyes widened in surprise upon closer inspection. Still, her response was unaffected. "Tamae?" she muttered casually. "Do you mean Tamae over at the Hanamiya?"

"How old is this Tamae at the Hanamiya?"

"Well, let's see . . . She's already past thirty, but she looks young. Is her complexion fair?"

"That's her. That's her," Kisuke replied eagerly. He had been right to come here, he thought. To make sure, he asked again if the name of the woman at the Hanamiya was Tamae.

"It's Tamae for sure," the woman said. "She's a really nice person." She paused and stared at Kisuke. "But you know, mister . . . Tamae, well, she's been sick."

"Sick?"

"Yeah, she had a cold that got real bad. I heard that she's been laid up in bed the whole time. Hasn't been working at all."

A cloud passed over Kisuke's face. "When you say she's laid up and doesn't go out, do you mean she's laid up at the Hanamiya?"

"Yeah, she's there." The woman put on a grave face to match Kisuke's worried expression. "She had several appointments at the hospital, but I heard she's at the Hanamiya. She's strong, but she got soaked in a heavy snow coming back from some trip. She caught cold, and it just got worse and worse."

Kisuke wanted to see Tamae as soon as possible. He impatiently received directions from the woman, then thanked her and hurried off.

The Hanamiya was a rundown two-story building just fifty meters further down the street. Kisuke arrived in moments, just as two young women had come out to sprinkle water around the entryway. They stared at him as he approached.

"Is there a woman named Tamae here?"

The women exchanged glances. Contempt for Kisuke's appearance showed in their eyes. "She's here, but . . ."

"I know she's been ill and in bed. I hate to bother you, but could you tell her that Kisuke from Takekami is here? If you tell her I'm Kisuke from Takekami, she'll understand."

Kisuke was agitated. Although the women looked upon his face and pouting lips with disdain, they withdrew straight away, their clogs clattering. After a moment, one of the women returned. "Please come in," she said and led Kisuke inside.

The light from the streetlamp was shining through the door's red and blue stained glass, casting colorful patterns on the hard-packed earthen floor of the entryway. Kisuke glanced from the floor toward a dimly lit hallway and let out a gasp. Tamae stood before him, a mere shadow of herself. Since he had last seen her in December, her face had become thin and wasted. She appeared weak, and her skin was pale and lusterless.

Tamae stared at Kisuke and pulled together the collar of her nightgown. As she spoke, the blood rose to her face. "How nice of you to come. Are you here on your own?"

"Yes, I came alone."

"Please come in," she said. "I'm taking a break from work. The place is a mess, as you can see, but come in."

Kisuke removed his rubber boots and followed after Tamae, whose red-striped nightgown dragged along the floor. This was Kisuke's first visit to a brothel. In the dark corridor, he passed a woman wearing nothing but a long under robe.

Tamae led him to a six-mat room at the back of the building. Because the eaves hung low over the windows, it was dark and gloomy, but it was thoroughly clean and seemed cheerful compared to Kisuke's house in Takekami. Against one wall was a red-lacquered vanity, a small desk and a chest of drawers made of paulownia wood. A futon had been laid out in front of the tokonoma alcove next to a doll case. Apparently this was Tamae's room. Kisuke hesitated at the door.

"You were a great help to me that time I visited you," Tamae said in a weak voice, placing a hand over her breast. "My right lung has gotten much worse since the New Year. I've been bedridden this whole time. I've gone to see the doctor repeatedly and keep taking the medicine he gives me."

She offered Kisuke a smile.

The woman at the first brothel had said Tamae had fallen ill after getting soaked in a heavy snowstorm. Now that Kisuke learned she had been sick since the New Year, he found it hard to look at her. Tamae had visited him in mid-December. The snow had been falling lightly when she arrived but the weather worsened by evening. Kisuke was certain she fell ill after walking home through that storm.

"Isn't this all because you came to visit my father's grave? It snowed heavily that night, didn't it? It's because you walked through a heavy snow that you caught a cold, right?"

Tamae raised her listless eyes to Kisuke and smiled. "I got to Takefu that day without problem. But after I boarded the train, I suddenly felt a chill. By the time the New Year arrived, I had developed a cough."

"If that's what happened, then it's just as I thought. Visiting my place wasn't good for you."

Kisuke felt that he was somehow responsible for Tamae's illness and a look of contrition shone in his eyes. Avoiding his gaze, Tamae added charcoal to the brazier and stoked the embers. At last she poured water from the iron kettle and made some tea. With pale, trembling hands, she held out a cup to Kisuke.

"Kisuke?" she said at last. "Do you know what that is?" Tamae pointed to the glass doll case sitting next to the alcove.

Kisuke had noticed it casually when he entered the room, and thought the doll it contained was unusual. Only now did he realize that it was made of bamboo.

"Your father made it," Tamae said, her voice warmly passionate. "I received it the same year I came here. That's ten years ago now. You were still a child then, Kisuke. You were still wearing a pipe-sleeve kimono, toddling along behind your father. He bought you a candy drop. Your father was always sweet to me. He even went to the trouble of making that doll for me."

Kisuke became transfixed on the doll and a strangely sensual light settled in his eyes. He had never seen anything like it before.

He opened the case and took it in his hands. It looked to be about a foot high, and was exquisitely crafted. Was it a courtesan of the Edo Period? Kisuke wasn't sure, but there was a lacquered wooden comb fixed in its hair, which was styled in a chignon. The doll's kimono looked like an unlined summer robe. The speckled pattern of the kimono was created with bamboo-shoot bark. The doll wore clogs with three supports made out of bamboo stems. Her large obi, knotted in front, was also fashioned entirely from bamboo bark. Looking at the back of the doll, Kisuke could see that her body was made of a split stem of bamboo grass; its delicate plastering peeped through in several places. It was the most elaborate piece of bamboo craftsmanship he had ever seen.

"I remember it was a winter day when your father gave this to me. He went out of his way to bring it here," Tamae told him.

Kisuke was astonished by the display of creativity in his father's use of bamboo for the doll's kimono. His heart soared. His father's spirit infused every inch of the doll and it was because Tamae looked after it so well that it remained in such pristine condition a decade later.

*Father was in love with Tamae. He must have loved her to have created such a work and to have traveled the snow-covered roads to bring it here . . .* Still Kisuke could not recall his father ever making a doll like this. *Father must have gotten up quietly after I was asleep to make this.* He had to fight back the tears.

"Kisuke?" Tamae called him back. "That doll is an *oiran*, a courtesan. I told your father about a courtesan who performed old ballads when I worked at the Shimabara in Kyoto. Your father made a doll of that woman. He told me that I'd become an *oiran* just as distinguished as she was, and then he made this doll."

Kisuke placed the doll back in the case and glanced at Tamae's profile. Her face was flushed. Stifling a cough, she asked, "Have you ever been to Kyoto, Kisuke?"

"Yes." His nose was running and he sniffled to prevent a drip. "My father took me to Kyoto now and then. But I never went to the Shimabara. When we talked in December, I told you that the only things I remember are the grove of *mōsō* bamboo in Uji and the *madake* grove in Ogurusu. There was also a very wide grove at the base of a hill covered in tea plants; it looked like an ocean."

"That's right, isn't it? There are lots of bamboo groves in Uji." Tamae smiled and her eyes narrowed.

Hearing her speak so familiarly about the bamboo groves in Uji made Kisuke increasingly nostalgic. Still, her emaciated frame, her pale face and her nearly translucent skin startled him. Tamae, who had looked so healthy before the New Year, had been transformed by her illness. It seemed to have aged her. Wrinkles had developed at the corners of her eyes. And while her lips had retained their shapeliness, the lines from her nose to the corners of her mouth made her look forlorn. Overall, her appearance created the impression of fragility.

If Tamae had worked in the Shimabara in Kyoto, she had endured years of hardship as a prostitute. Although Kisuke had no experience with women himself, he had heard of the Shimabara as well as other red-light districts. He had heard that both Sabae and Benten-chō, which was located along the Omote River in Takefu, had pleasure quarters that catered exclusively to soldiers. *Are all brothels enclosed in stained glass? Are they all divided into small rooms that get little sunlight because of the low eaves? Do women such as Tamae actually live in such places?*

From the moment Kisuke had entered the Hanamiya, he felt nauseated by the scent of the women and the acrid smell of carbolic acid. He had thought the latter must have come from the toilets, but its distinctive odor was present even in Tamae's room and he had no idea what carbolic acid might be used for.

Kisuke watched in silence as Tamae repeatedly warmed her hands over the brazier. When she loosened her collar and leaned over the weak charcoal embers, he could see the ribs on her chest. He suddenly felt that he had over-stayed his visit.

"I'll come again, Tamae," he said, standing up. "I really wanted to see you. I wanted to thank you for coming to visit the grave. A lot of people showed up at the Zuisenji in Hirose on the day of the funeral, but once they moved the grave to the bamboo grove, not a single person has come by to pay respects. You're the only one, Tamae, and you came a long distance to visit father's grave. He must have been rejoicing there in the earth."

"Kisuke?" Tamae suddenly asked with glistening eyes. "Is your father buried under the marker?"

Kisuke was surprised. Although he thought it a strange question, he answered straightaway. "His body was placed in a coffin and moved from the cemetery at the Zuisenji. Father sleeps on a hill covered with bamboo grass and *hachiku*. The spot gets good sunlight."

"Get well soon, Tamae," he said, starting for the door. "Then come again to Takekami and visit father's grave. Whenever I have business in Fukui, I hope you don't mind if I drop by to see you."

As soon as he uttered the words "drop by to see you," Kisuke fell silent. The Hanamiya was a brothel; it would not be easy for him to come see her.

On his way out, Kisuke passed another woman in the darkened corridor. From the hard-packed earthen floor of the entryway, he glanced back and saw Tamae coming hesitantly along the hallway with a group of three young women in brightly colored kimonos. Tamae was lowering her head in a bow.

Kisuke felt a twinge of regret. He wished he had stayed in her room a little longer.

# IV

Back in Takekami, Kisuke reveled in memories of his meeting with Tamae at the Hanamiya. All of the details were burned into his mind—Tamae's dimly lit room, her furnishings, and even the faces and movements of the women he had passed on his way in and out. Most unforgettable of all was the bamboo doll. It was the first of its kind that Kisuke had ever seen. Even more surprising was the fact that it was made by his father.

Kizaemon had used the striped bark of bamboo shoots to create the pattern of the courtesan's kimono and made fine cilia from the soft bark that grows at the core of the shoot to fashion her hair. The doll's hands and feet, the face—everything showed to advantage the luster of the bark, which had been meticulously polished with a scouring rush. The three-support clogs the courtesan wore had been carefully lacquered. Kisuke thought his father had been more than meticulous—he had poured his soul into the work.

His father had been a perfectionist. Once he had received a letter from the Daianji, the family temple of the Matsudaira clan in Echizen, requesting a tea whisk for the head priest, Sugita Shōsen. Kizaemon had been absolutely delighted, but he did not make the whisk right away—the sooty bamboo he had on hand would not do. Eventually a second letter arrived, in which the head priest once again asked about the whisk. Only after half a year had passed did Kizaemon complete the task; it was the year before he died. Kisuke had been anxious about the whisk. But his father had waited patiently for the perfect material from which to make it. Once he obtained it, he went into the workshop, took up his cutting tools, and forgot everything else.

No doubt Kizaemon had crafted the bamboo doll in the same manner, pouring his soul into the work. And because it was for Tamae, Kisuke was convinced that she had captured his heart. Kizaemon's devotion to Tamae showed in her face. When she spoke about the bamboo doll, Kisuke could not help noticing the color rise to her pale cheeks.

*Just how old is Tamae?*

Kisuke guessed she was about thirty-one or thirty-two. His father had died at the age of sixty-eight. Since he had given her the doll ten years ago, he must have begun seeing her when he was already in his late fifties. That being the case, his father had been drawn to a very young woman. Recalling the thin, wasted figure of his father in his final year, Kisuke wondered how it could have concealed such energy.

Kisuke could not clear his mind of Tamae, but he continued to work diligently. Rather than wait for the wholesalers to come buy his wares, however, he would load them on his back and make the trip down the mountain to sell them himself. He would bring along rice cakes or beans from his neighbor Yohei or from the other farmers in the neighborhood as a gift for Tamae, whom he would gather his courage to call on in Sanchō-machi.

Even by the time of his second visit, Tamae's health had improved dramatically; Kisuke could hardly believe it.

"I'm getting better because you came to see me, Kisuke," she told him. "I'm out of bed now, and just look how fat I've become!"

Tamae rolled up her sleeves to show off her plump white arms. Although her veins showed through her pale skin, her limbs looked young and healthy. Tamae seemed to have recovered the vigor lost after coming to Takekami to pay respects at Kizaemon's grave. Kisuke delivered his gifts and quickly went home.

During his visits to the Hanamiya, Kisuke felt proud that he wasn't a customer but also ashamed at the thought that he could never be one. When entering or leaving the brothel, the other women who lived and worked with Tamae would stare at him and his midget-like body. Their eyes would sparkle with a faint gleam of contempt. Kisuke, however, was accustomed to these types of stares.

It made him happy that Tamae never looked at him the way others looked at him. Truly, her eyes never betrayed a hint of disgust toward him. She always welcomed Kisuke like a younger brother.

By his third visit, however, circumstances had changed. The moment he stepped onto the hard-packed earthen floor of the entryway, he was brusquely told, "Tamae's with a customer." Kisuke had anticipated that Tamae's recovery would require a resumption of work. Since she had sold her body to the Hanamiya, she had no choice.

For a fleeting instant, Kisuke felt glad that Tamae was well enough to take a client. This, however, was quickly overtaken by feelings of anxiety—*Perhaps she's overdoing it. Perhaps she's not fully recovered and taking a client will only make her worse*—and then intense disgust—*How could she give her body to some random passerby she knows nothing about?*

Feeling irritated and unsettled, Kisuke bowed, left the Hanamiya, and wandered the streets of Sanchō-machi. After about an hour, he returned just in time to watch Tamae seeing off her customer. The man was a laborer, perhaps thirty-five or thirty-six years old. He wore a soiled flat cap and his dark, sunburned face was contorted. He trotted off in Kisuke's direction. Although Tamae waved after him, she hadn't noticed Kisuke standing there in the street.

"Tamae!" Kisuke called out just as she was about to step back inside.

"When did you get here?" she asked as he ran over.

"A little while ago. You had a customer, so I just walked around. Are you feeling better?" Kisuke held out the package of rice cakes he had brought for her. Tamae looked at him gratefully.

"As you can see, I've put on weight recently," she said. "Thanks to you, Kisuke, I've completely recovered." The light gray circles under her eyes twitched and she gazed at him flirtatiously. "Aren't you coming in?"

"No, not today. I'm on my way home now. I'm making a doll. My father won't outdo me. When it's finished, Tamae, I'd like you to take a look at it."

Tamae detected a strange look in Kisuke's eyes.

"You're going to make a doll to rival your father's? You'll win, Kisuke," she laughed, exposing her teeth. "Your father once told me that he was no match for you," she said and her eyes narrowed to threads.

Kisuke felt awkward hearing that his father had come to the Hanamiya and praised his skills. "Well, I should be getting home," he said. "I'll come by again when the doll is ready." Unsure of how to handle the lump that had formed in his chest, he retreated several steps.

Tamae nodded, and a dark shadow crossed over her moist eyes. "Please," she said, "make a beautiful doll."

Kisuke's expression darkened during the journey home. He couldn't stand imagining Tamae with a customer. He conjured an image of her pale face and lamented the fact that she had to bare her lusterless skin for a man she didn't know.

As soon as he arrived in Takekami, Kisuke went straight to his workshop and slammed the door behind him. He sat on the hollowed-out cushion his father always used and took up his cutting tools. Kisuke was fashioning a doll that resembled Tamae on the day she came to pay her respects at Kizaemon's grave. It would be dressed in loose work trousers with a shawl draped over its head. He would not make a courtesan like his father had. Awl in hand, he felt as if he were carving Tamae's very body.

# V

Kisuke split a stalk of thick *madake* bamboo into two pieces to fashion the doll's torso. Then he took the stems of bamboo grass and used them for the legs, which were slightly spread. He made the loose work trousers from the bark of bamboo shoots with a striped pattern. He soaked the bark in water until it was soft enough to cinch up the waist and cuffs of the trousers, which were ingeniously pleated. The kimono, too, was made of bamboo bark. Kisuke selected bark with a dappled pattern most appropriate for the robe, then he carefully fit it to the body of the doll. The collar and string ties of the short jacket worn over the kimono were also made of bark. After Kisuke had finished the ensemble, he applied lacquer according to a technique called *roiro-nuri*. His father had employed the same technique when making chopsticks and toothpick holders in the Wakasa style. It involved applying several layers of a whitish-yellow lacquer to the bamboo, then polishing it with charcoal and a powder made of deer's horn. The *roiro-nuri* method achieves lacquer ware of the highest luster.

Kisuke did not spend every day working on the doll alone. Rush orders for birdcages or fans would come in from wholesalers in Fukui or Takefu, so he could only work on the doll in the breaks between filling these orders and his regular work.

It wasn't until early May that Kisuke neared completion of the doll, which stood about a foot high. The light-green buds at the tops of the zelkova trees standing at the base of the mountain were just beginning to blossom.

Kisuke was shut away in his shed, bent over his coping saw, when he heard the sound of someone's approach.

"Is anyone home?"

It was not the voice of one of the village women. It sounded like Tamae. Kisuke's heart thumped loudly. Wiping the dust from his knees, he stood hurriedly to open the door.

"Hello," Tamae said. She was standing in the entryway, bowing her head slightly and smiling her toothy grin.

Kisuke's voice caught in his throat.

"The weather is so nice and I had the day off, so I thought I might come here to pay a visit to the grave."

Kisuke experienced a momentary panic. Would Tamae peek inside the dark workshop and see the nearly completed bamboo doll standing beneath the window? He had thought it best to have Tamae see the doll only once it was finished. Quickly, he directed Tamae to the main house.

"It's dirty here," he said. "Shall we rest over there?"

Something in her demeanor and the way she walked told Kisuke that Tamae had grown more comfortable with him since her first visit. Still, she could not hide the fact of her recent illness. A shadow of frailty showed in her face and her manner of speech.

Kisuke showed Tamae to the tatami room of the main house and opened the door onto the veranda. Then he lit the lamp in the family altar. Tamae faced the old, soot-covered altar, closed her eyes, and put her hands together in prayer.

"Kisuke?" she asked after a while. "Is this your mother's memorial tablet?"

Standing next to his father's tablet was a slightly shorter tablet of black lacquer. Carved in gold letters was the posthumous name

**Hōkō shun'en daishi.**

"Yes, that's Mother's," Kisuke said.

Tamae's voice immediately grew soft and solemn. "Do you remember your mother's face?" she asked.

"I never knew her. I was only three when she died. No matter how often I shut my eyes and try to recall her face, I can't."

"That's right, you wouldn't remember."

"She was carrying fertilizer to the bamboo grove when she collapsed. They say she died of a heart attack. She and my father spent their whole lives looking after the bamboo groves. Father would cut the bamboo and make the crafts, but I heard it was Mother who weeded the grove everyday, picked the bark from the bamboo shoots and trimmed the branches. She worked hard to make the groves thrive. Everyone says that the groves around our house are the best because of all the painstaking care Mother put into them."

"She must have been a good mother," Tamae said with a twinge of envy. Moving away from the altar, she stepped out to the edge of the veranda. For a while, she stood there silently listening to the rustling of the bamboo grass outside.

Gazing upon Tamae's profile, Kisuke was suddenly overtaken by an image of Tamae returning to Awara and taking a customer.

"How about your mother, Tamae?" he asked.

"My mother?" Tamae did not turn to look at him. "She lived in Chūshojima in Fushimi. But she's dead now."

"And your father?"

"I don't know my father," she said flatly. Her answer had a ring of carelessness.

"You said you don't know, but . . . is he dead?"

"I heard he died. It sounds a little irresponsible to say that I heard about his death, but I never knew my father's face. I was raised by my mother in Chūshojima."

Hearing this, Kisuke felt an even greater affinity and pity for her. *So Tamae had also been raised by a single parent.* Finally, he gathered the courage to ask what was on his mind.

"Tamae? How long will you go on working in Sanchō-machi?"

Tamae glared at Kisuke briefly, then immediately looked to the floor.

"If someone would have me as a wife, then I'd quit," she said dismissively. "But there's no one like that for me. My body belongs to the world of prostitution. I'm just a plaything, nobody who would ever consider marrying me. I'm an unmarried woman without a father . . . Kisuke, my path is set and there's no other way for me."

"But if you stay at the Hanamiya forever, Tamae, you'll ruin your health."

"Yes, I know that."

"Why did you come to Echizen from the Shimabara? From Kyoto?"

Kisuke thought of Tamae constantly while he worked. There were so many things he did not know about her, and all of his questions burst out in succession.

"I had my reasons, so I came to Echizen."

"Kyoto's better than Awara, isn't it?"

"Awara's a nice place too."

"Where did Father first meet you, Tamae, ten years ago?"

She paused a few moments before answering.

"We met in Awara. It was the tenth day after I arrived from the Shimabara. At that time I wasn't working at the Hanamiya but at a brothel called the Matsunoi. It was also an inn, and I started out as a maid there. I didn't do the sorts of things I do now."

Kisuke quickly understood the relevance of this information. Tamae had quit her job as a licensed prostitute in the Shimabara and come to Awara to find more respectable work. But she apparently reverted back to her old profession soon after moving to the Hanamiya, which wasn't all that different from a licensed establishment. Yet Kisuke could not help but think that something beside the death of her mother must have motivated Tamae to leave Shimabara and bury herself away in the snow-bound region of Hokuriku.

Kisuke couldn't bear to see Tamae struggle as she spoke of her past, so he did not question her any further.

After finishing her tea, Tamae made her way through the bamboo grass to pay her respects at Kizaemon's grave; Kisuke followed behind her.

Unlike during her last visit, the area around the gravesite was pleasantly warm. In front of the stone marker stood a pair of vases made from the tube-like stalks of young, green bamboo which were replaced every harvest time by Kisuke. A bright red double-camellia flower was placed inside each one.

"What lovely flowers!" Tamae cried. "Where do such camellias bloom?"

"Father was fond of this flower. Four or five camellia trees grow near the edge of the grove, but I think I'll transplant a couple of them here. Some years the trees bloom, and some they don't. This year, all of the trees are covered with large flowers."

Tamae lit some incense and placed it in an opening on the foundation stone of the grave. She floated some camellia leaves in a cup of water and then poured the water over the gravestone. She began to chant: "*Nanmandabu. Nanmandabu. Nanmandabu.*" Because she felt Kizaemon's presence as she prayed, she continued murmuring the *nembutsu* for a long time.

When at last Tamae was ready to leave, she told Kisuke, "Next time I come,

I'll help you transplant the camellia trees your father loved. Is that all right with you?"

Kisuke was ecstatic. The best time to transplant the tree would be in late June or early July. "I'll transplant it right after the rainy season," he said. "Do you think you could come then, Tamae?"

"I promise to come, if it's all right with you."

Kisuke was sure he could have the doll finished by then. He looked forward to surprising her with it.

Tamae left at the onset of evening. Kisuke saw her off as far as the entrance to the village. From there, he watched until her figure disappeared in the shadows of the large cedars. Tamae assured him that once she reached the village of Hirose she would board a carriage for the rest of the journey.

The following day, Yohei dropped by the workshop unexpectedly. Kisuke quickly covered the bamboo doll with a *furoshiki* cloth before inviting him in.

"You seem to be working really hard," said Yohei, taking in the sawdust and scraps of bamboo covering the workshop floor. Then, in his typically brusque manner he asked, "So who was that woman who came by here yesterday?"

Kisuke was stuck for an answer. "A customer from Fukui," he promptly lied. "The wife of a wholesale merchant."

"Is that so?" Yohei's deep-set eyes widened. "She looks just like her, doesn't she? I mean, that woman looks just like your mother, Kisuke."

Kisuke stared blankly into Yohei's face.

"Your mother, Oshima, had the same fair complexion and large earlobes. She had a pretty face with a wide forehead. Your guest looks just like Oshima."

Kisuke was dumbstruck. *Tamae looks like my mother?* The reason for his father's attraction to her suddenly became clear. Kisuke wondered if his father had recognized his mother's image in Tamae. Kisuke believed he now understood why his father had made the doll and taken it to Awara.

"Is that really true, Yohei?"

"I don't know anything about your guest's personality, but I was sure surprised to see how closely she resembled your mother. It was almost as if Oshima had come back to life. I'm not lying to you. You mother had fair skin and large earlobes," Yohei said. "I heard that your guest boarded a coach in Hirose to get home."

# VI

The words Yohei had uttered so casually stirred in Kisuke a powerful desire to marry Tamae and bring her to Takekami. He knew that she was unhappy in Awara. And because she believed no man would ever marry her, she felt she had no choice but to stay at the Hanamiya. When she explained this to Kisuke, he had sensed she was lonely. He thought of how happy he would be if she came to live with him in Takekami. He would throw himself into his work. He told himself he would treat her more preciously than anyone else in the world.

Kisuke earned a steady income through his bamboo work. He felt confident it was enough to support the two of them. His father had no savings when he died. He left only the house, the workshop and the bamboo groves— only about 350 square meters of land. But the groves had been painstakingly cultivated and included more than ten varieties of bamboo. The soil was so well fertilized by their various roots that no matter how much bamboo was harvested, each new season brought forth new shoots. Kisuke could afford to get by on his crafts work alone. His income had increased several-fold after he began spending more time making expensive furniture and elaborate birdcages and less on cheap items like baskets and colanders. His skills and his labor earned him everything he needed. By working hard and using the materials left to him by his father, Kisuke believed he could amass more money still.

As he lived alone, he had no reason to be extravagant with food or clothing. Even when his work clothes became torn, he continued to wear them. When they threatened to come apart, he would take a needle and sew them himself, despite his lack of skill. The villagers gossiped among themselves about Kisuke's lonely lifestyle and said they had to find a wife for him soon. Because Kisuke's parents were already dead, his household was considered an easy place for a bride to join. Yet there was not one young woman of the village who would go there willingly. Not only had Kisuke inherited the gloomy disposition of his father, he was also short and stingy. A few folks had tried to arrange a match for him, but in every case the other party broke off the negotiations.

Although he hadn't the slightest idea where his bride might come from, Kisuke expected to marry after turning twenty-five. If Kizaemon had managed to win Kisuke's beautiful mother, he reasoned, then he was certain to find a woman to marry as well.

Once he laid eyes on Tamae, however, Kisuke could think of no other woman but her. He fantasized constantly about their marriage, but worried over whether she would really agree to come live with him. He reckoned there was a fifty-fifty chance. Tamae, after all, had been fond of his father despite his unusually small size. But if she'd had a physical relationship with him, could she ever consider marrying his son? Although she worked as a prostitute, the arrangement might prove too disturbing. Still, the possibility could not be entirely ruled out. If Tamae loved the father, surely she would love the son. And Tamae had such affection for Kizaemon that she crossed snow-covered roads to remote Takekami to pay respects at his grave. Kisuke entertained the possibility that she felt the same affection for him.

Still, Kisuke placed little hope in his dream. For one thing, Tamae might not want to live in such a rural environment. Surrounded by bamboo groves, Kisuke's house was dark and gloomy. Bluish-green moss covered the damp thatched roof. The snow was much heavier here than in Awara. Takekami was poor and shabby. You couldn't go see a movie or a play. To live in Takekami was to be completely cut off from outside culture. A woman who had lived in the Shimabara in Kyoto or the pleasure quarters of Awara could not be expected to put up with life in such a place, not even for a day.

Although discouraged by such thoughts, Kisuke did not feel that he should simply abandon his hopes. Tamae had said she would come after the rainy season to help transplant the camellia trees to his father's gravesite. Before then, he planned to ask her if she might not come to Takekami and marry him.

All day long, Kisuke thought of Tamae. Even while at work on his bamboo crafts, he couldn't get her out of his mind. A woman who so resembled his mother, he felt, belonged in the Ujiie household. He spent his waking moments mulling how he could bring her to Takekami to stay.

.

Kisuke finally broached the subject with Tamae at the beginning of June. He dropped by Awara on the way home from a folk arts exhibit in Fukui. Upon seeing the healthy Tamae he felt unsure about going back to her room just to talk. So he entered as if he were just another customer, leaning forward and nodding his head. Because Kisuke looked unusually tense, Tamae wondered if something had happened.

As soon as they entered her room, Kisuke burst forth with his proposal.

"Tamae? Will you come live at my house? If you come and look after father's grave, I'll make you a room of your own. And not just the room, either. If you want, you don't have to do anything. If you could just look after my food and clothes, I won't mind if you just spend the time idling about. If you come live with me, I'll work harder than ever to earn money. Tamae, once I saw you, I haven't been able to get you out of my mind. Please come to the house in Takekami."

Tamae was touched by the sincerity of Kisuke's speech, but she was stunned by its suddenness. "You mean you want me to be your bride?" she responded jokingly. But on seeing how serious he was, she caught herself.

"If you don't want to be my bride, I don't mind if you don't marry me." Kisuke had to catch his breath and took a moment before he continued. "If you go on working in a place like this, taking several customers a day, you'll ruin your health. You'll end up dead. My house is much better than this place. Come to my house and be a mother to me, Tamae."

The intense desperation in his eyes was overwhelming, and Tamae had to avert her blushing face.

"Thank you for your kindness, Kisuke. But I can't give you an answer right away. I like you, Kisuke. You're just like your father, a master craftsman through and through. I like that about you. But no matter how much I like you, if I go to Takekami to live with you . . . well, the villagers will always be watching us."

"I don't care what the villagers say," Kisuke said, sidling closer. "The villagers are all strangers to me. In their hearts, they all look down on me. Honestly, I can't open my heart to any of them.

"The moment I saw you, Tamae, I liked you. I've come to love you as if you were my mother. I don't remember being caressed by my mother. If you came to live with me, I'd feel as if being born into this world had meaning. Whenever I look into your face, I feel my frozen heart beginning to thaw. Tamae . . ."

Large tears were falling from the corners of Kisuke's eyes.

"I understand how you feel," Tamae replied. "You've made me so happy, telling me these things. I'm as alone as you are, Kisuke, so I could never consider you a stranger. When your father was still alive, when you must have been about ten or eleven, I dreamed about becoming a mother to you. Your father, however, was concerned about your welfare and wouldn't allow me to come to the house in Takekami."

"Concerned about my welfare?"

"That's what your father said. He didn't care what the villagers thought, he thought only of you."

"Concerned about me!" Kisuke grew angry over his father's excessive devotion. "Father was foolish. Foolish!" Kisuke stared at Tamae, his fists clenched.

"I'll think it over carefully, Kisuke," Tamae said, attempting to soothe him. "You said you would transplant some camellia trees after the rainy season. I'll think over your proposal and come give you my answer when it's time to transplant the trees. There are so many things I have to take care of. You can ask me to come with you, but I can't just fly off like a bird."

Kisuke bowed his head in agreement. "I'll move the trees some time around the end of the month. Will you definitely come with an answer by then?"

Tamae nodded.

Seeing her damp face, Kisuke felt his chest puff out. "All right then, I'll head home. I'll be waiting for you, Tamae." With that, he stood and hurried out.

Kisuke knew that it was customary throughout Echizen to plant trees at the end of the rainy season. Because the ground was so wet, the roots would rot if planted before it was over. It was said that late June or early July was the best season to transplant a tree because the ground was soft and the sunlight relatively warm. Kisuke envisioned the double-flower camellias that grew at the edge of the grove as he left the row of brothel houses and boarded a coach bound for Fukui City. *I hope the rainy season ends early. When it's over, I'll transplant those camellias . . .*

As soon as Kisuke got home, he went straight to his workshop and picked up the unfinished doll. He was determined he would have it completed by the time Tamae arrived.

.

On the first of July, Kisuke transplanted two camellia trees from the edge of the grove to Kizaemon's grave. He had waited as long as he could for Tamae, but she had not turned up by the end of June. The rainy season had lifted and if the sunny weather continued the ground would soon become too hard for transplanting. Kisuke decided he would undertake the job on his own. Taking his time so as not to knock the soil off the roots, he carried the trees up to the grave on the hill and planted one each on either side of the marker. The overall effect was beautiful. *Now Father can always gaze on the flowers he loved.* But although the completion of the project made Kisuke happy, he was still disappointed that Tamae had not come.

It occurred to Kisuke that Tamae might have fallen ill again. People with tuberculosis had to be careful during the rainy season and when the buds were blooming. He grew worried but he was busy weeding and fertilizing the rice paddies in the lower section of the valley. Because he had no time for his bamboo work, he also had no business that might take him to Awara.

Every evening, exhausted and stinking of sweat from his work in the fields, Kisuke would fall into bed without even bothering to clean himself and slip into a death-like sleep. *She said she'd come with an answer around the time I transplanted the camellias. She told me to wait for her until then . . .* Even when he slept, he couldn't escape thoughts of Tamae. In his dreams, he'd cry, *It's fine if you don't marry me. Just be my mother. Just look after me at the house in Takekami!*

Just after noon on July 5, Kisuke was working determinedly in his shed during a break in the fields when his neighbor Yohei, a cloth wrapped around his head, stuck his grimy face through the doorway.

"Kisuke? I was just down at the seedling patch under the big cedars and I saw a visitor coming into town on a cart. She's coming to your house, isn't she?"

Kisuke looked over at Yohei in surprise. "Is that true?" he said loudly.

"Do you know who she is? She's got an awful lot of baggage. The cart is filled to the brim. What's she coming here for?"

"To be my bride," Kisuke shouted and flew out of the shed, ignoring the blank look of amazement on Yohei's face.

*Tamae's come. She's finally here.* Kisuke ran around to the back of the shed. From there he could see the large cedars at the edge of the mountain. Because the leaves of the trees blocked his view of the road, he went further up the hill. Upon reaching his father's gravesite with its newly planted camellia trees, he stretched his back briefly before peering down through the groves to the white, one-lane road below. A single horse-drawn cart could be seen winding its way slowly toward the hamlet. A woman in a crimson kimono was riding atop the freight cart, and a man was sitting motionless behind the horse, his shoulders hunched over and his head covered with a cloth.

Kisuke stared intently at the cart. It was definitely Tamae. She was seated atop a cushion with one of her knees drawn up and smoking a cigarette. Among the pile of luggage, Kisuke recognized her paulownia chest of drawers and her vanity.

"It's Tamae," Kisuke shouted. "She's come here for me!"

He bowed low before Kizaemon's grave, his forehead nearly touching the stone marker, then scampered back down the hill without stopping to rest.

The date was July 5, 1923. Orihara Tamae was thirty-two years old when she entered the household of Ujiie Kisuke to become his wife. It was the summer of Kisuke's twenty-second year.

# VII

Never before had the hamlet of Takekami experienced a wedding like that of Orihara Tamae and Ujiie Kisuke. It had not even involved a go-between. The ceremony consisted of nothing more than Tamae casually bringing her things to the house where Kisuke had previously lived alone.

Still, Kisuke could barely breathe when Tamae's cart stopped at the entrance to the hamlet. With that amount of luggage, there was no doubt Tamae had come to live with him permanently.

"Kisuke, I've made my decision," she told him. "Will you let me stay here as you promised?"

Dumbfounded, Kisuke stared wide-eyed into Tamae's blushing face. Finally, his voice cracking with excitement, he said, "Please come in. I've waited a long time."

"You said you'd come in June, so I waited to transplant the camellia trees. But because you never sent word, I was sure you had been toying with me so I went ahead and transplanted them next to father's grave on my own."

"Is that right?" Tamae could see the happiness in his eyes despite his tone of reproach. "In that case you should take me to the grave. I want to let your father know I've come here. Let's go together."

Once the cart driver had finished unloading the luggage, Tamae handed him some money wrapped in calligraphy paper and hurried through the grove toward Kizaemon's grave.

Kisuke had placed the camellia trees about half a meter to the right and left of the stone marker. The mounds of fresh soil at their roots gave off the scent of red clay. Covered in thick black leaves, the branches cast dark shadows over the upper part of the grave. Overall, the atmosphere seemed suited to the grave of a master bamboo craftsman.

Tamae sighed when she saw it. "It's a beautiful gravesite," she said. "You cleaned it up so well." Then she put her hands together and closed her eyes to pray the *nembutsu*: "*Nanmandabu. Nanmandabu.*"

Once this was finished, she bowed her head toward the gravestone and whispered the following words:

"Father, I finally quit the Hanamiya in Awara. I've come to live with Kisuke. Is that all right? Is it all right that I've become Kisuke's bride? I came to help look after your grave . . . Is that all right, too? Please, Father, will you give us your blessing?"

Tears were streaming down both of Tamae's cheeks. She had been staring at the gravestone for some time, talking to Kizaemon as if he were still alive. At last she turned back to Kisuke, who had been standing behind her the whole time.

"I don't want to be any trouble to you, Kisuke. If you ever come to dislike me, I'll leave anytime you want."

Kisuke's heart pounded with joy but his impatient expression was meant to discourage any formalities between them. He pointed to the camellia trees. "Tamae, the tree on that side is a double-flowering camellia. The one on this side is a white camellia."

"White camellia? You mean white flowers bloom on it?"

"Yes, really big ones. I thought white flowers would be best for a gravesite. I planted them myself. We won't know for sure until we see them next spring, but the blooms should definitely be big. I clearly remember stringing flowers together when I was a little boy, alternating red and white ones to make a necklace. Those were camellia flowers. They grew around the edges of the grove. Father loved them, so I planted the red one on the right and paired it with the white one on the left."

"Is that how you did it?" Tamae said and turned her cool eyes toward the flowers. Both the new leaves of this year and the old leaves from last year looked like they had been painted with the same black-green lacquer. They overlapped each other like the scales of a fish. Just the right amount of shade fell around Kizaemon's gravestone. The spot was so perfect it was as if he had chosen it himself. It seemed that neither Kisuke's damp house nor his workshop were as dry as this particular plot of land. It was easy to imagine Kiza-emon sitting here among the flowers.

After some time, Tamae finally made her way back to the main house.

"The inner storage room is nice, Tamae," Kisuke said. "I was told it's the room where my mother stayed. Could you please make this your room?"

Tamae opened the door off the living room and peeked inside. It was a long, narrow space about five tatami mats in size. New floorboards of pine, or perhaps some other wood, had been laid, and fresh white wallpaper hung on the walls. It was clear to Tamae that Kisuke had fixed up the room in anticipation of her arrival.

Tamae carried her chest of drawers, futon and various bundles into the room and slid open the shōji doors that looked onto the garden. Two azalea bushes had been planted just outside her doors, and beyond the landscaped hill she could see the *madake* leaves swaying gently in the wind.

"What a wonderful place," she said. "Where will you sleep, Kisuke?"

"I can sleep anywhere. There's the room where father used to sleep."

As if possessed, Kisuke watched quietly from the doorway as Tamae put away her belongings. Because she was constantly moving, completely absorbed in her work, he could observe her without reservation. She had a fair complexion. Her face was round and the bridge of her nose was straight. According to Yohei, she had the face of his mother.

By evening, Tamae had all of her things beautifully arranged along the walls of the storage room. Then she set about preparing dinner. She lit the portable clay stove that sat next to the dark stone oven and boiled rice. Then she picked some greens from the vegetable patch beyond the grove and made soup. She and Kisuke ate dinner together, but as soon as they were finished he went out to his workshop.

Night fell and a first-quarter moon rose in the sky, visible in the fan-shaped opening between the mountains over Takekami. Still, Kisuke did not come back from the workshop. Shortly after nine o'clock, Tamae slipped on her clogs and went to look in on him. Kisuke was hunched over his lathe making a birdcage.

"Aren't you coming to bed, Kisuke?" Tamae asked, sidling up to him.

He glanced up at her briefly, his eyes ablaze, but he immediately returned to his work.

"Leave it for later. Let's go back to the house and go to sleep."

Kisuke refused to look at her. "Tamae, you go ahead and go to sleep. I'll finish this work in a little while, then I'll go in and sleep."

Gazing at Kisuke's profile, Tamae sensed he was being bashful. She spent a few minutes inspecting the various tools lining the walls—the knife, the coping saw, the hatchet, the rip saw—then returned to the house alone.

Back in her room, she spread out her futon—red silk with a chrysanthemum pattern—and waited for the sound of Kisuke's approaching footsteps. All she could make out, however, was the turning of the lathe. Tired from the day's journey, she fell into a deep sleep. When she woke the next morning, she found herself alone in bed. This had been Orihara Tamae's first night as Ujiie Kisuke's bride.

In fact, Kisuke yearned for Tamae. But what he sought from her was a substitute for the mother whose face he could not recall. He felt for her a pure, unsullied attachment.

*If you continue to work here, your illness will only get worse. Your body will waste away completely. If you come to my house, I'll treasure you. I'm alone in my house. Since you'd be the only other person there, I'll always be able to support you. If it's all right with you, come and marry me. I really like you . . .*

Kisuke had spoken these words to Tamae in her dark room at the back of the Hanamiya, but even then he had not tried to embrace her. Perhaps he had hesitated because of a subconscious awareness of Tamae's recent illness. Kisuke couldn't stand seeing her look so ill, nor could he stand the paleness of her neck right after she had been with a customer. Yet, even now, after Tamae had brought all of her belongings to the house in Takekami, Kisuke made no effort to go to bed with her.

Tamae thought it was peculiar. Even though he had begged her passionately to be his bride, when she finally came to him, he gave her the cold shoulder. Did the thought of embracing her disgust Kisuke? On her fifth night in Takekami, she couldn't stand it anymore and ran to the workshop, where he had retreated after supper as usual.

"Kisuke? Am I a nuisance to you? Deep in your heart, you're annoyed with me, aren't you?"

Kisuke's body tensed and he found it difficult to breathe. He had a habit of hanging his head in such a way that made his body appear as if it were shrinking inward. This was the first time Tamae had seen him this way. The closer she came to him, the further his head fell, until his shoulders were straining.

"You don't like me, do you?"

Having suddenly gathered his nerve, Kisuke dropped his lathe and looked up at Tamae.

"It's not that. I like you, Tamae. Why would I dislike you? Since one of the villagers told me you resembled my mother, I've grown more and more fond of you. I never knew what my mother looked like. Whenever I look at you, I feel I'm seeing her. That's why I can't do anything with you. I'm really happy you came here. I'm really motivated to work and I'm making progress on my dolls and birdcages. Please understand, and please stay with me. I don't want you to hate me, Tamae."

Tamae looked utterly deflated. Staring into Kisuke's pleading eyes, she was reminded of a child. "But I came here to be your wife, Kisuke," she told him flatly. "I'm not your mother."

"I know. I really do understand. If you could just leave me alone, just a little longer. Please don't feel constrained by me. Use the house and live here however you like. I'm happy just watching you do anything—cleaning the house or going out front and walking about. You've brought me back to life, Tamae. Please stay with me always."

Kisuke's lips quivered as he spoke, and Tamae had to resist the urge to embrace him.

"All right, then," she said, "it doesn't matter to me. I'll be a substitute mother. I don't mind being a surrogate. But I'm lonely. I came here to be your wife. It's lonely sleeping all by myself in the storage room. Starting tonight, can't we at least sleep together?"

Kisuke thought intently before nodding his assent. "If we're just sleeping in the same room, then I'll sleep with you."

"Really? Are you telling me the truth?" Tamae narrowed her eyes until they were like threads. "You'll definitely come to me when you've finished working?"

"I promise I'll go to you," he said and, avoiding her gaze, went back to work.

With a look of regret, Tamae returned to the main house and once again climbed into her futon alone. It wasn't until after eleven o'clock that she heard Kisuke quietly enter her room. Tamae hadn't slept a wink and she watched wide-eyed as Kisuke stripped down to a single shirt and slid into the futon next to hers. Moments later, she could hear his soft, muffled snores. By the light of the moon, Tamae gazed upon his small body and large head—more than a child, but less than a man—and was reminded of Kizaemon.

Tossing and turning, Tamae finally called to him—"Kisuke?"—but he didn't stir. Kisuke had fallen into a deep sleep as soon as his head hit the pillow. This too reminded her of his father. Only moments after they finished making love, Kizaemon would begin snoring.

Although Tamae was lonely, she never considered leaving Takekami.

*This place will do for me. Didn't I spend all those years as a prostitute? I've been allowed to bring my defiled body into a proper household. I don't mind being a surrogate mother. I'll live the rest of my life with Kisuke . . . The day will come when Kisuke visits my futon. After all, he is his father's son. If I just patiently wait for that day to come, everything will turn out for the best . . .*

Comforting herself in this way, Tamae finally fell asleep.

# VIII

There wasn't a single person in Takekami who wasn't surprised by Tamae's sudden appearance in Kisuke's home. Not only was she was simply too beautiful to be his bride, she appeared to be about seven or eight years older. Where had Kisuke found her? That was the first question on everybody's lips. One of the villagers recognized Tamae from her first visit to Takekami right after Kizaemon's death. She had lost her way in the snow and had asked him for directions to Kisuke's house. "Kisuke must have seized the opportunity to take her into his home that time she came to visit his father's grave," the village man said. "His body may be small, but he seems to have a quick hand when it comes to women."

Although stories like this were exchanged in a joking manner, all of the villagers looked upon Kisuke with envy. How did he manage to bring such a beautiful woman into his home? "She looks like his mother," one of the elders said, implying that Kisuke's attraction for her must have been irresistibly strong.

No one knew where Tamae had come from. This was natural because only a few people in the hamlet visited the crafts wholesalers in Takefu or Fukui as Kisuke did. Although Kizaemon had initiated them all into the art of bamboo crafts, none of them relied on it as their sole means of livelihood. Crafts were merely a second source of income. Between working the rice fields and making charcoal, it was all they could do to fashion baskets and bamboo furniture to sell in neighboring villages. Only Kisuke would go so far as to leave the hamlet and solicit orders for his work. The impoverished men of the village had probably never set foot in places like the red-light district of Awara. And even if a few had visited the brothels in Sanchō-machi, it was unlikely any of them would have been a client of Tamae.

Whenever Kisuke ran into one of the villagers on the road, they would always ask him about her. But he felt no need to bring up Tamae's past. "Thanks to the help of some people in town, I was able to find a bride," he would say before heading off into the groves. The villagers could only watch him go, shaking their heads in amazement.

Tamae herself felt no need to hide. Whenever she met anyone on the village road, she would bow her head charmingly and greet them. Her friendly, open manner made everyone marvel over her all the more. All the other village wives had dark, sunburned faces. Not even the young girls had skin as white as hers. It was natural that everyone should feel envious of this woman who had flown in like some butterfly.

Tamae spent most of her day at home. She would do the laundry or mend clothes. She and Kisuke managed to get by without having to work the fields. Kisuke's crafts became well-known in Takefu and Fukui City and orders for his work poured in from wholesalers and merchants. Not a bad word could be said about the union between the hard-working Kisuke and the beautiful Tamae.

.

About three months after Tamae joined him in Takekami, Kisuke debuted a pair of bamboo dolls of superb workmanship. He completed the dolls in his spare time between filling orders for birdcages and tea implements. Initially, Kisuke had intended to make only a single doll in the likeness of Tamae on her first visit to the hamlet. This doll was nearly complete by the time Tamae arrived in summer. Once she moved in, however, Kisuke felt just the one doll wouldn't do. He began work on a couple representing a man and wife.

This proved to be challenging work. Kisuke's yearning for Tamae and his appreciation of her beauty were so intertwined that it was difficult for him to contain his feelings for her in his work. Keeping in mind an image of his father's courtesan doll, he made several attempts at the dolls until he was finally satisfied.

The completed dolls represented an old man and an old woman, each a little more than a foot tall. They wore large silk robes like those used as dance costumes on the Noh stage. To make the robes, Kisuke had used nothing but the bark of young bamboo shoots. The bodies were fashioned from a cylinder of *madake* bamboo cut to height. He made the hair by slicing bamboo bark as finely as the hairs of a writing brush and dying it white, giving it the sheen of a goddess's. It wasn't clear where he learned to do this. He tied back the hair with a white cord and left it hanging down the dolls' backs. Around the multi-layer collars of the necklines, he wrapped necklaces made of bamboo root. To the faces, he attached small Noh masks purchased at a doll shop in Fukui City.

A buyer from the Iwataya department store in Fukui City let out a cry of amazement when he saw the dolls displayed on the staggered shelves of Kisuke's workplace. He was about forty years old and wearing a business suit. "What extraordinarily elaborate dolls!" he exclaimed. "Would you let me display them for you at our exhibition?"

Kisuke smiled bitterly. He had made the dolls for his own pleasure and he couldn't mass-produce them. Public display, he said, was unthinkable.

"But you don't have to produce a lot of them," the man assured him. "We only want our visitors from Kyoto and Osaka to know that Echizen bamboo crafts include works of such delicacy. It'll be a source of pride for us."

That night Kisuke spoke to Tamae about it over dinner.

"A man from the Iwataya showed up today and asked if I could submit my dolls for an exhibit. Do you think I should?"

"That's wonderful," Tamae replied at once. "You should do it. I know everyone will praise them."

"You think so?" he asked.

Kisuke's expression indicated some doubt. Unlike with his first doll, he had not tried to hide this project from Tamae. She would visit him in the workshop whenever she got bored and had seen Kisuke working on the dolls numerous times. She had been the first to express admiration of them when they were finished. It had occurred to Tamae that it would be a waste to keep such beautiful dolls buried away in Takekami.

"Your father brought his doll to me," she told him. "Your dolls are much better than your father's. If you exhibit them, you'll certainly win praise."

Tamae's words seemed to sway Kisuke.

The man from the Iwataya returned to Takekami a few days later. He told

Kisuke he wanted to submit the bamboo dolls for display in the Folk Arts Exhibition. This time he brought with him a formal commission.

Kisuke entrusted the dolls to him.

·

The Folk Arts Exhibition opened December 1, 1923, in an events hall on the second floor of the Iwataya department store in Fukui City. Among the many displays were the experimental dolls of Ujiie Kisuke. This marked the public debut of the bamboo dolls of Echizen.

Although there were many fine works of lacquer ware, pottery and cutlery on display from the villages around Takefu, the bamboo dolls, which were in a glass case at the center of the hall, elicited the most astonishment. The craftsman had put to best advantage the various types of bamboo and displayed remarkable judgment in his choice of technique. The dolls possessed an inexpressible elegance. The glow of the polished dappled bamboo bark seemed to fill the space surrounding the dolls with stillness. It truly seemed as if the dolls were alive.

The sponsors of the exhibition had written up display cards explaining the works. This is what the card for Kisuke's dolls said:

BAMBOO DOLLS
ARTIST: UJIIE KISUKE

*These bamboo dolls are a rarity, making use of bamboo unique to Echizen. They are a delicate expression of the richly elegant quality of bamboo work. From the time the Way of Tea flourished in the Ashikaga Period, the province of Echizen has shipped bamboo tea utensils to other provinces. Although the name of master craftsman Taniguchi Hikozaemon was known throughout the nation, this tradition died out, putting an end to the production of bamboo folk arts and crafts. Then, near the end of the Meiji Period in the hamlet of Takekami in the county of Nanjō, a man named Ujiie Kizaemon began making his own bamboo crafts. From his youth, Kizaemon showed an interest in this folk art. He would go on pilgrimages throughout the nation to seek materials. He planted more than a dozen types of bamboo around his house and worked skillfully at his craft. The artist who made these dolls is Kizaemon's son. Inheriting his father's vocation, he has perfected the first bamboo dolls in our nation.*

*Clothing—bark of young bamboo*
*Body—stalk of madake bamboo*
*Hair—fibers from the bark of bamboo grass*
*Obi—bark of bamboo grass*
*Neck Ornament—root of black bamboo*

*Note: Green bamboo has little natural durability, and because it will discolor quickly when exposed to direct sunlight, a weak gelatin solution has been applied as a preservative. The bamboo is stained with a thick alkali solution.*

Among the attendees that day was the governor of Fukui Prefecture. His name was Ikeda Kashichi and he was the tenth governor since the prefecture's formation. Accompanied by his secretary and aides, he was strolling through the exhibition hall when he suddenly stopped to stare at Kisuke's dolls. He seemed utterly transfixed as he read the commentary.

"Where's this place, Takekami?" he asked.

"It's a hamlet tucked away in the mountains beyond Takefu," one of his aides answered.

"Are there rare bamboo groves in that area?"

"Yes."

Because none of the aides had actually seen the bamboo groves of Takekami, they could provide no further details.

Samejima Ichijirō was following close behind the governor. Samejima was the owner of an arts and crafts gallery called the Heikodō, which was located at the north entrance of the intersection of Shijō and Nawate avenues in the Higashiyama Ward of Kyoto. Samejima was similarly amazed by the workmanship of the bamboo dolls. In a low voice, he asked one of the locals, "How long is the road from Takefu to Takekami?"

The man tilted his head and replied, "I think there's a bus or a horse-drawn carriage, but I hear it's way up in the mountains. They have really deep snow up there. I don't think you could make it up there in a day."

Samejima jotted down the artist's name in his notebook. How had this man Ujiie Kisuke made such exquisite dolls? He wanted to have a look at his workshop. Private business interests motivated Samejima.

"You can't find dolls like these even at the Tentoku in Kuramae, Tokyo. I've never seen dolls like this at any of the wholesalers in Kyoto or Osaka." His voice was filled with admiration.

Samejima Ichijirō visited Ujiie Kisuke in the hamlet of Takekami at the end of March, during the first signs of spring. The peaks of the Nanjō range were still white, but only patches of snow lingered in the lower-lying villages. The snowmelt sent water pouring down the mountain and crashing into the rivers in a haze of mist.

Samejima rode in on a horse-drawn carriage from Takefu, accompanied as always by his head clerk, Seshita Shigematsu. Seshita was a short, hunch-backed seedy-looking man in his fifties. His boss was tall and lanky with a long, horse-like face. Samejima was obsessive about his work and was constantly traveling the nation on business. Because he always wore a black, double-breasted suit and rimless glasses, he looked less like an arts dealer and more like some elegant gentleman recently returned from Europe. It was almost noon when the two men alighted from the carriage and entered the hamlet.

Samejima asked the first villagers he met on the road about the home of "the master doll maker, Ujiie Kisuke." One of the men cocked his head and politely pointed to the damp thatched roof of Kisuke's house in the shadow of the mountain. The weathered house was, as expected, surrounded on all sides by bamboo. Samejima recognized several types, including bamboo grass, black bamboo, *madake* and *mōsō*. He and Seshita immediately made their way to Kisuke's door.

Upon reaching the main house, Samejima called out in greeting but there was no sign of anyone. He called out a few times more, but again to no reply. Finally, in the shadow of the low *shikoro*-style eaves of the house, he spied the shed. Hearing the creaking sounds of the lathe, he went over to take a look. Peeking his head through the entryway, he saw a tiny figure hunched over a lathe in the dark interior of the room. Samejima opened the door and called out politely, "Excuse me!"

The man quickly turned toward the door and seemed to glare at him. Although he was childlike in stature, his small face was quite mature, creating a grotesque appearance. Samejima couldn't conceive that this was the man responsible for creating those beautiful bamboo dolls.

"Is Ujiie Kisuke here?"

"That'd be me."

Samejima was startled. Could the master doll maker really be such a shabby-looking man? He was tiny—just over four feet tall. Was he deformed in some way?

"I'm an art dealer," he explained. "I'm the owner of a gallery in Kyoto called the Heikodō, which is at the bottom of Yasaka Hill."

Kisuke waited silently for him to continue.

"Your bamboo dolls are extraordinary. I've been thinking that I'd like to take a look at your workshop. Since I had the opportunity to visit Echizen, I decided to take advantage of the trip and call on you."

Because Samejima spoke so politely and was so properly dressed, Kisuke let down his guard. Slowly he released his hands, which were threaded through the cord of the lathe.

"You've sure come a long way. You said you wanted to visit my workshop, but it's a pretty messy place, as you can see. Let's go back to the main house. There's no place to sit here." Kisuke rose and moved toward the door.

Samejima took in the scene with curious eyes. The earthen floor of the workshop was crowded with piles of rough bamboo. Mountains of sawdust and shavings stood here and there so that the cushion upon which Kisuke worked appeared set in a valley by comparison. Following Kisuke to the main house, Samejima regretted that he could not inspect the workshop a little more.

Having shown his guests inside, Kisuke called hoarsely in the direction of the storage room and veranda. "Hey! Hey!" he cried. Samejima assumed that Kisuke was calling for his wife, but he recognized no sign that anyone else was there.

Using only his eyes, Samejima signaled Seshita to set down the can of *Yatsuhashi* biscuits they had brought as a gift next to the threshold of the living room.

# IX

Once his two guests were seated around the hearth, Kisuke brought down a blackened teakettle and kindled a small fire with a spill. As the flames spread in the hearth, the wood began to crackle and pop and issue billows of white smoke.

Though the light of the fire brightened the room, Samejima found the house to be rather gloomy. A blackened canopy was suspended over the hearth. The rope on the trammel hanging from the canopy was also black from smoke. The kettle, which Kisuke had placed atop the ashes of the dying fire, had blackened right up to the handle, which was wrapped in twine. Never before had Samejima seen a house like this one hidden away in the recesses of the mountains of Hokuriku. To his appraiser's eyes, it was like an antique work of art, and he began to observe it more closely. The ramshackle living room contained nothing more than a few mats spread out on the wooden flooring. The room was extremely dark. Only the front door beyond the packed-earth floor of the entryway and the rear doorway were fitted with shōji screens; and those screens, combined with the steep triangular roof, helped create Samejima's impression of having stepped into a half-open parasol. Beneath the triangular roof, bundles of fresh bamboo were piled in the *tsushi* loft. A thick straw rope had been wrapped around the ladder leading up to it to prevent it from slipping.

"Do you store your bamboo up there, too?" Samejima at last broke the silence.

"I bring in the bamboo I harvest in the autumn and put it up there in the *tsushi*. It dries by itself with the heat from the hearth. That way it gets really hard."

Kisuke's expression suggested his mind was elsewhere. He had said little since they entered the house. Samejima assumed Kisuke had a naturally taciturn disposition. He asked his questions in the friendliest way possible.

"When did you start making dolls?"

"I started by trial and error in May last year."

"Had you ever seen bamboo dolls made by anyone else before or did you invent them yourself?"

"My father made a doll once," Kisuke said and once again retreated to his thoughts.

Samejima was surprised. He had thought that Kisuke's father had only crafted tea utensils, confectionery trays and the like. When he heard that Kizaemon had also made dolls, he felt even greater respect and admiration for the two generations of craftsmen who had lived under this dark thatched roof. He came to believe that Kisuke's ability to fashion such exquisite dolls derived from the spirit of diligence and hard work he had inherited from his father.

The water in the kettle began to boil. Kisuke opened the lid with a practiced hand, scooped out some hot water with a bamboo ladle, and poured it into the teapot beside him. The aroma of brewing tea filled the room. Kisuke didn't have teacups. Instead he used cups fashioned from the cylindrical tubes of *mōsō* bamboo. He handed one each to Samejima and Seshita.

"It's not much, but please drink up," Kisuke said politely.

The more hospitably the craftsman behaved, the more Samejima was puzzled by his manners and appearance. Kisuke was so short and his head so large. Samejima had visited lacquer ware makers in places as far off as Aizu or the Noto peninsula; he had visited with potters in Tagawa in Kyūshū. Crafts makers who resided deep in the mountains, he found, were for the most part good-natured people. Having naturally acquired the manners of their native region, they were hospitable to guests.

Only Kisuke was different. Perhaps this was due to his grotesque appearance. His body was so unusually small that he looked deformed. His eyes were set deep within his large head. His ears were big, and he had a swarthy complexion. His fingers were small like a child's, yet thick. The work jacket he wore appeared to be made of rough hemp. And his pants had been mended so often it was difficult to tell if they had originally been *hakama* or work trousers. Overall, his appearance was off-putting. It was hard to approach him. Only after much hesitation did Samejima broach the subject of business.

"Actually, the reason I am here is because I saw your bamboo dolls the other day at the Iwataya department store. They were so magnificent that I came here to ask if you might sell them to a wholesale shop in Kyoto owned by my younger brother, Masujirō.

"The shop specializes in Kyoto dolls and is at the corner of Muromachi and Anekōji Street. You may know it. It's called the Kanetoku. It's an old business that traces its lineage to Kaneda Tokuemon. Along with the Tentoku in Tokyo and the Yamadaya in Hakata, it's a shop of long-standing with clients all over the nation. I was hoping you might permit us to sell your Echizen bamboo dolls . . ."

The white smoke from the fire stung Kisuke's eyes and he was forced to squint. But although he said nothing, he was listening carefully.

"I plan to send the head clerk from the Kanetoku here soon to request formal permission to sell your dolls. I hope you welcome him and give him a favorable response. I've traveled through many provinces, but I've never seen such elaborate dolls before. Really, I am genuinely impressed."

A faint smile drifted across Kisuke's face and his eyes softened. Naturally, he was overjoyed to receive such praise from a Kyoto art dealer.

"Are the dolls really the kind that a Kyoto dealer could sell? I can't judge the quality of the dolls myself; I just make them for pleasure in my spare time. I'm surprised to hear that they are something people might buy. Of course, I'm happy to hear such praise, but if it turns out that the agent can sell them, then I'll have to mass-produce them, won't I? There's no one in the village I can contract out for help. If I had to make them on my own, I'd never be able to keep up."

Samejima smiled.

"Good dolls are rare," he said. "Master craftsmen don't mass-produce their works. Whether it's lacquer ware or pottery, the fewer the works, the better the price, Kisuke."

"If it's just a few dolls, then the agent is welcome to come for them. However, I don't have any models yet; the only ones I have are that old man and old woman."

Excited to have received Kisuke's consent, Samejima bowed his head. "That's fine," he said.

At last, Samejima could consider his visit to Takekami worth his effort. He had known that his brother would be interested in the Echizen dolls. On all of his business trips, whenever Samejima found a *kokeshi* or carved wooden doll in the provinces, he would put in a good word for the Kanetoku. The shop maintained these connections over the years and continued a thriving business in a variety of dolls.

After finishing his tea, Samejima made his excuses to leave but asked if he might inspect Kisuke's workshop and groves first. Because Kisuke saw no reason to refuse, he led the two men out of the house and back into the workshop.

"Right now, I'm working on birdcages," Kisuke said, pointing to a mountain of cages piled next to a floor cushion. Samejima reached for one to inspect it. The long thin bars of the cage had been cut and rounded precisely, and all were evenly spaced. Each cage Samejima examined had clearly been crafted carefully. They were, he thought, a testament to Kisuke's conscientious nature.

Next, Kisuke pointed to the tools lining the shed's walls. "Here's a small awl, a round blade, a triangular blade . . . That tool there with handles at either end of the blade is called a flat chisel. It's no different from the one used by people who make clogs or buckets. Over there are a small three-point, a four-point, and a half-rounding file, next to a rounding file and a fluting gouge. That over there's a vise. Here's something unusual—a bending rod."

Samejima focused his eyes on the single oak rod stuck into the earthen floor. He had never seen anything like it. A large, one-and-a-quarter-inch square notch had been bored into its upper section. Kisuke picked up a piece of bamboo lying at his feet, thrust it through the notch and, gripping both ends firmly, bent it into a bow shape.

There was a clay stove next to the bending rod. Grooves were worn into the metal grille stretched over its top. "First you start a fire and pass the bamboo over the heat. If you do that just once, even new bamboo will bend," Kisuke explained, bending two or three rods of green bamboo in quick succession.

All the tools that Kisuke demonstrated had been used by his father and were well-worn. The grime accumulated over the years had lent them a glistening sheen.

After surveying the various tea utensils and confectionery trays, Samejima stepped out to inspect the bamboo grove at the rear of the house.

He had never seen such a beautifully maintained grove. A thin layer of green moss carpeted the ground, and not a single fallen leaf littered it. *Madake,* bamboo grass, black bamboo, *mōsō* bamboo—the various species had been arranged systematically, growing in rows like the teeth of a comb.

"There's just about every kind of bamboo here," Kisuke said.

As he gazed down the rows of bamboo, Samejima was startled to discover a woman heading in his direction. Was she the one Kisuke had been calling for earlier? She was dressed in work trousers over a black kimono and was carrying a broom. Apparently she had been sweeping the grove. As she drew near, she removed her crimson sash and bowed her head low in his direction.

"This is my wife," Kisuke said.

Slowly shifting his gaze toward her face, Samejima stifled a gasp. She was beautiful. Against the backdrop of bluish-green bamboo, her pale skin seemed to steal out of the grove. She was tall and slender but nicely curved. And her eyes, which turned up slightly at the corners, held a seductive glimmer.

*Can this man have such a beautiful wife?* Samejima wondered if she had been the inspiration for his exquisite dolls. Lost in his admiration for her, Samejima said nothing in the way of greeting. The sun fell like rain onto the moss-covered ground, streaming between the rows of bamboo. Tamae stood before him like a bamboo nymph, her back turned to the golden threads of sunshine.

No one knew that Samejima's visit to Takekami would prove to be a major turning point in Tamae's life. As always in spring, the wind blowing through the newly sprouted bamboo leaves recalled only the song of a panpipe.

# X

Sakiyama Chūbei, head clerk of the Kanetoku doll shop in Kyoto, arrived in the hamlet of Takekami at the end of June. Spring was over and the snow on the Nanjō mountaintops had melted into a milky white haze. The dark green leaves at the tops of the zelkova trees lining the mountain road were bathed in sunlight, and the fresh golden leaves of bamboo around Kisuke's house swayed in the breeze.

By the time he reached Kisuke's door, Chūbei's heart was pounding with excitement. Although he had come to purchase the bamboo dolls, he had heard about the doll maker's beautiful wife and was eager to see her. Samejima had instructed him to look for Kisuke in his dimly lit shed, but Chūbei had returned to the main house after finding no sign of him there. Sticking his head through the entryway, he cried, "Excuse me! Is anyone home?"

From the back of the house, Chūbei could make out the faint sounds of coughing followed by approaching footsteps. After a while, a tall woman with a fair complexion emerged from the dark interior. Chūbei instinctively cried out in astonishment.

"So-Sonoko?" He stood stiffly in the doorway, his legs frozen.

Tamae regarded Chūbei suspiciously. She couldn't make out his small, pinched face very clearly because it was obscured by the light streaming in around him. She squinted.

Chūbei was convinced that the woman standing before him was Sonoko. He had met her in the pleasure district of Shimabara fifteen or sixteen years ago, and the two had been on intimate terms.

"Aren't . . . aren't you Sonoko?" His voice was filled with amazement.

As if doubting her ears, Tamae arched her eyebrows and peered into his face. A glint in her eyes suggested she recognized him, and she quickly looked down. "Mr. Sakiyama?" she said in surprise. "You are Mr. Sakiyama, aren't you?"

"I can't believe I found you in a place like this. It must have been fated for us to meet again." The corners of Chūbei's eyes crinkled and his thin upper lip stuck out as he stared fixedly into Tamae's face.

"I'm head clerk for the Kanetoku doll shop," he said. "It's at the intersection of Shijō and Nawate avenues. My boss sent me here on the advice of Mr. Samejima to buy your bamboo dolls. Is your husband here?"

Hearing Chūbei's voice made Tamae nostalgic. She swallowed once, an expression of regret on her face.

"My husband left for Fukui and won't be back till evening. He went to collect money from some of his clients," she apologized.

"Is that right? So he's not here? That's too bad. By the way, your husband does make dolls, doesn't he?"

"Yes, he makes dolls," she answered. "Mr. Samejima sent a letter after he went back to Kyoto. There was also a letter from the owner of the Kanetoku. Ever since those letters arrived, my husband has been putting all of his effort into the dolls. He's completed about ten so far. But I can't just hand them over to you while he's away. What will you do? Could you come again?"

Chūbei focused his gaze on Tamae's mouth as she spoke and it made him all the more nostalgic. He recalled her as she was just after reaching womanhood—her plump, soft body and her full, white throat. She had just begun working in the Shimabara then and went by the name Sonoko. Seeing her again, he thought she had changed very little. No, he reconsidered, the woman before him was even more beautiful; she had about her the sensual air of a mature woman.

"Sonoko," Chūbei said in an excessively familiar tone. "May I come in? For us to meet in a place like this after such a long time . . . well, it must mean there is some special bond between us. Did you tell your husband . . . Kisuke, isn't it . . . about your past? And how in the world did you end up coming to such a remote mountain village to marry? May I come in?" Chūbei bowed low and looked up at her with an air of restraint.

After a moment's hesitation, Tamae at last said decisively, "Please come in. My husband is away, but he'll be angry with me if I don't ask you more about your business here . . ."

Seeing her behave this way, Chūbei felt Sonoko had been completely transformed. She was no longer the woman he once knew but a doll maker's wife through and through. "How old are you now, Sonoko?" he asked as he crossed the threshold and into the living room.

"Me? I'm thirty-three."

"Really?"

"And how old are you, Mr. Sakiyama?"

"I'm forty now. Exactly forty. I'm finally established as the head clerk at the Kanetoku. I've been thinking I'll ask my boss to open a shop for me once the term of my contract is up. I've been working hard and the owner of the shop has taken a liking to me. He and I understand each other really well when it comes to business. But as always, I can't stop myself from playing around, so I'm still treated like I'm just one grade above the apprentices . . . I dragged my sandals all the way to this out-of-the-way place just for business."

Chūbei sat down next to the hearth and fixed his gaze once more on Tamae. "You're young," he said. "You haven't changed at all." He repeated this several times out of genuine surprise and admiration.

Tamae hadn't been nearly as buxom when she first started working under the name Sonoko at the San'yō brothel, but her round face and pleasingly symmetrical features secured her a steady line of customers. Chūbei had become intimate with her three months after she left her home in Chūshojima to go work as a prostitute in the Shimabara.

"How's your mother back in Chūshojima?"

"She's dead now," Tamae said, as she set the kettle next to the hearth and lit a fire.

"And your father?"

"He ran away a long time ago. He wasn't even around when I was in the Shimabara."

"And so you quit the Shimabara . . . And since then you've been here?"

"No, that's not how it was at all."

Tamae's joy over being reunited with this old companion—and of simply having someone to talk to—showed in her face. Her eyes seemed to have taken on a sparkle that wasn't there when she met Chūbei at the door.

"From there, I went to Miyagawa-chō, and then later returned to the

Shimabara again. By that time, you had stopped coming. I wasn't at the San'yō then. I was at a place called the Tachibana. I worked there for two years. There was a big argument among the women, and it was difficult for me to stay on . . . I was already sick and tired of Kyoto, and was thinking that it might be better to go somewhere far away. While I was searching for a place, Kiyoko, a friend of mine who had gone to Awara, told me that it was a good place. She said it made no difference whether I went to Miyagawa-chō or Hashishita, since they were all the same. So I decided to go to Awara."

"Awara? That's a hot springs town, right? In northern Echizen?"

"That's right. It's on the way to Mikuni from Fukui City."

"What were you doing there?"

Tamae smiled, revealing her white teeth.

"As usual, I worked as a prostitute. I wanted to get a serious job, but there wasn't any work for me. I worked for a little while as a hostess at a brothel called the Matsunoi, but that got dull so I moved to a house called the Hanamiya."

"Is that right?"

Chūbei stretched out, narrowed his eyes, and sighed—just as in the old days. He was a good-natured man. His eyebrows were thinning and the corners of his eyes were creased with lines, but his skin was still fine and velvety like a woman's. He still possessed the same sensual aura he had all those years ago. Seeing him now, Tamae recalled her time in the Shimabara and felt her breast grow warm.

"So what fate brought you here?" Chūbei asked. "Did you meet Kisuke through the Hanamiya?"

"Yes."

As she said this, Tamae conjured up an image of Kisuke's face and was struck by a sense of guilt. Her husband was away on business, and here she was talking with a man she had been intimate with long ago. On the other hand, Tamae had not completely resolved her doubts as to whether Kisuke could really be called her husband. Even though he slept beside her, not once had he reached out for her body. And when Tamae reached for him, he always shrank away from her. Although they spent their nights this way, he always spoke to her in a familiar manner. She knew very well that he yearned for her as he did for his mother.

Perhaps these powerful feelings of longing had been the driving force behind Kisuke's exquisite crafts. Kisuke had said himself that Tamae was his incentive for work. For her part, Tamae also worked hard. She never allowed a single fallen leaf to clutter the grove behind the house, and she never failed to keep fresh flowers on Kizaemon's grave.

So many times Tamae had told herself, *This is good enough for me. If my life ends like this, that's fine with me.* She never expected her relationship with Kisuke to change. She intended to lavish the love she had felt for Kizaemon on his son as well. But Chūbei's unexpected visit changed everything. Seeing this man with whom she had once been intimate, Tamae suddenly found herself returning to the past.

"I met a man named Kizaemon. He was a bamboo craftsman from Takekami. He was fond of me. He was an intimate customer of mine for a long time. I was a companion to him." Tamae spoke simply and honestly. "Kizaemon died in November the year before last. Right after that, I fell ill and was laid up at the Hanamiya, unable to work. One day Kizaemon's son Kisuke showed up out of the blue."

"Really?" Chūbei's eyes grew wide.

"But that wasn't the first time we had met," Tamae continued. "I came here to pay my respects after Kizaemon was buried on the hill behind the house. That was the first time I ever saw Kisuke. He's a lonely man . . . No, he's more solitary than lonely. At first I thought he was creepy, but after coming here to live with him I have discovered his good points. He has a pure spirit, he's like a child."

Tamae saw that Chūbei's eyes were gleaming.

"I feel sorry for him. There's something indescribable about him. Mr. Sakiyama, I don't know what the gentleman from Kyoto who came here told you, but to me Kisuke has the soul of a master doll maker. He's really skilled at making birdcages or tea utensils or fans, but his expression changes when he's crafting a doll. He's a tiny man, and he may look like a hunchback, but at times it seems there's a halo above him. You must meet him. The dealer from Kyoto had told him someone from the shop would be calling on him, and he was really looking forward to it. What a shame he went to Fukui today. I'm sorry he's away. Truly, Mr. Sakiyama . . ."

Chūbei watched the color rise to Tamae's cheeks and saw in her flushed face the same pliant woman he had known those many years ago. A feeling of warm nostalgia mixed with specific memories of the nights they had spent together in her dimly lit room at the San'yō. His heart was in turmoil.

"You found a good husband. Since you speak of him so proudly, then what you say must be true. Kisuke's a lucky man to have a woman like you fall in love with him."

Chūbei's eyes had taken on a peculiar glow. With each flicker of the flames in the hearth, Tamae's white face shimmered seductively before him. Her bewitching eyes pierced his very heart. The interior of the house felt like the inside of a dingy parasol. Chūbei drank several cups of tea, but his throat still felt dry. He found himself overtaken by desire.

"Sonoko," he said and quickly sidled across the tatami. "Have you already forgotten all those nights we spent together?"

Ignoring the pair of tongs she was holding, he placed one hand over one of her own and wrapped his other around her narrow waist. Pulling her toward him, he pressed his lips to her ear, which was covered by limp strands of her hair, and whispered, "I never dreamed I'd meet you in a place like this, Sonoko."

Tamae clamped her mouth shut and recoiled her head. Panicked and still gripping the tongs, she tried to break free of his hold. Breathing heavily, Chūbei attempted to overwhelm her with kisses.

"Sonoko . . . Sonoko," he murmured repeatedly.

Tamae had endured a year without sex since coming to Takekami, and she felt her body grow hot.

"Stop it . . . stop it!" she cried, but she was unsure if this were directed at Chūbei or her own heart. Then suddenly she pictured Kisuke's cold, distorted face. It was outrageous the way he rejected her every night; her mind raced with thoughts of revenge.

"Sonoko, Sonoko," Chūbei repeated as he pushed her onto the floor and sent the tongs flying. Chūbei was strong. He seized Tamae from behind and dragged her along the mat. At once, he was on top of her like some animal. She went limp.

The fire crackled and the hems of Tamae's kimono and red underskirt flickered in the light of the flames. White smoke encircled the bundles of bamboo in the sooty storage space under the roof.

As she felt her body being tossed about, Tamae in her heart called out Kisuke's name. *Kisuke, Kisuke! You don't care about me. I'm not bad, am I? I'm not bad. You're the one to blame . . .* Tears poured down her cheeks, and she found it difficult to breathe.

Strengthening his grip, Chūbei told her, "No one can see us. Only the gods know. It's best not to tell Kisuke. And I won't say a word to anyone. So don't worry, Sonoko . . ."

Tamae lowered her head, her sobs quietly seeping into the tatami.

# XI

Kisuke returned from Fukui just as the sun was setting and the ridge of the Nanjō range was starting to take on a dark red tinge. Sakiyama Chūbei had taken his leave a mere two hours earlier, saying that he would be staying at an inn in Takefu. When her husband arrived home, a pale-faced Tamae greeted him at the door. He handed her a paper package secured with a cord. "I brought some Habutae rice cakes," he said.

Kisuke's good mood showed in his face. After stepping inside, he immediately made his way to the hearth and began to tell Tamae how he had spent the whole day discussing his work with his clients. Still she was at a loss as to how to bring up the fact of Chūbei's visit. Not much time had passed since he had left, and unpleasant feelings—guilt or regret, she wasn't sure—still lingered within her. It wasn't until after they finished supper and were sipping tea together that she finally mentioned the visit.

"The head clerk for the doll wholesaler in Kyoto showed up today," she began.

"He came here?" Kisuke's eyes widened in surprise. "He came while I was out? What happened? Where'd he go?"

"He said he definitely wanted to purchase your dolls. He told me he would stay at an inn in Takefu tonight, and that he'd come again tomorrow. He asked that you sell him the dolls you've already finished. Then he left."

148

"Really? What sort of person is he?"

"Just a clerk. He's short with a round face. About forty."

"Did he come alone?"

"Yes, he was by himself." Tamae stole a glance at Kisuke's profile, but of course there was no way he could have suspected anything.

"Is that right?" Kisuke appeared to regret having gone out. "You say he's staying at an inn in Takefu? Do you know which one?"

"When he left he said he'd be staying at a place near the station. He said he'd come here again straight away."

"In that case, I wonder if it's the Hinokan? That's where merchants who buy knives and cutlery stay. I know," he said excitedly, "I'll take the dolls to the clerk myself tomorrow. It was bad of me to be away the first time an agent turned up to buy the dolls. He's an important client. I'll make it up to him by bringing them to him myself. Did you get his name?"

Tamae was startled, and her heart beat wildly. "His name is Sakiyama," she told him, her face slightly downcast.

"Sakiyama? All right, then, I'll go and ask for him at the Hinokan since it's close to the station. I'll take just the dolls I've finished. He's an important customer. I'll feel bad if he has to go to the trouble of riding that carriage over the mountain roads again."

Kisuke was in a good mood, his business having gone well that day. Naturally, Tamae did not oppose him. Chūbei was unlikely to tell Kisuke what had happened that day. So long as he didn't reveal too much of their shared past, there was no way Kisuke would ever suspect anything.

*No one saw us. Only the gods know. If you don't say anything, no one will find out. I won't say a word, so don't worry . . .* Chūbei's words echoed in her ear. Recalling them now, she was overcome by feelings of fear mingled with hatred.

"But what if you miss each other on the way? You'll have wasted a trip."

"Then I'll have to get up and leave early in the morning, won't I?"

Kisuke abruptly stood up, slipped on his sandals and made his way out the front door. Shortly after, the light of a lantern could be seen spilling out of his work shed. Tamae could hear the high-pitched squeak of bamboo being rubbed with a scouring brush and wondered if Kisuke was polishing the dolls he would take with him.

Minutes later, as Tamae was finishing up the dishes, Kisuke called to her from the front door.

"Could you give me a hand?" he asked, his voice betraying his excitement. "This will be the first time I put my dolls up for sale, so I want to make sure they are well made. I'm sorry, Tamae, but after I'm done with some finishing touches, could you polish them?"

Tamae nodded. Kisuke had taught her how to polish bamboo before, and she often helped with the confectionery trays and tea utensils. She had even polished some finished works. She thought that if Kisuke worked on his own, he might not have the ten dolls ready before dawn, so she left her chores and hurried over to the shed.

Kisuke was sitting on his cushion, a doll stand between his legs. With shoulders taut, he skillfully wielded a small blade. He was utterly absorbed in his work. Tamae took a seat beside him and began to polish the bodies and stands of the dolls that Kisuke had already completed.

The lantern cast a circle of light just big enough to enclose the area of the workshop in which they sat. Whenever a breeze penetrated a crack in the wall, the light flickered. Watching Kisuke's profile, Tamae sensed he was in an unusually good mood. Her feelings of guilt and regret gradually changed to a feeling of relief. In her sincerest voice, she told him, "At last the dolls you crafted will go to Kyoto."

The thought of this made Tamae truly happy. When she worked in the Shimabara, she had once looked inside one of the large doll merchants in the area around Shijō and Kyōgoku. She could hardly believe one of Kisuke's bamboo dolls would be placed in a glass case and grace the gorgeous storefront of one of those shops.

Kisuke, too, was happy. Of all the bamboo crafts he had made thus far, only these ten dolls had won his genuine devotion.

"If my dolls sell well, then let's go to Kyoto together next time. You and me," he said abruptly.

"That would make me so happy," Tamae cried. "Would you really take me with you?"

"Yes, I really will. I haven't done a thing for you since you came here. You do the laundry and cooking, you tend the grove, but I haven't done anything nice for you in return. To repay your kindness, I'll take you to Kyoto."

Hearing him say this, a feeling of joy welled up in Tamae's throat. Kisuke's eyes, too, seemed to be strangely ablaze. She recognized it as the same curious look he wore at the Hanamiya the year before. At the time, she couldn't tell if it was shyness or desire, but now she saw in his eyes an undeniable light. Tamae suddenly felt that she was in love with Kisuke. Her body turned feverish. *He seems somehow different today. If I reach for him in bed tonight, then perhaps he'll at last embrace me.* Tamae swallowed hard to fight back such thoughts.

By the time they completed their work, it was already past eleven o'clock. Tamae helped wrap the dolls in paper and place them in a basket. Kisuke placed the basket in the entryway of the main house so that he could easily shoulder the load just before his early morning departure. It was almost midnight when they finally laid out their pillows.

.

Tamae could not sleep. In her mind, she reviewed the events of the day and recalled the pleasure she took in exercising vengeance toward Kisuke as Chūbei had his way with her. If she were honest with herself, however, she had to admit this did not reflect her honest feelings.

By the light of the moon streaming in through the shōji, Tamae stared at Kisuke's closely cropped head lying beside her. Although he'd had a long day on the road and in the workshop, he was not snoring as usual. Her throat dry, she suddenly recalled that moment under the light of the lantern when Kisuke's eyes had blazed with that peculiar fire.

"Kisuke? Kisuke?" She slid toward him, but he didn't answer. "Are you awake?" The instant she slipped under his futon and pressed her body up against him, Kisuke jumped out of bed.

"Kisuke, why are you running away?" Tamae's heart was pounding. She made no effort to redo her nightgown. "Won't you please come here, Kisuke?"

Crouched in the shadows on the tatami, Kisuke sighed loudly. "I'm afraid to touch your body, Tamae," he said.

"Why? Are you afraid of me? Please tell me. After all, I am your wife."

"Ever since we married, Tamae, I've thought of you as my mother. Whenever I think I want to have sex with you, my body goes weak. Please forgive me, Tamae."

Kisuke, his head shrinking away, continued.

"Please sleep over there. I think of you as my mother . . . I want to continue living together with you, Tamae, so please sleep over there."

Feeling as if she had been slapped, Tamae retreated to her own futon and crossed her hands over her feverish breast with tears streaming down her face. A few moments later, Kisuke climbed back into his bed.

Tamae didn't sleep at all that night. She was in a state of agitation. Her mind was haunted with images of the brutish Chūbei, who had forced himself upon her, and the innocent Kisuke, who had pushed her away.

·

The next morning, Kisuke got up at five, ate breakfast with Tamae, checked the contents of his basket and set off to meet the clerk from the doll shop. He had completely forgotten the awkward incident of the night before. Tamae's face was swollen from lack of sleep, but Kisuke's eyes sparkled with excitement over the new day's business. "I'm on my way," he called to Tamae before leaving.

To reach the village of Hirose, Kisuke had to cross the bridge at the bottom of the hamlet and traverse the Nanjō Pass. In the faint light of sunrise, Tamae watched him zigzag along the road, the basket swaying on his back, until he disappeared into the forest.

*I'll never do that again* . . . Tamae was overwhelmed by a deep sense of regret. *With Kisuke's childish heart, there's no excuse* . . . *I'll never do that again.*

# XII

Just as Samejima Ichijirō had predicted, Ujiie Kisuke's bamboo dolls sold out on the first day they were displayed in the Kanetoku's showcase windows. The merchants of Kyoto were, as usual, hungry for original works. The owner of the Kanetoku, Samejima Masujirō, pulled his head clerk Sakiyama Chūbei aside for a talk.

"These dolls have an incredible reputation," he told him. "Ten of them aren't enough. Can't the doll maker produce more?" Since he did not know the circumstances surrounding the dolls, he couldn't help feeling that Chūbei had been remiss in purchasing only ten of them.

"Well," Chūbei replied, "Ujiie Kisuke is the only doll maker in his village. There are other households that make bamboo crafts, but he's the only one who makes dolls."

"Is that so?" Masujirō sighed in admiration. "Do you think we could get him to subcontract his work to increase production? Our clients will be unhappy if this is all he can make. Ask Kisuke if he can make ten dolls a day. Go and tell him that orders are going to start flooding in."

His prediction proved right. Retailers who saw the dolls tried to place orders with the Kanetoku by phone the very next day, and each time the Kanetoku was forced to refuse them.

All new dolls usually sell briskly at first, but because Kisuke's bamboo dolls were so unusual and exquisitely fashioned, Masujirō knew from his many years of experience that demand for the product would remain high. He ordered his head clerk to work out an arrangement to increase the production of the dolls immediately. And once again, Chūbei left Kyoto and set out for Echizen.

It was the middle of July when he turned up at Kisuke's door for the second time. Although the doll maker was likely in his workshop, Chūbei first peered into the main house in search of Tamae. When he found no sign of her there, he went out back to the shed, where Kisuke was working on a doll. After they exchanged greetings, Chūbei explained the purpose of his visit.

"Your dolls have a tremendous reputation in Kyoto. They're a real success. Could you take on an assistant and, at the very least, double the pace of production? My boss sent me here to encourage you to do just that. What do you think? Isn't there anyone in the village who could learn your techniques?"

Kisuke was overjoyed at the proposal. With a wholesaler backing him in this way, he explained, he should have no trouble convincing one of the local craftsmen to help work on the dolls. Satisfied with this answer, Chūbei packed up the four dolls Kisuke had recently completed, paid for them in cash and made to leave. Just as he was stepping out of the workshop, he turned back and narrowed his eyes. "How is your wife today?" he asked.

"She must have gone to the grove," Kisuke replied easily. "The bamboo shoots are coming out right now. This is the season when the new bark falls. New bark is best for making the dolls' *hakama* trousers."

Before leaving, Chūbei looked for Tamae behind the main house. When he could not find her there, he pictured her collecting bamboo bark in the groves. It would have been nice to see her, but he wasn't going to go out of his way for her. Chūbei was a lecherous man, and he considered her nothing more than a careless fling. He had to admit that he was inferior to her husband, who had the aura of a master despite his grotesque appearance, and so he felt a vague sense of regret for having violated her. Chūbei left the village praying that Kisuke would be able to make arrangements to increase the production of his dolls.

As soon as his visitor had gone, Kisuke immediately called on the three most gifted craftsmen in the village—Takichi, Matsunosuke, and Eizaburō. Although all three were familiar with Kisuke's dolls, they were surprised to learn of their high monetary value. Naturally they wanted to learn Kisuke's techniques if it would secure them a greater income. The craftsmen didn't earn much making the baskets and farming implements they sold in the neighboring villages, and there was little pleasure in the work. Word soon got around, and two more villagers—Kohei and Daishirō—joined them. From morning to night, they studied the art of doll making. Kisuke was a kind teacher, and he lent his tools to those who didn't have them. Because the five men were already skilled in the basics of the craft, they picked up Kisuke's techniques quickly.

Production of the bamboo dolls increased considerably after that. By the summer of 1924, the craftsmen had to use the carriage from Hirose to ship out their products. The dolls were widely praised in Kyoto, and their fame spread to Osaka and Nagoya, where they were sold at the fashionable art galleries that were cropping up at that time in the bustling shopping districts. Customers even began traveling to Takekami to place special orders for the "Bamboo Dolls of Echizen" that were quickly becoming famous throughout the Kansai region.

By then, fourteen craftsmen in the village had switched to making bamboo dolls and working from Kisuke's shed. Because they could barely keep up with orders, they began bringing their lunches with them. Tamae became increasingly busy. It was her job to serve the workers tea and to keep the accounts, something that had never been required before. Keeping the accounts meant simply recording in a large ledger book the names of customers and the price of each doll sold. At the end of each month, she would total up the numbers and request payment for accounts receivable. For Tamae, the work was a lot more challenging than the responsibilities she had when she first arrived in Takekami.

Kisuke's household income rose very quickly. Because the bamboo used to make the dolls grew in the surrounding area, they were cheaper than Hakata or Gosho dolls, whose clothes were made of pure silk. Nonetheless, the bamboo dolls were highly prized because they were so labor intensive to produce. A set of Okina dolls sold for two yen in the Kyoto shops, making the Bamboo Dolls of Echizen among the highest class of dolls.

All of the craftsmen in the hamlet enjoyed coming to Kisuke's shed to work. Not just because of the extra income it earned them, but because it brought them closer to Tamae. Up to that time, they had only had the chance to speak with her when they met her on the village road. Now she brought them tea, sometimes with rice cakes or sweets. All of the men grew attached to her; "Miss Tamae," they called her.

One day in August, Tamae's complexion suddenly lost its glow. Kisuke was the first to notice.

"Are you okay?" Kisuke asked worriedly over dinner one evening. "Is all the extra work tiring you out? You look pale. You've got to take care of yourself."

Tamae shook her head.

"There's nothing wrong with me. My complexion is naturally pale. Look at how much I eat!"

Although she tried to dispel Kisuke's worries with a laugh, her voice sounded somehow weak. Kisuke recalled an image of Tamae laid up in her room at the back of the Hanamiya in Awara.

"You're not as sturdy as the villagers here," he told her. "Because you were ill before, you have to take care. You should have a doctor look at you."

In fact, Tamae had felt unusually tired and sluggish recently. When she got up in the mornings, her body would be soaked with sweat. She didn't have a fever, but her whole body felt like lead. She didn't want to bother Kisuke with these things because he was so busy.

"Please don't worry about me," she told him. "Every time I think about the Hanamiya, this place feels like heaven. My body has grown strong."

"You may not have to work as much here, but you still don't get enough sunlight. You have to take care. Next spring, I'm going to build you a room that gets good sunlight. If I extend the roof, I can make your bedroom bigger. I'm going to work hard to make enough money to build it for you. Please be patient for a while longer."

A genuine love showed in Kisuke's eyes as he gazed into Tamae's lusterless face. She quickly looked down, her own eyes blurred with tears.

In October, Tamae began to lose weight. Her breasts lost their plumpness and the area around her hips, which had been round and full, seemed to lose muscle. Her appetite had diminished.

"You should go see a doctor," Kisuke scolded her. "If you take the carriage from Hirose, you can be in Takefu in two hours. Have a doctor in town take a look at you and then get some medicine."

Tamae remained silent. She was mortified, for she had suspected since August that she was pregnant. Although she had kept it a secret, Tamae hadn't had a period since July. This was not entirely unusual. Because of her years of work as a prostitute, she had grown accustomed to having an irregular menstrual cycle. Once, when she was younger, she went six months without a period. Its recent delay had not worried her. On top of this, she hadn't had sex with anyone since Chūbei. She didn't believe she could have possibly gotten pregnant from just that one time. Even though some of her customers had refused to use condoms, Tamae had not once gotten pregnant in all her time as a prostitute.

Now, however, Tamae feared the worst. Small lumps had developed on the undersides of her breasts, which were normally smooth and plump, and her nipples had darkened. She would suffer nausea and terrible heartburn. She had learned about morning sickness from magazines and from a fellow prostitute who had given birth, and she recognized the symptoms.

Tamae had seen Chūbei only twice since the incident. Both times he had come to purchase dolls, and he never let on that anything had happened between them. She felt such hatred for him. If she really were pregnant, she could never hate him enough. If only she had tried harder to resist him, she thought, everything would be fine. But she was resigned to her fate. It was too late for regrets.

With Kisuke insisting she see a doctor before the onset of winter, Tamae set off for Takefu on October 20. It was the first time since she arrived in Takekami that Tamae left the hamlet on her own. Although the sky was clear blue that day, Tamae was in a dark mood. What would she do if the doctor told her she was pregnant? She was overwhelmed by anxiety.

Tamae boarded the carriage at Hirose. The sixty-year-old driver, a man named Chōshichi, was the same man who had carted Tamae's luggage to Takekami after she left Awara. On seeing her, he snuffled loudly to clear his runny nose and struck up a conversation.

"You came to Takekami in the summer, isn't that right?" he began affably. "The persimmon trees were blooming then." Chōshichi tapped the horse's rump with his whip, and Tamae smiled quietly, her hands pressed to her heavy stomach.

The carriage was made of oak and had metal wheels. Once they reached the gravel road, it began to sway and pitch. All at once Tamae felt like she was going to throw up. Grasping the side of the freight wagon, she tried desperately to hold it in. From time to time, Chōshichi would look back to check on her. Just as the rows of houses on the streets of Takefu came into sight, he noticed that all the color had drained from her face. He slowed the horse's pace.

"Are you all right? Are you sick, ma'am? You're white as a ghost."

"It's nothing," Tamae replied as cheerfully as possible. "My stomach's a little upset, that's all. I'm going to see a doctor, so please don't worry." She did not want the driver to notice her anxiety.

There were many doctors in Takefu and Tamae wanted to find one who would not know her by sight. From the station, she took a nearby alley and found herself at the entrance of a square, whitewashed building with a sign out front reading **Yoshida Internal Medicine**. She would have preferred to see an obstetrician, but she would have been unable to explain to Kisuke her reason for doing so. Just as she was feeling discouraged, she spied the word *Gynecology* in small characters at the bottom of the sign. She stepped inside feeling glad that at least she had found a suitable doctor.

Fortunately the doctor had no other patients and was free to see her. He was thin, about forty years old, and wore round, Harold Lloyd-style glasses on his swarthy face. He led her into the empty examination room where Tamae explained her condition.

"When were you married?" the doctor asked.

"July of last year."

He checked her eyes and tongue, and had her disrobe to her undergarments so he could listen to her heart with his stethoscope. Next he had Tamae lie down on the examination table. Lightly squeezing the left and right sides of her lower abdomen, he closed his eyes tightly and thought for a moment.

"How old are you, missus?" he asked casually as he put away his instruments.

"Thirty-three."

The doctor removed his glasses, returned to his desk and slowly reread his notes on Tamae's medical chart.

"When did you say your period stopped?"

"In July."

"Then it stopped in your thirteenth month of marriage . . ."

The doctor smiled, and the downward sloping corners of his eyes wrinkled.

"Missus," he told her, "you're pregnant. No doubt about it. You're in your fourth month. The baby is growing splendidly, just splendidly."

# XIII

Back in 1924, it wasn't as easy to get an abortion as it is nowadays. Whenever an abortion was performed, a report had to be filed with the government. Because midwives were sometimes hired to perform secret abortions, the government enacted an extremely strict law that banned from practice those who did, and set severe penalties for the mother. Did the government pass this law because it so greatly cherished human life?

These days, contraceptives are openly displayed in drugstores, and an obstetrician, claiming the well-being of the mother, can create a thriving career with his curette. In the old days, if a woman became pregnant the law determined that she had to carry the child to term. Adultery, of course, was also a crime. But perhaps the only reason it was considered a serious problem was because the legal system made abortion nearly impossible.

Tamae, however, was less afraid of giving birth than she was of telling Kisuke of her pregnancy. How could she explain it to him? If she told him who the father was, would he ever forgive her? Tamae knew Kisuke well enough to know he never would. Because he adored her the way a child adores his mother, he was more possessive of her than the average husband. There was no question he would be upset. No, not just upset—insanely angry. Tamae couldn't bear imagining the look in his eyes should she tell him.

With heavy feet, Tamae left the doctor's office and trudged back to the station where the driver from Hirose was waiting for her. Even if she invented some disease to explain her illness to Kisuke, her stomach would eventually give her away. There was nothing she could do. Wearily, Tamae boarded the carriage, her face pale and waxen.

"How'd it go, ma'am? What did the doctor say?" the driver asked with a look of concern.

"He said there's something wrong with my stomach," she lied, taking a seat on the mat. "Because I neglected it so long, the lining of my stomach has weakened. He told me to take care of myself and to start eating gruel."

As the carriage left the town of Takefu, the wave-shaped peaks of the Nanjō range gradually came into view, clouded in a milky mist. On either side of the white road were dry rice paddies; the straw stalks left after the harvest resembled rows of bristles on a brush.

Tamae recalled that day the previous summer when she traveled this same road on her way to Takekami, her luggage piled high in the back of the carriage. As the mountains drew near, she felt those memories recede into the distant past.

*I'll have to do it so Kisuke will never know . . . so he won't be hurt and sad . . . When I start showing, I'll have to leave Takekami . . . I'll have to leave home . . .*

With these thoughts in mind, Tamae conjured an image of the house with its triangular roof and the carefully cultivated groves of bamboo grass and black bamboo that surrounded it. She shuddered over the fact that a single lapse could so greatly affect her body, and she was assaulted by feelings of deep regret and loneliness. She lowered her head and listened to the grinding sound of the carriage's iron wheels.

"It's going to snow soon, ma'am," the driver said. "The snow bugs are swarming."

Looking up, Tamae saw hundreds of the insects flitting in the breeze like a cloud of pure white down. As she sat exposed atop the carriage, one or two brushed against her tear-stained cheeks.

·

By the time Tamae reached home, all of the workers had already left for the day. Hearing her approach, Kisuke rushed out of the workshop brushing the sawdust from the knees of his trousers.

"What did the doctor say? Is it anything to worry about?"

Tamae trembled, but she maintained her composure. In as casual a tone as she could muster, she repeated the story she had told to the driver.

"He said there's something wrong with my stomach. He doesn't know for sure without X-rays, but he said it's probably my stomach and intestines. I'm throwing up because my stomach can't digest what I'm eating. He told me I need to start eating gruel and that I shouldn't overwork my stomach."

"Is that right?" Kisuke's face broke into a smile of relief. "If it's your stomach, then you'll be all right. You just watch what you eat and you'll be fine."

Kisuke's good-natured response made Tamae feel guilty, but she was relieved to have passed this first hurdle. Now if she threw up, she had a good excuse.

Still, the child inside her would continue to grow with the passing of each day. She was safe for now because the cooler season called for lined kimonos. But by the sixth month, she wouldn't be able to disguise her belly so easily. Back when she was in Awara, a fellow prostitute had gotten pregnant. Tamae recalled how the woman was forced to retreat to her dark room once her belly got too big to hide. Tamae had to do something before she reached that point. If only she could force a miscarriage. She couldn't possibly seek an abortion in Takefu. If the doctor refused, word would get around; it was a small town. And since Kisuke made monthly visits to Takefu, Sabae and Fukui City, he was bound to hear the rumors. Even if Tamae found a doctor to perform the procedure, she risked being caught and prosecuted.

Tamae was deeply troubled, but in the end decided it would be best to go somewhere far away to take care of it. If her plan failed, she would have no choice but to leave Takekami. There was no way she could remain in the hamlet if she gave birth to a child Kisuke refused to recognize.

Suddenly, Tamae thought of Chūbei. He had not come to Takekami that month to buy Kisuke's dolls but had sent an assistant in his stead. Recalling his narrow forehead and sly expression, she felt a surge of hatred. The thought that he was keeping his distance from her made her nauseous. Yet, because he was the baby's father, she felt it was safe to confide in him. Perhaps he might help her find a doctor in Kyoto to take care of it.

*All right, then, I should go to Kyoto.*

In Kyoto, there were people Tamae could consult with about various things. She no longer had family in Chūshojima, but she had an aunt who worked as a procuress in Mukōjima. She also had acquaintances there from the days when she worked in the Shimabara. Unlike Takefu, Kyoto was a big city with lots of doctors. She thought Chūbei might be willing to arrange for an obstetrician to help. Not only was he responsible for Tamae's condition, it might cause him serious problems if his boss found out. Once he heard about her distress, he couldn't ignore her; he had to help.

Tamae thought it best to carry out her plan as soon as possible before Kisuke found out about her condition.

*I've got to come up with a good excuse to go to Kyoto*, she told herself.

·

By December, the northern region of Echizen had grown bitterly cold. Because Takekami was situated in the northern section of the Nanjō range, the wind would buffet the thatched roofs and the bamboo groves in the hollows day and night. In the early morning, snow-covered Mount Hakusan could be seen in the clear northern sky.

Kisuke, however, had no time to think of anything but his dolls. With the New Year approaching, orders were flooding in, not only from the Kanetoku in Kyoto but from the Sakaeya in Osaka, from Jinroku Dolls in Nagoya, and from the Tachikawaya in Gifu.

Since October, the number of villagers making dolls had increased to sixteen and the narrow workshop was filled with cushions. Kisuke worked frantically to ensure that all the work was up to his standards. Because he refused to sell imperfect dolls, he naturally fell behind in his shipments.

Tamae continued to keep the accounts, tend to the groves and serve the workers tea and miso soup at lunchtime, but she visited the workshop less and less frequently. Her complexion was getting worse by the day, and her cheeks and eyelids were puffy. Because of this, she often kept her face turned down when in the presence of the workers.

One day, one of the old hands, a man by the name of Daishirō, couldn't help but comment on the change in Tamae's appearance.

"Kisuke, is your wife expecting?" he asked. "She looks really pale."

Kisuke dropped his scouring rush and glared at him. Tamae couldn't possibly be pregnant. They had not had sex even once since she arrived in Takekami. Even still, Daishirō's comment had caught him off guard.

"Does she look pregnant to you, Daishirō?"

"It's been more than a year since she came here to be your bride. There's nothing strange about her being pregnant. Everyone in the village has been waiting, wondering when it would happen. Given the way she looks, it's hard to imagine it's anything else but a baby, Kisuke."

Kisuke cocked his head and laughed quietly.

"She went to a doctor in Takefu who told her she had some stomach problems. She's been eating nothing but gruel lately. That's why her face is so puffy. She's not pregnant."

All the workers turned to look at Kisuke with doubting eyes, and a look of shyness washed over his face.

"If she's pregnant, then I'll be happy," Kisuke said and quickly turned back to his work.

The people in the hamlet knew nothing of Tamae's former life. They would have been surprised to learn she had once worked in a brothel. Kisuke had heard an old wives' tale that said it was unusual for prostitutes to become pregnant because they mistreated their bodies. Whatever the case, he didn't think Tamae could possibly have gotten pregnant without having sex.

Although Kisuke couldn't accept Daishirō's theory, the remark bothered him. That evening, after all the workers had gone home, he spoke with Tamae about it.

"Your complexion isn't very good these days. Daishirō was chatting about it, and he wondered if you were pregnant . . . I turned red with embarrassment."

For a moment, Tamae stared silently at Kisuke's downward-turned face.

"It would be so wonderful if I were pregnant," she said, a tone of rebuke in her voice. "I'd be so happy if I could have your child, Kisuke."

Although she spoke dismissively, there was a certain truth in her words. As soon as she said them, she instinctively lowered her head in shame.

Kisuke's expression turned sour and the house filled with a chilled silence. Seeing him this way, Tamae felt an urge to confess the truth and free herself of the torment she had been enduring.

A few moments passed.

"Kisuke, there are a lot of unpaid receipts from the Kanetoku," she said. "I told the clerk who was here recently, and he said he wanted us to come to the shop to collect the money, just like we do with the other wholesale retailers . . . If it's all right with you, I'd like to go myself. The New Year will be here soon, and we'll have to give the workers their bonuses so they can buy their winter provisions. I should be all right if I go now, before it gets too cold. Will you let me go to Kyoto to collect the money?"

Kisuke snapped his head upright and stared into Tamae's face. His gaze was so intense that Tamae had to look the other way.

"In addition to going to the Kanetoku, I have a selfish request as well. May I go to Chūshojima? My parents are dead, but I have an aunt who lives in Mukōjima, and she works at the Katsuragirō. It's in front of the Benten Shrine in the licensed quarters. I'd like to see her to let her know what good fortune I've met with. May I go?"

Kisuke was deep in thought. Then his face suddenly broke into a grin.

"Is that right? Is the Kanetoku's unpaid balance really so large? If they've asked us to come and collect it, then I guess we have to go. That way, you can also go see your aunt in Mukōjima. But I wonder if it wouldn't be better for me to go with you. I did promise to take you to Kyoto . . . Unfortunately, I'm really busy with work and I can't put it aside. I have to send dolls right away to the Jinroku in Nagoya and to that dealer in Osaka."

"Then let me collect the money for you," Tamae said. "It's the only way I can help, so please let me do that much. Please, take me with you to Kyoto in the spring."

Tamae had given considerable thought to these words and spoke them with a feeling of great desperation. She studied his face and waited in a state of suspense for his reply. Finally, Kisuke nodded in agreement.

"All right. Given how things are, I'll have you go for me. Still," he added uneasily, "I'm worried about your health."

"I'll be fine. It's only a two- or three-day trip. It's nothing. And it's important we collect the money. I'll take care of it quickly and come right back."

Although Tamae felt tremendous relief that the conversation had gone so smoothly, she was filled with despair for the future. If she failed to find a doctor in Kyoto, this might be the last time she would be able to see Kisuke's face. She would have no choice but to send the money to Takekami and disappear. In her heart, she desperately wanted to return, one way or the other. She wanted to help Kisuke build his reputation as a master doll maker.

Tamae left Takekami on December 15. She was dressed in a vertical-striped kimono tucked into a pair of navy blue trousers; her head was wrapped in a large shawl with an embroidered fringe. Kisuke saw her off.

Before boarding the carriage in Hirose, Tamae secretly stopped by the post office to withdraw money from her savings account there. She had accumulated a decent sum over the years she worked in Awara and planned to use it to pay the doctor in Kyoto. Kisuke poured his soul into his dolls and she couldn't bear the thought of using the same money earned from their sale to pay for an abortion necessitated by her carelessness.

After leaving the post office, Tamae boarded the carriage that would take her to Kyoto. A light, powdery snow was falling and the wind was bitterly cold.

# XIV

The Kanetoku doll shop was located on Anekōji Avenue, just above Muro-machi in Kyoto's Nakagyō Ward. It was nestled among the rows of large, prosperous-looking double-roofed buildings that housed kimono shops with wide frontage to the street, their names written in thick brushstrokes on signs hung outside their sparkling clean doors. Hundreds of obi and Yuzen silks in the latest patterns lined the shelves of the shops' tatami interiors, which were visible through large glass windows. Clerks and young apprentices dressed in aprons could be seen bustling in and out of the shops and onto the street, which was cluttered with bicycles. Although the street was narrow, it had a lively appearance.

The Kanetoku was well known throughout the Kansai region as a business of long-standing. It was located in a rather timeworn building. Despite the low appearance of the second floor facing the street, however, it was broad in expanse, and included a large inner garden and a mud-walled warehouse. From the outside, the shop looked no different from the kimono shops, but beyond the glass doors, which had the shop's name painted on them in gold leaf, was a large thirty-mat room lined with cases of beautiful dolls.

Tamae stepped across the threshold of this shop in the late afternoon of December 15. When she announced that she was from Takekami in Echizen, the shaven-headed apprentice immediately retreated to the back of the store. Not long after, Chūbei's wrinkled face and narrow forehead peered out to her

165

from behind a dimly lit desk. Tamae felt an unexpected wave of relief. She was tired from the long train ride, and she felt lonely. Although she ought to have been repulsed by the sight of him, she welcomed him as someone she could rely on.

"It's been a long time." She bowed her head and smiled, revealing the dimples in her cheeks.

"This is certainly a rare occasion," Chūbei replied, crinkling the corners of his eyes. "It's good of you to have come all this way."

With mincing steps, he led her through the accounting office, past the desk, to an inner eight-mat room reserved for customers. After showing her through the lattice door and stepping up into the room, he bent over and arranged her clogs at the entryway. Then he sent the apprentice to fetch some tea.

"I've come to collect the year-end accounts," Tamae said after the apprentice withdrew. "After I receive the money, Chūbei, then I have a request to make. Will you hear me out?"

Chūbei's face twitched cunningly. "The year-end accounts are prepared at the desk in the accounting office," he began in a low voice. "We have money ready at the accounting desk, so we are always prepared to make payments when clients come here.

"But what is it? What did you want to ask of me . . . ?"

He stared at her sharply. Her face was haggard.

"Sonoko," he continued, calling her by her old name from the Shimabara. "You've gotten awfully thin. Aren't you feeling well?"

Tamae looked at him fixedly. Chūbei was clever. Behind his words lurked the same man whose beast-like face had blazed up beside the hearth at the dark house in Takekami. Surely he had not forgotten what he had done then.

"I can't speak about it here," she said at last. "What time do you finish work this evening?"

"I usually finish the books by seven," he replied, "but I'll have one of the apprentices take care of it so I can leave at six."

He swallowed.

"Sonoko, where will you be staying tonight?"

"I haven't decided yet," she answered honestly.

After arriving at Kyoto Station, Tamae had boarded an electric trolley and come straight to the Kanetoku. She wanted to collect the money before it was dark. She placed Kisuke's business before her own body. For Tamae, this was the most important task.

"In that case, how about this? There's an inn I know on Oshikōji in Nakagyō Ward. They have separate rooms there, very private. Doll makers from all over stay there when they come to Kyoto."

It would be nice if Chūbei could help her arrange lodgings at the inn, but the fact that it was frequented by doll makers worried Tamae. Kisuke might stay there himself. If she found a doctor to perform an abortion, she would need a couple of days to rest. An inn where she didn't know anyone would be more convenient.

"Chūbei," Tamae said. "Instead of a fancy inn, do you know of a small inn for businesspeople somewhere? The location doesn't matter, but I don't like the idea of staying at a place where a lot of doll makers stay. It makes me uncomfortable, somehow. Isn't there some small inn you know?"

Chūbei's deep-set eyes widened. He tilted his head and gave her a lecherous smile.

"If that's the kind of place you want, there are a lot of them. Leave it to me, Sonoko," he said, his tone even lower than before. "May I take care of things for you?"

"Yes, anywhere's fine with me."

Tamae decided it would be best to explain to him her situation at the inn. Although she worried what kind of face he would he make when she told him, she felt she had no other choice. She agreed to go ahead on her own and wait for Chūbei to meet her.

It was just after five when Tamae left the store. She had received from the accounts desk a payment of sixty-two yen in cash for the dolls that Kisuke had supplied to the Kanetoku that year.

·

Chūbei had placed a call to the Taneyasu inn in Horikawa, Nakadachiuri, and drawn a map for Tamae. Although she had never been in that area before, she had a pretty good idea of where it was because of the time she had spent at the Shimabara. She walked from Muromachi Avenue to the Horikawa, where the low, black river flowed. From there she boarded an electric trolley. It was a small train, an old-style clang-clang trolley that looked like a wooden toy. It jostled Tamae as it rattled along the stone walls of the Horikawa embankment, moving away from the watchtowers of the old shogun's palace, the Nijōjo, which were tinted by the light of the sunset. The trolley took a sharp turn at Nakadachiuri, where the dye-stained waters of the Horikawa continued as far as the eye could see in the direction of the river's headwaters.

Tamae got off at a station next to the riverbank. Following her map, she walked east and found the Taneyasu Inn, which to her relief was enclosed by a black, board fence. Truth be told, she wanted a quiet place that was out of sight. Still it seemed strange how Chūbei happened to know such an out-of-the-way inn in such a bustling city. Tamae chose not to dwell on the matter.

She walked across the paving stones, which had been sprinkled with water, and approached the entryway. A fat woman in her mid-thirties greeted her at the open door. As she knelt on the floor, Tamae could see a red collar peeking out from under her kimono.

"Are you the guest from the Kanetoku? We received a phone call."

The inn looked small from the outside but extended a long way back. An interior garden, which contained a granite lantern and a pond drained of water, divided the building into a main wing and an annex. A narrow, well-worn corridor passed alongside this garden, connecting the two sections of the inn. As they walked across it, the floorboards creaked.

"Do guests of the Kanetoku stay here sometimes?" Tamae asked.

"Yes." The woman's eyes protruded from her single-fold lids, and when she spoke she rolled them to expose their whites. "The head clerk often uses our inn."

As the maid had encouraged her to do, Tamae bathed immediately, put on a padded kimono over her thin yukata and retired to her room. She had been tense before collecting the money and felt some momentary relief after the task was complete. When she considered the more difficult task ahead, however, she became overcome with exhaustion.

Perhaps at Chūbei's instruction, the maid did not bring her meal right away. Finally, at about seven o'clock, Tamae heard restless footsteps coming down the corridor. The shōji door slid open and Chūbei peered in. He was dressed in a kimono of fine cotton tied with an obi in gray vertical stripes. Smiling, he entered.

"I kept you waiting a long time. I was all set to leave, but then something came up. Now look at the time. It's late. I'm really sorry."

He gave her a fawning look and then quickly turned to the maid who arrived with tea. "Hurry up and bring some dinner," he barked.

The maid grinned familiarly. "Would you like some sake?" she asked. Apparently Chūbei was a frequent guest.

"Now that you mention it, maybe you should bring in a flask. We can relax a little then."

Chūbei took a seat before the low ebony table. After the maid left, he leaned in toward Tamae and said, "This is a nice, quiet inn, Sonoko. After I eat dinner, I'll go home and you can rest."

"All right, thank you."

Chūbei's overly familiar manner stirred a violent hatred in Tamae's heart, but given the circumstances she knew she could not openly display her true feelings.

The maid brought a ceramic bottle filled with sake and set out the side dishes. Once she had gone again, Tamae began her appeal.

"I have a request to make of you, Chūbei."

Chūbei froze with the sake bottle in hand.

"What do you mean by request?" he asked with a piercing stare. "Let's at least have a drink first."

He forced Tamae to take a cup and poured her a drink. Gathering her courage, she set the cup on the table and began again.

"Earlier you asked if I wasn't feeling well, but there was a reason I couldn't answer you then. I'm pregnant, Chūbei. I'm in my sixth month."

"Oh, is that right?" Chūbei said as he sipped at his cup, a note of surprise in his voice. "That's wonderful news, isn't it?"

"There's nothing wonderful at all about it. The baby inside me is yours."

The tips of Chūbei's hairy fingers trembled. Still clutching his sake cup, he glared at her. Then the corners of his mouth twisted, and he let out a weird laugh.

"What are you talking about? You're joking, right?" He raised his hand level with his nose and waved it back and forth several times.

"My child? That's ridiculous. Tamae, I had sex with you only that one time . . ."

Tamae drew in her chin and stared hard at Chūbei. Her anger boiled over, but she remained silent.

"I had sex with you just once. You're Kisuke's wife, aren't you? It's his child you're carrying in your belly. What do you think you're saying? Who's going to believe you?"

"Chūbei," Tamae cut in, trying to suppress her tears. "I've never slept with Kisuke. Not once. The only man I've had sex with since coming to Takekami is you. Just you, Chūbei. I don't expect you to believe me when I tell you such a thing, but it's the truth. Chūbei, you're the only man I've had sex with."

Chūbei's expression changed—not because what Tamae said had a whiff of truth about it, but because he suddenly sensed the urgency of the matter. He lowered his chin and looked into Tamae's teary eyes.

"Tamae, you say you haven't slept with Kisuke. Who'd believe such a thing? And in any case, what reason do you have to believe I'm the father? Is there any proof that it's my child?"

"Proof?" she shot back. "As a woman I'm the one who knows best about this. It was near the end of June when it happened. It was when you first came to the house to buy dolls. It was strange when my period stopped the next month, but I used to work as a prostitute so I thought, Well, this can't be. So I relaxed. Then I started getting heartburn, and my food started tasting odd, and the lower half of my body felt weak.

"I thought I should see a doctor, so I went to Takefu. I asked the doctor what he thought was wrong with me, and he told me that I was pregnant. That I was already in my fourth month. He said the child was healthy and sleeping in my belly. I was shocked. Since I've never once had sex with Kisuke since we married, I could hardly tell him. I've been torturing myself ever since, worrying every night, wondering what I should do.

"Chūbei, you have to believe me. I didn't come here to ask you to take responsibility. When I was working in Awara I managed to put aside some money. I never told Kisuke. I thought I might need it someday, so I secretly deposited it in a post office account. I withdrew the money and brought it with me. Chūbei, can you take me to a doctor somewhere and help me get an abortion? There are lots of doctors in Kyoto. Can you introduce me to one? That's all I came here to ask of you. Please do this for me."

Chūbei had been holding his breath the whole time and words failed him. He stared blankly at Tamae as tears streaked down her face. What was this woman telling him? He was overwhelmed by a feeling he couldn't identify— was it shock or disdain? All at once, a look of anger spread across his face.

*Who ever heard of such an idiotic story? A married woman gets pregnant then comes crying to the man with whom she cheated on her husband once, insisting that it's his baby and that he help her get an abortion . . . Even supposing Tamae's story were true, what man in his right mind would honestly believe it? Any man who believed such a thing was a fool.*

Chūbei was also gripped by fear. He knew very well that abortion was illegal. Just the previous month a maid from Kamigyō Ward aborted a five-month-old fetus and buried it in a bamboo grove. She was caught and brought to trial. Because the child was illegitimate, she was also charged with adultery.

It was in all the papers. Everyone in Kyoto was shocked when they read about it.

*If I do what Tamae asks, there could be terrible consequences. Even if I try to help her out of sympathy, no doctor will agree to abort the baby if the father doesn't acknowledge it. And why should I have to admit to being the father? It was a one-time mistake. There's no way I'll act as a scapegoat for her husband . . .*

Witnessing this spectacle, however, made Chūbei partially regret ever having committed adultery with this outrageous woman. Just maybe Tamae really never had sex with the doll maker. He recalled how startled he had been by Kisuke's small face, his sullen, sunken eyes, his tiny body—he wasn't even five feet tall. Chūbei had wondered if Kisuke weren't deformed. He recalled how the art dealer in Nawate, Samejima Ichijirō, had described him with great relish to his younger brother, the owner of the Kanetoku.

*He's a really short man. Just like a child. Even so, he makes wonderful dolls. Then there's his wife. She's really beautiful and with such fair skin. When I saw her in the groves, I thought she was a fairy of the bamboo . . .*

His words were right on target. When Chūbei visited Takekami, never in his wildest dreams did he imagine the woman Samejima spoke of was the same woman he had known from the Shimabara. But it was Sonoko after all. When he saw her, Chūbei felt the days and months of more than a decade disappear in an instant. Sonoko was lovelier than ever. And she just happened to be the wife of the very man he had come to visit . . . Overcome by lust, he took advantage of Kisuke's absence and forced himself on her. She clung to him and her body trembled just like in the old days. Why would a woman like Sonoko marry that deformed doll maker? It was queer. And why would she yield her body to another man?

*Maybe it's just as she said. Maybe she has no physical relationship with Kisuke. So she yielded her body to me. And after just that one time she got pregnant . . .*

If this were in fact true, then Chūbei thought he had drawn the short straw. Sonoko had worked in a brothel until she got married. To get a woman like her pregnant was just unbelievable.

"What a mess," he said.

Tamae didn't bother to wipe the tears from her cheeks.

"Please believe me, Chūbei. I don't know how many times I've thought about killing myself. I thought about asking a doctor in Takefu or Sabae, but I don't know anyone there, and besides, Echizen is a small place and people in the village would find out. I came here because there are lots of doctors in Kyoto, and I thought if I asked you, then maybe I could find a good place that would help me."

"You can say that, but . . . I don't know any midwives or doctors." Chūbei thrust his lips out in a pout. "I'm still a bachelor after all these years. I've never been married. I've never gotten a woman pregnant before. You're asking me to help, but I don't have the slightest idea what to do. I'm completely in the dark."

To halt his retreat, Tamae began to plead with him.

"Chūbei, I know you don't believe me, but you really are the only one I had sex with. When I saw your face that day, it truly brought back memories. But I never thought you would act so rashly. If I had been firmer with you and kicked with all my strength, none of this would have happened. But I've never slept with my husband and because I worked as a prostitute for so long, I suddenly felt lonely. I knew it was wrong to let you do what you wanted, but my body was burning in opposition to my heart. Chūbei, I'm a bad woman. Now I'm being punished for it."

Tamae leaned her elbows on the table and shook her head in a pleading manner. Her eyes were bloodshot, her eyelids were pink and her cheeks were hollow. She seemed a shadow of her former self. From time to time, her face twitched. Chūbei caught the scent of her hair and thought he could hear the crackling of the firewood in the hearth of that gloomy house in Takekami.

*This woman is an utter fool. She has a husband she doesn't sleep with. She comes here saying that she cheats on him one time and gets pregnant. To top it off, she comes here begging for help to abort the baby. She's a fool . . .*

This doll maker's wife, this Tamae, suddenly struck him as an idiot of no interest. But since she was being so foolish, he felt the urge to use her for his own amusement.

"Sonoko?" Chūbei narrowed his eyes. "I understand. I'll think it over. Come here."

He moved the table aside and seized Tamae's arm. He put his other arm around her neck, its bluish veins visible beneath her white skin, and pulled her to his chest. Unable to breathe, Tamae stared up at Chūbei with moist eyes.

"There are a lot of doctors in Kyoto," he told her. "Early tomorrow morning I'll go around and check for you. I don't know how things will turn out, but I'll do my best. So don't worry. If you show the doctors your money, you'll find one who can perform a good abortion. So don't worry. In this world, money solves everything."

Chūbei pressed his bearded cheeks against Tamae's face. "I love you," he murmured gently. "Ever since we met that day in Takekami, I haven't forgotten you."

A spark of hope appeared in Tamae's vacant eyes. *Chūbei will try for me. I'll get the abortion* . . . She felt a brief surge of joy. Then Chūbei pulled her to him. With one hand, he rolled up the hem of her striped kimono in the same way bamboo is stripped of its bark.

"I'll go all over Kyoto tomorrow looking for a midwife. All right, Sonoko? So don't worry."

Panting heavily, Chūbei forced open Tamae's thighs. She was shaking now, and he imagined he could smell the musty scent of the child inside her. But since he had already given himself over to his sexual desires, he went ahead and straddled her slightly distended belly.

"I've always loved you. I love these qualities of yours. I love you, Sonoko."

The Kanetoku clerk rubbed his bearded face against the trembling doll maker's wife, who shut her tear-stained eyes as if resigned to her fate.

# XV

Tamae had indeed been a fool that night. Unable to read the true intent behind Chūbei's words, she forgot herself and allowed him to toy with her exhausted body. At the sound of the maid's footsteps, he abruptly thrust her aside and hurriedly made to leave without touching any of the dinner that was served. He promised Tamae he would find her a doctor the next day. As she watched him go, she desperately wanted to believe him, even if she were grasping at straws.

The sliding door to the adjoining room was open, and Tamae staggered over to the futon that had been laid out there. Her body was exhausted but her mind was active. She worried about the next day's operation and she couldn't sleep.

Images of Takekami and its groves of bamboo filled her head. Kisuke was probably in his workshop hunched over his awl. The workers would have all gone home already. Kisuke had to pay them their salaries and year-end bonuses so they could buy their New Year provisions. She had come to Kyoto in order to collect that money. No doubt Kisuke was waiting impatiently for her to return with the cash. She pictured him in profile polishing a doll with a scouring brush, completely absorbed in his work. Tamae was determined to get back to Takekami just as soon as the child she was carrying had been aborted.

*Kisuke's so different from Chūbei. He yearns for me as if I was his mother.*
*He doesn't reach out for my body. He reaches out for my spirit. If I weren't there,*
*he might go insane. I have to deal with this baby, no matter what. I have to get*
*back to Takekami . . .*

As the night wore on, the sound of the trolley ceased, the sound of the
water in the Horikawa rose, the tears on Tamae's cheeks dried, and at last she
fell asleep.

·

The next day, Tamae got up early. The maid from the previous evening had
brought her breakfast, but it was a dreary, lonely meal. Tamae waited for
word from Chūbei, but no news arrived all morning. She became increasingly
anxious.

Finally, at a little past noon, the maid reappeared. "There's a call for you,"
she said.

There was a phone located in the alcove of Tamae's room. She picked up
the receiver and pressed it to her ear. Chūbei's raspy voice came through on
the other end.

"Sonoko, I'm really sorry about last night," he began. His voice seemed to
come from far away and his tone was humble. "You see, the thing is . . ."

"Did you find a good doctor, Chūbei?" Tamae cut him off.

"You see, I tried three doctors this morning, but with the way things are,
none of them listened to me."

His words assaulted Tamae's ears; they penetrated so deeply.

"I forgot to tell you last night, but recently in Kamigyō Ward there was
a maid who worked at the house of a director of the Gas Company. She got
pregnant with the director's child and had an abortion. The story just broke
in the papers. . . . They buried the baby in a bamboo grove, but the police
arrested the midwife who helped them, and the consequences were terrible.
They were prosecuted. Now all the doctors in Kyoto are nervous about that,
and when I asked them they all looked like I was asking them to touch something fearful. They wouldn't listen to me."

Tamae swallowed hard.

"What do you mean, Chūbei? . . . Are you giving up? What about the
promise you swore to me last night?"

"That's why I tried everything I could think of . . . I even went to a couple
of midwives I had heard about."

"And?"

"Listen, Sonoko. It's no good. It was hopeless from the start. The midwives said they can't abort a child if they don't know who the father is. If you . . . well, if there's proof of paternity, then they'd do something for you, but when they heard your story . . . that you're properly married . . . that the baby isn't your husband's . . . Well, to ask for an abortion for such an absurd reason . . . It's clear nowadays to everyone that abortion's a matter for the police. They're all afraid. It's just not a reasonable request. I spoke to them for you, but no one will do it."

Chūbei's words took on a careless ring.

"Sonoko, it's because you came to Kyoto with an unreasonable request from the beginning. If you're going to get an abortion, you have to get permission from Kisuke. So go back to Echizen and explain to Kisuke what happened. Get some kind of proof of his permission, then come back to Kyoto. How about it? The midwives told me that if you have proof of your husband's consent, there's a loophole in the law and they have a way to deal with the abortion. I think that's the best way. How about it?"

Tamae felt her world turn black. If she had been able to discuss the matter with Kisuke, she never would have come to such a place nor make such a humiliating request.

"Chūbei, I can't go back to Echizen in this condition. If I can't get an abortion, then I don't want to go back. I'll have to ask you to take the money I collected from the Kanetoku and deliver it to Kisuke. He has to pay the workers and give them their year-end bonus. He's waiting for the money. I'll take care of things somehow on my own. But I'm not going back to Echizen. At the very least, you can take care of the money for me, can't you?"

Chūbei remained silent. She could picture his expression.

"Chūbei, can I count on you to do that much for me?"

"But . . ." Chūbei drew the receiver away from his mouth momentarily. "If I take the money to him, it's going to be awfully strange because the Kanetoku has already delivered the money over to you. If I take it back and send it by transfer, won't that seem odd? You could ask someone else to do it, but you wouldn't be able to tell them why. And if you don't explain why you're sending the money, you won't find anyone willing to travel as far as Echizen to take it for you.

"On top of that, it's a lot of money. If you just hand it over to someone you know nothing about, he may run away with it. Sonoko, it's best if you take the money home yourself. It's money that Kisuke earned through the sale of dolls he labored hard over. Asking someone to take it for you is wrong. If you ask me to do such an unreasonable thing, I can't help you."

Tamae understood Chūbei's argument. All the same, she felt as though she was being pushed away, and was at her wit's end.

"So that's the way it is?" Clutching the phone to her ear, she heard the sound of a trolley passing by.

Was Chūbei calling from a public phone somewhere near a tramline? At last, Tamae recognized the insincerity of his words. She was crestfallen. Before she knew it, she had hung up the phone.

*I have no choice but to go see my aunt in Mukōjima and plead my case to her. Chūbei is a stranger to me. But my aunt is family, so perhaps she'll be kind enough to help. I'll leave the inn and go see her right away.*

Investing her last hopes in this plan, Tamae quickly readied to leave. She settled her bill with the maid and left the Taneyasu a little after one P.M. She carried her personal effects, which were wrapped in a *furoshiki* of Fuji silk, under her arm.

Tamae boarded the empty early-afternoon trolley and took a seat. Images from the night before haunted her mind. She pictured Chūbei as he forced himself on her and the soiled red futon that had been laid out in the adjoining room. Had he planned all of it from the very beginning? She seethed with an even greater hatred of him.

*I'm an idiot. I've been completely fooled . . .*

The Nijōjo came into view. The castle's stone walls appeared angular above the moat, and the white-walled watchtower was outlined sharply against the gray, smoky sky. On the south side of the castle, Tamae could see black-tiled roofs layered one on top of the other. The Shimabara district, where she had lived years earlier, lay in that direction. Tamae stuck her face out the window and gazed at the scenery. All at once, she felt a dull pain in her lower abdomen. Instinctively, she put her hand to her belly.

*The baby's angry . . .*

Tamae went pale as she felt the faceless baby moving inside her. Each time the trolley jerked, the pain became more severe.

*Your father is a cunning, dishonest man. He tricked and toyed with me, and then broke his promise with a phone call . . .*

It occurred to Tamae that Chūbei had never even bothered to look for a doctor. Although the thought made her furious, at least his call served to warn her about the recent scandal. It was a bad time to seek an abortion. Even so, Tamae convinced herself that had Chūbei really walked all over Kyoto looking for a doctor, surely he would have found someone somewhere willing to listen. He had simply given up.

*I'll ask my aunt. She works as a procuress in Chūshojima. She's worked in brothel districts, so she may have some kind of connection.*

Tamae recalled her aunt's face—her thin jaw and her sharp eyes, which turned up at the corners and narrowed when she laughed. Tamae hadn't seen her in more than ten years; she was her sole living relative.

By the time the trolley arrived at Kyoto Station, the pain in Tamae's lower belly was flaring up every five minutes. It felt like something was squeezing her insides.

*The baby is angry. It's angry.*

Tamae got off the trolley, crushed by thoughts of anger and regret that she could share with no one.

# XVI

The venerable pleasure quarters of Chūshojima were located in Fushimi Ward in the southern part of Kyoto, just north of the 16th Division's military training grounds in the town of Fushimi, which spreads out along the flats that stretch as far as the Yodo Plain.

As its name—Chūsho Isle—would suggest, the town was cut off from the mainland by a river called the Ujigawa, which flows south as it passes under the Kangetsu Bridge. A fairly swift-flowing current, the Ujigawa merges with numerous other streams, either inlets or branches of the river, as it flows into the Yodogawa. The pleasure quarters of Chūshojima were located on the delta near the confluence of these rivers.

The town was originally frequented by men who worked for the sake merchants and breweries in the vicinity. It was situated along Misu Inlet, a man-made channel built to accommodate boats transporting rice—sake's key ingredient—to the breweries. The boats would enter from the Ujigawa and drop off young men from neighboring towns. There were about two hundred brothels—the largest with thirty women or more—housed in two-story buildings with balustrades lining both sides of a single long, narrow street. The eaves of the tiled roofs resembled open parasols reflecting off the surface of the river. Each brothel had a small pier that jutted out into the water to attract customers.

Restaurants such as the Amifusa and the Minamitsuru, which specialized in freshwater fish, had been erected in a district called Misu Mukōjima, which was situated along the river across from Higashi Yanagi-chō. It was a lively area with a lot of geisha who could dance and play the samisen.

Tamae's aunt, Sakita Mon, was a procuress for a brothel called the Katsuragirō. For many years, Mon had lived in a house in the middle of some fields in Mukōjima, which was cut off from Chūshojima by the river. It was her custom to leave for work after five o'clock. Because it was still early afternoon, Tamae decided to go straight to the house in Mukōjima. It would be a far better place to talk about arranging an abortion. She'd never be able to discuss such a thing in front of the Katsuragirō.

The dull pain in Tamae's lower abdomen continued to worsen. After arriving at Kyoto Station, she took a moment to rest in the waiting room. She had left Takekami the previous morning, arrived in Kyoto in the late afternoon and was violently raped by Chūbei that evening. That shock on top of her exhaustion must have upset the baby. The pain was like nothing she had ever experienced before. It felt as though a drill was piercing her middle. Every five minutes, she experienced another contraction of pain. Tamae did her best to endure it. Seated on a bench, she doubled over at the waist and hung her head low. She absolutely had to get to the house in Mukōjima before her aunt left for work. When the station clock struck two, she gathered her strength, walked across the station plaza and boarded the train for Chūshojima.

By the time she arrived at the village of Mukōjima, it was past three-thirty and the wind had picked up. Because her memory had faded, she had trouble navigating her way.

Mukōjima was also situated along the Ujigawa, and there were many farmhouses spread out beneath the embankment. Some of the larger structures were surrounded by bamboo groves or stands of cedar trees, but most were smaller, zinc-roofed dwellings. The Sakita house was just such a one. Mon had left the Orihara household to marry the second son of the Sakita family, a man named Yūjirō who worked as a rickshaw puller. She lived in a small branch house located about 120 meters away from the main house in the middle of some mulberry fields. Yūjirō had died five years earlier. Mon, who was probably about sixty by then, needed to find some means to support herself, so she started commuting to Chūshojima.

Tamae hadn't seen Mon since she left the Shimabara, but she recalled her aunt's greedy disposition and rather cold expression. Still, she was a relative, and surely she would do her best to help once she saw the pain Tamae was in. At worst, she would bluntly refuse to help and Tamae would be unable to return to Takekami. If it came to that, Tamae would ask if she could stay until the baby was born and then go to Chūshojima. If she could not return to Kisuke's place, she thought, she had no choice but to resume work as a prostitute.

In her heart, Tamae wanted desperately to return to Takekami. As she walked along, she became consumed by despair. At last the roof of Mon's house came into view, offering Tamae some sense of relief. Mount Daigo could be seen in the distance shrouded in mist. The brown, desolate field rose gradually toward its base. The mulberry fields Tamae crossed were filled with needle-like trees with only a few yellow leaves. Tamae gazed beyond the Ujigawa embankment toward the town of Fushimi. The outlines of the sake warehouses that dotted the skyline seemed to dissolve like ink sticks into the horizon.

"Aunt Mon? Aunt Mon?" Tamae called as she reached the entryway of her aunt's dilapidated home with its crumbling eaves. Large *daikon* radishes were hanging to dry here and there; off to the side were some baskets of *daikon* that had been thinly sliced.

There was no reply so Tamae tried the door. Was it locked from the inside? It wouldn't give.

"Aunt Mon? It's me, Tamae," she called again, but still there was no answer.

At last she noticed the slips of mail jammed into the door and she knew that Mon wasn't home. Tamae's tension deflated like a balloon, and her strength drained away. Exhausted, she crouched on the ground in front of the door.

"Aunt Mon! Aunt Mon!" she cried.

Because Tamae's belly began to ache again, she contemplated waiting for her aunt to return. It was already evening, however. The pleasure quarters would just be coming to life, and her aunt probably wouldn't be back until dawn.

*I'd better go to Chūshojima. I have to meet my aunt. She'll be at the Katsuragirō for sure . . .*

Once she found her aunt at the Katsuragirō, she would ask her to go to the Benten temple grounds where they could talk about the abortion. With these thoughts in mind, Tamae made her way back through the stand of mulberry trees, which against the darkening sky resembled a forest of needles.

# XVII

Tamae set out from Mukōjima toward the Ujigawa embankment, where she could board a ferry to Chūshojima. She couldn't possibly have reached the main bridge to Fushimi on foot. Because she used to ride the ferries with her mother, she was familiar with the port, but it took her a long time to walk anyway because of the severity of her pain. By the time she climbed up the embankment, which was covered in withered grass, and could see the ferry crossing, it was nearly dark. There were no signs of passengers, and she could see only a single boat moored to the pier. The boatman was an older man wearing a headband. He was staring intently at the surface of the river. Tamae gathered herself and descended the zigzag path of the embankment.

At the tip of a slight sandbar was a small rest station that was nothing more than an old-fashioned, weathered hut with a single stool. There were no customers there either. After the main bridge had been completed, fewer people used the ferries. The pier, which was low to the water, had decayed so badly it looked as though it could be swept away at any moment. The single boat docked there was extremely humble. Feeling utterly helpless and alone, Tamae called out to the boatman, who was crouched over with his back to her.

"Mister! When does your boat leave? Will you take me to Chūshojima?"

The man stood up. He was about sixty years old and had a close-cropped haircut. His complexion was dark from the sun, but the way his narrow eyes were set in his round face made him seem good-natured. Tamae felt as if she had been rescued.

"Are you by yourself?" the boatman asked.

"Yes, I'm alone."

The boatman nodded his head, stepped quickly toward his boat and began to loosen the mooring rope from its post.

"Thank you," she said.

Tamae walked gingerly across the pier, which was swaying under the weight of her body. Her white tabi were completely soiled. The thongs on the new clogs she first put on in Takekami were also covered with dust. She was struck by a feeling of embarrassment as well as a desire to offer a prayer of thanks to the boatman. Lifting up the hem of her kimono, she lightly stepped into the bow of the boat, which he had pulled up close to her. A mat had been laid over the duckboards, and in a corner was a pile of three thin cushions whose cotton filling was bursting its seams.

"Spread the cushions out and sit on them," the boatman directed her.

"Yes."

With a quick glance at Tamae's lower belly, he skillfully maneuvered the punting pole and pushed the boat away from the pier.

The waters of the Ujigawa are deep, and the current swift. The current reflected in Tamae's eyes took on the darker colors of the ocean and seemed to be pressing in on her. She had heard when she was little that if a boatman isn't used to the current, he won't make it across. The old boatman seemed taciturn by nature. Each time he worked his pole, the boat would tilt left and right, sending a spray of water up the sides, but he never looked around. He remained silent until they came to the middle of the river. Suddenly he turned to Tamae.

"Heading home to Chūshojima?"

"Yes."

The boatman again glanced at Tamae's belly. It wasn't clear to her if his expression was one of pity or of contempt. Then a kind, friendly glow settled into his eyes and his mouth broke into a grin.

"Did you go to Mukōjima?"

"Yes."

As the old man pushed off his punting pole, the shoulders of his patched, knitted shirt pulled taut and the boat swayed. Trying to keep her pain under control, Tamae clung to the boat's sides. Then suddenly the boat pitched heavily and she was overcome by a stabbing sensation; she clutched her middle with one hand.

"What's wrong with you? Your belly hurt?"

The old boatman's language was rough, but his words contained an echo of kindness. He stopped punting.

"Yes," said Tamae. Her face went a deathly pale and sweat smeared her forehead.

"What's wrong? Does it hurt? Does it hurt?" the boatman cried.

His voice reached Tamae from far away. The boat was listing heavily. She felt the baby twist inside of her and drop. Tamae groaned as the pain worsened. Placing both hands on her belly, she tried to bear up, but with the rocking of the boat and the way she was sitting, she couldn't. She broke into a sweat and gasped for air; then she felt a thread of something warm and slimy move down her thighs. No longer able to control the pain, Tamae curled up on her side like a shrimp. She felt a heavy lump press against her pelvis. Tamae grabbed at the duckboard and stared out onto the surface of the river. She thought she saw the water rise slowly toward her, its purple color deepening. Then she lost consciousness.

The boat was swaying. Tamae heard a keening squeak, like the sound she heard whenever Kisuke was hunched over the spinning lathe in his workshop. The boatman had put away the punting pole and switched to sculling, pushing the oar at the back of the boat through the water. Beyond the darkening sky, Tamae saw the hamlet of Takekami tinted in a red light. She watched a fragment of a cloud that looked like a flower drift by. At last she had some relief from her pain. She heard the gush of warm blood spreading slowly over her lower body. She fell into a pleasant sleep.

*Kisuke, Kisuke . . .*

The evening sun dyed the bamboo groves of Takekami an orange tint. That image was transposed over the sky that opened like a fan above the Ujigawa, whose waters reflected the shadow of Mount Daigo.

·

"Are you awake?" The boatman was smiling down at Tamae, his wrinkled face leaned in close to hers.

While she was unconscious, the boat had moved away from the center of the current and come to a rest on a quiet bank. Tamae felt a cold breeze at the hem of her kimono, and at last came back to herself.

"You're awake. Good. Good." he said gently. "The baby dropped. The baby's not in your belly anymore. Look there at the beautiful current. It flowed away cleanly. You were sitting here."

The boatman grabbed a crude mop made of bamboo and straw and began swabbing the duckboards, which were slicked with fishy-smelling blood. After scrubbing for a while, he would grab a bucket and bail the soiled water over the boat's sides, soiling his hands in the process.

"The baby has been washed away in the river. No one is at fault. The baby just wasn't fated to be in this world. Will you return to Chūshojima now?"

Tamae remained silent.

"The baby wasn't meant for this world. Now you can work again."

The boatman's voice seemed to echo inside Tamae's pitiful body; his warm voice wrapped around her ears like silk floss. She stared at the boatman with tearful eyes.

*The baby's been washed away in the river . . .*

Suddenly, Tamae's eyes widened in surprise. The water the boatman bailed stained the waters of the Ujigawa a rose color—the same tint the evening sun was now giving to the peak of Mount Daigo.

"I'll go home to Echizen. I'm a prostitute who worked in Echizen. I was on my way to Chūshojima where my aunt works as a procuress. I thought I'd ask her to help me get an abortion. Then . . . then . . . by chance I got on your boat, and this is how it turned out . . . I've caused you a lot of trouble, mister. Please forgive me."

The boatman put down his bucket and stared into Tamae's face. Smiling, he wiped the sweat from her face. His expression was even more soothing.

"All right, then it's just as well. I thought about showing you the baby, but if somebody saw us, there'd be hell to pay, so I took the liberty of washing it away in the river. No one knows. No one saw. The waters at Uji are very swift, so they've carried your baby far out to sea."

Tamae lowered her head.

"I'll never forget your kindness, not for as long as I live. Mister, could you take the boat back? If I go on to Chūshojima and someone sees this bloodstained kimono, there'll be a big fuss. I'm sorry, but I should go back to my aunt's house in Mukōjima. Can you take the boat back?"

The old boatman nodded at once and reached for his punting pole.

The Ujigawa becomes the Misu Inlet on the west bank at Minami Fushimi. Compared to the main river where the current is swift, the inlet is calm and smooth as a mirror. Now the surface of that inlet looked like a distant sea glowing in the crimson sky at dusk. The ripples sparkled as if sprinkled with glass powder. The boatman deftly maneuvered his pole to redirect the boat toward Mukōjima.

"I owe you, mister."

Grasping the soaked hems of her kimono, which had chilled in the breeze, she listened as the old boatman propelled the boat through the Ujigawa's scarlet-speckled waters.

"Let's go back to the hut. I'll get a fire going. You're chilled to the bone," the boatman said and began to row faster.

# XVIII

Tamae returned to the hamlet of Takekami early on the evening of December 17, the third day of her journey. Work had already finished for the day, and there was no one in the workshop. Kisuke was back at the main house jointing *mōsō* bamboo beside the hearth.

To joint bamboo, you tap a hard, pointed iron rod into the knot of the bamboo and then pop the joint, all the while being careful not to scratch the bark. After that you pass a slender rod of bamboo grass wrapped in shark-skin through the inside to smooth the joints. Anticipating Tamae's return sometime that evening, Kisuke had placed a pile of bamboo beside the hearth. From time to time, he would poke at the smoldering firewood.

Kisuke expected that Tamae had collected the money at the Kanetoku right away and then headed to Mukōjima. After spending the night with her aunt, she would have started home. *If she hasn't forgotten her home here, Tamae will certainly be back tonight . . .* Suddenly the front door opened onto a deep purple evening and a voice called out, "I'm back!"

Overjoyed, Kisuke tossed his rod beside the hearth and stood up to greet her.

"So you're home?"

He stepped down onto the earthen floor, slipped on his sandals and moved quickly to the entryway.

The sight of her stopped him in his tracks. Tamae was pale. No, her skin was translucent. Could she have changed so much during her short trip? Tamae's face had undergone such a transformation that Kisuke could only stare at her, breathless.

When she left the house, the flesh around her cheeks had seemed drawn and lifeless. Now her skin glowed with the sheen of white snow. A few strands of hair fell down around her ears, and her shoulders were slumped and sagging. He thought it may have been due to exhaustion from the trip, but for some reason she also looked taller. Kisuke detected a voluptuous look in her eyes.

"What happened? I hope you didn't strain yourself. Are you all right?"

A faint smile drifted over Tamae's face, exposing the dimple in one cheek.

"It's nothing," she said. "It was a long train ride, and my lower back hurts. That's all. It was a really long, long train ride. Kisuke, I brought a lot of money from the Kanetoku."

She moved to the hearth and stoked the fire. After the flames blazed up with a crackle, she sat down at her usual place and slowly unwrapped the bundle in her Fuji silk *furoshiki*. She handed Kisuke the account book and a packet of cash wrapped in paper.

"Sixty-two yen. Kisuke, this is the money you earned. You can pay the workers with this, and give them a year-end bonus."

Kisuke took the packet from her, his hands trembling. After staring at it for a while, he muttered to himself and raised it twice to his large forehead. Next he went to the family altar in the dimly lit tatami room. He struck the small prayer bell and put his palms together. He was making an offering to the spirit of Kizaemon.

Tamae watched Kisuke as he prayed and recalled with relief all that had happened on her trip. How she had washed the skirt of her blood-stained kimono on a strand of the Ujigawa and warmed herself by a fire the boatman built to dry her clothes. How she had spent the night in her aunt's storage shed and then visited with her for about an hour the next morning before returning home.

What stayed with her most was not the image of her gray-haired aunt, whom she hadn't seen in so long, but the face of the old boatman, who had disposed of the fetus and afterbirth in the river. The face of the boatman was forever burned into her memory.

Tamae never learned his name. No doubt, he had worked for years as a ferryman. He had lit a fire in the hut at the ferry crossing, and they talked about various things while they waited for her clothes to dry. Tamae had been warmed by his compassion. Theirs was a random encounter, but he had brought her back to life. Tamae felt an enormous sense of gratitude toward him, but was even more relieved to be back home with Kisuke. Tears filled her eyes. In her mind, the fire from the hearth mingled with the flames of the fire at the ferry crossing.

*I must never tell Kisuke. I must act as though nothing happened . . .*

After Kisuke returned from the altar, she told him about her trip, and then prepared dinner. Although only three days had passed, she felt as if she had been away for ten or twenty years. The experience convinced her that she belonged here.

"It's a beautiful store," she told Kisuke as they ate. "There's a large room covered with tatami mats. The walls are stacked with shelves filled with dolls of celluloid and alabaster—Gosho dolls, Ichima dolls. Lined up on the top shelf are the bamboo dolls you made, Kisuke. When I saw those dolls, tears came to my eyes. They were described on a card as the '*Bamboo Dolls of Echizen.*' I was so happy seeing them standing on the tallest shelf, in a glass case with a lacquered frame, among the work of doll makers from all over the nation . . . I was so happy, I felt like crying. Everyone treated me kindly."

Kisuke's eyes sparkled.

"Mr. Sakiyama and the owner? Are they doing well?"

Tamae glanced downward, but answered him right away.

"Yes, they're all well. They have a lot of apprentices, and they welcomed me in one of the rooms they use for clients."

Kisuke grinned broadly and nodded his head repeatedly.

"And there's nothing wrong with you?"

"There's nothing wrong. I don't know why, but when I went to Kyoto, my stomach felt better. Please don't worry about me. I'm fine."

Tamae wanted to burst into tears. Fighting to retain her composure, she set down her chopsticks and lowered her face.

"What's wrong, Tamae? Is there something wrong?"

Tamae arched her eyebrows and saw his worried, innocent eyes blinking at her weakly.

"It's nothing. I'm just happy. I was so happy seeing the dolls you made. They were so beautiful, as if they could never be outdone. And I'm happy to be back here, Kisuke. When I saw you waiting here looking so lonely for me, it made me happy. It's all right if I cry, isn't it? If it's all right, then I'll cry. Kisuke, I was lonely traveling by myself. I was lonely."

Her voice cracked, and she threw herself down beside her dinner tray. Her shoulders were convulsing. Kisuke watched anxiously as her black hair shook against her white collar.

"Please smile for me, Kisuke. I'm happy. I'm happy . . . so I'm crying."

She raised her tear-stained face and smiled. Her translucent skin was aglow, as if she had been transformed. Kisuke's eyes gradually began to sparkle.

Kisuke's workshop became even livelier after Tamae's return. She resumed serving tea to the workers and looked more beautiful than ever. Her health had returned, and her mood was bright and cheerful.

The figure of Tamae waiting on Kisuke was enough, as always, to make the young men of the village dream about her. And she would smile brightly at the people she met on the village road.

.

Overnight the Nanjō range was completely covered in snow that resembled pure cotton. The snow piled up in the grove, and you could hear the stalks of bamboo cracking under its weight. Even so, the number of workers in Kisuke's workshop continued to grow. A group of older men wanted to quit making charcoal during the winter and turn their efforts to making dolls. Kisuke's narrow shed was filled to bursting with people. Some merchants even braved the winter roads to come buy the dolls. Tamae continued helping with clients and managing the accounts. In February, however, she fell ill again.

She caught a cold and developed a fever. In a single day, her fair skin lost its luster while her eyes lost their sparkle and began to droop. Despite her fits of coughing, she continued to come to the workshop to serve tea. Kisuke and the workers urged her to stay in bed, but Tamae wouldn't listen.

"You've got to rest, Tamae," Kisuke would scold her in front of everyone. "One of the young men can make the tea. You lie down in the *kotatsu*. If you think a cold is nothing to worry about, it'll just get worse. Go lie down!"

Tamae would drop her head and return to the house, only to return soon after to take care of something else.

After several days like this, Tamae began coughing up blood. It was February 18 and a storm raged in the Nanjō mountains. Tamae had gotten up early as usual and was preparing to boil water from her seat at the end of the hearth. Just as she was reaching for a thick piece of chestnut wood to add to the fire, she was struck by a terrible fit of coughing and a sharp, stabbing pain in her chest. Everything began to fade to a deep purple and the kettle hanging from the trammel began to spin. She collapsed on the floor and bright red blood flowed from her mouth. Unconsciously she pressed her hands to her mouth, and the blood oozed between her fingers.

"Kisuke, Kisuke."

Kisuke had gone out to the workshop after washing up and was about to light a fire in the portable clay stove when he heard her smothered cries. He hurried over, his knees shaking.

"What's wrong, Tamae? What's wrong?"

Seeing her face smeared with blood, Kisuke paled. Using all his strength, he lifted her up and carried her to the bedroom. Then he called his neighbor Yohei, who ran to fetch a doctor.

Yohei ran almost five miles over the snowy road to the village of Hirose, where Dr. Chikaraishi had opened a weekend clinic, and brought the doctor back to Kisuke's gloomy house. After completing a routine examination, the doctor calmly gave Tamae a large injection of a gelatin and salt solution to stop the bleeding.

"It's her lungs," he said and placed a hand on his closely cropped hair, which was wet from the snow. "It's pretty bad. She coughed up a lot of blood. Given how much blood there is, it means one of her lungs is completely infected. She has to rest quietly. There's no other way to handle a lung disease. Tuberculosis spreads if you move around. So if you don't move, the tubercular bacillus will harden. That is, they'll calcify. Whatever you do, don't let her move around. Please watch her carefully."

Kisuke was kneeling by Tamae's side, his head hung low.

"When the snow melts," the doctor continued, "move her to a room that gets more sunlight, Kisuke. It's cold here. And it's terribly damp."

The room had a wooden floor with nothing but a mat spread over it. The doctor looked at Tamae's thin red futon mattress, and contorted his face.

"Please make sure she rests," he said and made to leave.

In 1925 there were no effective medicines to treat tuberculosis—no strep-tomycin or para-amino salicylic acid. The disease was particularly fatal in the poverty-stricken mountain villages. Fukui Prefecture was once known for having the highest rate of lung disease, and because it was a rural prefec-ture treatments arrived there last. All Dr. Chikaraishi could leave for Tamae was something to reduce her fever. She remained quiet and inactive, and she stopped coughing blood. But she was drastically weakened.

Tamae lost weight and her appearance changed. The bones behind her ears began to show and the back of her neck appeared emaciated. Because her natural complexion was like white wax, she developed a greenish hue whenever the blood drained from her face. All day long, she would stare up at the ceiling, her eyes puddling with tears. She remained silent because whenever she tried to speak, Kisuke would scold her. Around the end of February, however, she mustered all of her strength to speak.

"Kisuke," she told him in a low voice, "I've caused you a great deal of trouble again. I'm really sorry."

Even though Tamae was ill, she still spoke to Kisuke in this formal way. It made Kisuke feel sorry for her, because otherwise she had completely changed. She was no longer bright and cheerful. She was depressed. He wanted somehow to cheer her up.

"Kisuke, I'm going to die soon," she told him one day when he stepped out of the workshop to check on her. "But it's all right if I die. I worked so long in the red-light districts as a prostitute. People would point at me behind my back. Then I had the good fortune to come here. It's been like paradise to me. Since I came to Takekami, I've had the happiest time of my life. It's been two years already, hasn't it? I want to live until the camellias next to your father's grave bloom. But I wonder if I'll live that long. I have a feeling somehow that I'm going to die. Kisuke. I'm sorry, but will you let me stay here until I die?"

Although her voice was listless, she sounded as if she were pleading with him. Then she stretched out her arm, which was so thin she resembled a praying mantis, and pointed to her dresser.

"Kisuke, there's a savings passbook in my dresser, in the small drawer on the second row. That's money I saved when I worked as a prostitute. Use that money to put my grave next to your father's. I'll be your father's bride. I came here to be your bride, but you wouldn't let me. Instead you treated me like your mother. To tell the truth, Kisuke, I came to think of you as my child. There were days when I thought of you as the child I had with your late father. Kisuke, please bury me next to your father. I'd like to rest there so I can enjoy the bamboo grass that's been cared for so beautifully."

Kisuke watched the tears flow from the depths of Tamae's sunken eyes. All their former beauty had vanished. While she had once recalled a fairy, Tamae now looked like a withered tree. She was an invalid whose movement was restricted to her dry, purplish lips. Kisuke slid over beside her and spoke into her ear.

"Tamae, I don't blame you if you resent me. From the beginning I thought of you as my mother. From the day we met in that back room of the Hanamiya in Awara, when I recognized your face in the bamboo doll my father created. All the bamboo dolls I made, Tamae, they're all you. It's all because of you that my dolls have become famous. You mustn't die. Please get well for me. If you die, I won't have the spirit to make dolls anymore. I'll lose all desire to work. So don't lose hope. Get better soon and show me your cheerful face. If you stay positive and rest, the doctor says you'll get better for sure. I'll do anything for you if it helps you get better. Anything. You're my mother. You're my mother. You can ask anything of me."

Kisuke took Tamae's bony hand.

"Kisuke, this is the first time I've touched your hand."

Tamae closed her eyes, her cheeks glistening with tears.

·

Kisuke sent a messenger to Takefu to fetch some expensive medicine and bought raw fish, the kind caught in small numbers in the rough waves off the cape of Echizen. He fed Tamae nutritious food and stayed up around-the-clock watching over her. He poured his heart and soul into nursing her, and by the end of March she seemed to have regained some of her former vitality. Then on the evening of April 2, she coughed up a large amount of blood and fell into a coma.

Tamae died in the middle of the night five days later; it was April 7. Kisuke was sitting at her bedside peering intently at her sleeping face when she suddenly opened her eyes halfway and began to babble.

"Ah, ah, ah, ah." The sounds didn't quite form words.

"What is it?" Kisuke said.

Exhausted from lack of sleep, he blinked his eyes rapidly and brought his face near hers. It sounded as if Tamae were faintly calling to someone.

"Who? Who are you calling?" Kisuke was overjoyed to hear Tamae say something. He listened intently, desperate to hear her voice.

"Kyoto . . . Uji . . ." she said and turned her sad eyes toward Kisuke.

Kisuke drew his ear to her mouth but she said nothing more.

Kisuke recognized the change in Tamae's face when death finally came. It was the first time in his life he had experienced true grief.

"You mustn't die. You mustn't die," he cried and searched Tamae's eyes for a flicker of life.

Smiling faintly as her fingertips lightly touched Kisuke's hand, Tamae died.

"Mother!"

Kisuke pressed his face to her cheeks, his cry piercing the dark ceiling of the bedroom like an awl.

# XIX

The grave of Tamae, wife of Ujiie Kisuke, is located in the family burial ground in the hamlet of Takekami, Nanjō County, Fukui Prefecture. Her short granite marker is carved with the inscription, **Ujiie Tamae**. It sits to the left of a tall stone marker inscribed with the words, **Ujiie Kizaemon, Master Bamboo Craftsman**. To the right is a third stone marker that reads, **Ujiie Kisuke, Master Doll Maker**. The three gravestones are hidden in the shade of a grove that is slightly more elevated than its surroundings.

The spot gets good sunlight, but the grove behind the Ujiie house, which has since disappeared, is now overgrown with weeds. There is no trace of the old days when the bamboo was divided up in orderly fashion—bamboo grass, black bamboo, *mōsō* bamboo, *Iyodake, hachiku*—and the floor of the grove was swept so meticulously that it looked just like a carpet.

Left untended, the bamboo grew haphazardly, and now stalks of tall bamboo grow alongside stalks of thick bamboo. Together they cast large shadows over the gravesite.

Only the two camellia trees planted at the gravesite continue to flower in the spring. Their large red and white blossoms give off a subtle, secret scent.

It's said that Kisuke, the master doll maker, lost his mind after the death of his wife and stopped making bamboo dolls altogether. He hanged himself just three years after her death.

The motive for his suicide was unclear, but the people of Takekami said it was the result of loneliness and madness. Even today, the truth of this is not known.

The people of the hamlet tended to the three stone markers to memorialize the short period in which doll making flourished in Echizen. But as history has shown, the elaborate bamboo dolls that were once famous throughout the Kansai region fell into obscurity following Ujiie Kisuke's death.

Recently mass-produced dolls made of *madake* have appeared on the market under the name Echizen Bamboo Dolls. These works have no connection to the hamlet of Takekami.

It is not certain if today's bamboo dolls are successors to so-called Kisuke Dolls.

However, if you go to the hamlet of Takekami, deep in the Nanjō range, you will find camellias blooming at a gravesite encircled by a grove of wild bamboo that still trembles in the breeze.

# TRANSLATOR'S POSTSCRIPT

Tsutomu Mizukami (1919-2004) was a writer whose works resist simplistic classifications. He was widely known in Japan for his popular fiction (*taishū bungaku*), but he was also honored with numerous prizes that recognized him as a master stylist of serious or pure literature (*junbungaku*). He wrote in a variety of modes—detective fiction, social realism, naturalism, biography, memoir—and on a sweeping range of subjects, but he often mixed these various elements within a single work. He was a regional author who made heavy use of dialects, but he also freely adapted the themes and techniques of many of the great writers of modern Japan in order to imbue his art with a mythic aura that had national appeal. Given the protean quality of his work, then, it seems somehow fitting that even the most basic marker of his literary identity, the characters for his family name, Mizukami, should have an alternative reading, Minakami.

The complexities of Mizukami's fiction are undoubtedly a reflection of his own remarkable personal background. He was born on March 8, 1919 in Wakasa, which was part of the village of Hongō in Fukui Prefecture. Fukui, together with Toyama, Ishikawa, and Niigata prefectures, is part of the Hokuriku region, an area on the coast of the Sea of Japan that faces northeast Asia. This region has historically been physically isolated because of both the rugged terrain and the cold, snowy climate. At the time of Mizukami's birth, the region as a whole was also far less developed economically than the urban areas on the Pacific coast that had modernized rapidly in the late nineteenth and early twentieth centuries.

Much like Appalachia in the United States, the Hokuriku region has long evoked ambivalent, contradictory emotions. For local residents, this has meant intense pride in their isolation, a sense of independence and endurance mingled with feelings of grievance toward the nation's cultural and political centers. For outsiders, Hokuriku has invited both scorn and sympathy. It was a symbol of a backward past that modern Japan decisively rejected, but it was also a haunting reminder of a culture—one that was more authentic, more truly Japanese—that had been irretrievably lost. These ambivalent reactions have been the source of many great works of literature, most notably Kawabata Yasunari's *Snow Country*.

For Mizukami, the privations of life in Hokuriku would eventually provide inspiration for his art, but that inspiration was grounded on material circumstances that profoundly shaped not just his aesthetics, but also his view of life. Mizukami's father was a carpenter who worked mostly for temples and shrines. The family was extremely poor, and the year Mizukami was born coincided with an especially severe downturn in the national economy. He attended the local elementary school until he was nine, but because of the family's poverty he began working in a local temple. The following year, in 1929, he was sent to the Shōkokuji, a Zen temple in Kyoto, where he began training for the priesthood. He eventually became an acolyte (*shami*) and went through the ordination ceremony.

Life for a young boy experiencing Zen training would be difficult under any circumstances, but Mizukami had a particularly unpleasant time of it. He moved from branch temple to branch temple, eventually ending up at the Tōjiin in the fall of 1932. The following year he began studying at the Hanazono Middle School. He graduated in 1936, but his turbulent relationship with the head priest, whom Mizukami considered corrupt, worsened and he found he could no longer bear temple life. So in May he left the Tōjiin.

For a while Mizukami supported himself doing odd jobs—he worked at an uncle's *geta* (clog) shop, and was even a peddler selling *Mugiwara Poultice*. In April 1937 he entered Ritsumeikan University and tried to continue his studies while working. However, he could not manage his schedule and withdrew in November. In 1938, with full-scale war now raging in China, he found a job with an international exporting firm and was sent to Manchuria to serve as an overseer for Chinese manual laborers. He soon fell ill, however, and had to return to his hometown in early 1939 to convalesce. During this period he began to study literature and for the first time in his life became seriously interested in writing.

During the height of the war, between 1940 and 1945, Mizukami led something of a nomadic existence, taking on a number of different jobs around Japan and managing to stay out of the reach of the military draft. He had an intense hatred of the military, which had been nurtured by his experiences in middle school, but avoiding service during this time forced him to lead an isolated and anxious lifestyle. The one thing that kept him grounded was the work he did for a wide variety of coterie magazines (*dōjinshi*). The network of connections he made through these small journals also helped him meet a number of important writers, including Fukuda Tsuneari and, most importantly, in 1945, Uno Kōji.

Uno became a mentor to Mizukami, and his highly personal, naturalistic style proved to be a lasting influence. With Uno's help, Mizukami published his first major work, an autobiographical novel titled *The Song of the Frying Pan* (*Furaipan no uta*), in 1948. The book sold well enough, but it was not a major success. He was discouraged by the reception of the novel, and he was beset with family problems at the time. His young daughter had serious medical problems, and his wife, who was depressed by their circumstances, left him in 1949. He would later remarry in 1956, but because of the personal and professional pressures he faced, Mizukami did not write another major work until 1959.

The 1950s witnessed a remarkable efflorescence of literature and art in Japan. The publishing industry was booming, older established writers were producing some of their best work, and extraordinary new talents were emerging on the scene. One of the more interesting and popular trends was a new style of detective fiction best represented by the work of Matsumoto Seichō. His novel *Points and Lines* (*Ten to sen*), for example, is a model of this style, in which the narrative begins with two or more seemingly unrelated events (points) that would eventually be joined through the process of detective work (lines). What gives this style its special tension is the way it combines naturalist techniques for establishing setting and historical context with depictions of social and political issues.

Inspired by this trend, Mizukami once more began to actively pursue his writing career, publishing *Fog and Shadow* (*Kiri to kage*) in 1959. This work was both a critical and commercial success, and it marked the beginning of an enormously productive five-year period. In 1960 he brought out another detective work, *The Sea's Fangs* (*Umi no kiba*), which provides a harrowing account of the victims of Minamata disease and a searing critique of the social costs of pollution. Mizukami's skill in weaving social issues into a work of popular fiction won him the Japan Detective Writers' Club Prize that year.

As well received as these novels were, it was the detective novel *Starvation Straits* (*Kiga kaikyō*, serialized in 1962 and published in 1963) that cemented Mizukami's reputation as a popular novelist. The story begins with two seemingly unrelated events—the capsizing of a ferry between the islands of Honshu and Hokkaidō (an event based on an actual disaster) and a murder at an isolated spot not far from the scene of the accident. Although the novel presents a dark, even sinister view of postwar Japan, Mizukami's taut, tense style and sweeping melodramatic narrative found a receptive audience. It is a testament to his popularity and stature during this period that *Starvation Straits* was adapted to the screen in 1965 in a masterwork directed by Uchida Tomu.

Compared to these works, which explicitly combined elements of detective fiction and social commentary, *The Temple of the Wild Geese* (*Gan no tera*), which won the Naoki Prize when it was published in 1961, and *Bamboo Dolls of Echizen* (*Echizen takeningyō*), which was published in 1963, signaled a new direction in Mizukami's fiction. Nevertheless, they still bear traces of the mature style that their author had developed through the medium of the detective story. *The Temple of the Wild Geese* draws heavily on Mizukami's boyhood experiences to give the reader a vivid sense of life at a small Zen temple. The immediacy achieved by a naturalist style, which Mizukami so admired in the writings of Uno Kōji, is tempered by a detached narrative voice that reveals the most intimate of details while still keeping its distance. The chilling effect Mizukami achieves may be compared to that in the fiction of Patricia Highsmith, or François Mauriac, in that while the psychology of the characters is artfully drawn, and the circumstances of murder are rationally laid out, the dark sources of the sexual obsession, exploitation, corruption, loneliness, and hatred that drive the actions of Satoko, Jikai, and Jinen are never fathomed. For all the recognizable literary elements that make up *The Temple of the Wild Geese*, their combination in Mizukami's hands results in a kind of realistic clarity that paradoxically acts to ensure that the essential mystery will never be fully disclosed.

*Bamboo Dolls of Echizen* is a very different kind of story, but it too demonstrates the skill Mizukami possessed in bringing together disparate literary elements. He makes use of a number of literary types: the craftsman, the central figure in a subgenre called *shokuninmono* that celebrates the authenticity of folk art; the young woman (a geisha, a prostitute, or a widow) whose beauty is enhanced by her suffering; the callous middle-aged male villain. But as he did in so much of his fiction, Mizukami contextualizes those archetypes by the use of naturalistic settings and by a critique of social institutions—prostitution, village and school, family, an unjust legal system—that trap individuals and destroy their chance for happiness. The result is a story that is part folktale and part social realism. The character Tamae is perhaps the perfect embodiment of this technique. She is the archetype who serves as the muse for Kisuke (and for Mizukami); and yet the novel does not flinch from describing her flesh-and-blood suffering. *Bamboo Dolls of Echizen* achieves a balance between reinvigorating essential cultural myths and undercutting those same myths to show the humanity beneath them. It remains one of Mizukami's most beloved works in Japan.

In certain respects the early 1960s were the defining moment of Mizukami's career. This is not to downplay his subsequent achievements, for he remained an active and prolific writer up to his death on September 8, 2004. He produced a large number of other important works, including *Gobanchō Yūgirirō* (*The Yūgiri brothel at Gobanchō*, 1963), *Kinkaku enjō* (*The burning of the Golden Pavilion*, 1979), and *Utsutake no fue* (*A hollow bamboo flute*, 2002). He also authored highly regarded biographies of Uno Kōji, the medieval Buddhist poet-priest Ikkyū, for which he won the Tanizaki Prize in 1975, and the priest Ryōkan. Still, for all his notoriety in Japan, unlike many of his peers, he has not been widely translated into Western languages. It is therefore appropriate that the first full-length translation in English is of two novellas that date from the moment when his talents were first fully realized. Together they capture the essence of the techniques and themes that made Tsutomu Mizukami such a significant figure in contemporary Japanese literature.